THE YEARS
OF FEAR

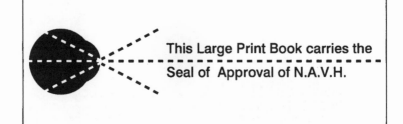

THE YEARS OF FEAR

A WESTERN STORY

FRED GROVE

WHEELER PUBLISHING

Published in 2004 by arrangement with
Golden West Literary Agency.

Wheeler Large Print Western.

The text of this Large Print edition is unabridged.
Other aspects of the book may vary from the original edition.

Set in 16 pt. Plantin.

Printed in the United States on permanent paper.

Library of Congress Cataloging-in-Publication Data

Grove, Fred.
    The years of fear : a western story / Fred Grove.
        p. cm.
    ISBN 1-58724-570-1 (lg. print : sc : alk. paper)
    1. Petroleum industry and trade — Fiction.   2. Osage
Indians — Fiction.   3. Oklahoma — Fiction.   4. Large
type books.   I. Title.
PS3557.R7Y43 2004
    813´.54—dc22   2003062158

THE YEARS
OF FEAR

As the Founder/CEO of NAVH, the only national health agency solely devoted to those who, although not totally blind, have an eye disease which could lead to serious visual impairment, I am pleased to recognize Thorndike Press* as one of the leading publishers in the large print field.

Founded in 1954 in San Francisco to prepare large print textbooks for partially seeing children, NAVH became the pioneer and standard setting agency in the preparation of large type.

Today, those publishers who meet our standards carry the prestigious "Seal of Approval" indicating high quality large print. We are delighted that Thorndike Press is one of the publishers whose titles meet these standards. We are also pleased to recognize the significant contribution Thorndike Press is making in this important and growing field.

Lorraine H. Marchi, L.H.D.
Founder/CEO
NAVH

* Thorndike Press encompasses the following imprints: Thorndike, Wheeler, Walker and Large Print Press.

PROLOGUE

It was the Roaring 'Twenties, and they came among the oil-rich Osage Indians of Oklahoma like a swarm of locusts: jackleg lawyers, hijackers, thieves, "dope" doctors, prostitutes, bootleggers, card sharks, oily merchants, drifters, killers-for-hire, fortune hunters determined "to marry me a rich Osage," preying on naïve Indian girls, and ostensible guardians whose clients never seemed to get out of debt.

The booming oil fields gave birth to a litter of tough little towns, and among the toughest of all was Whizbang, aptly named after a World War I shell, said to have connections with the Kansas City underworld.

Unsolved Indian homicides grew at an alarming rate. Officers of the law found it difficult to get witnesses to come forward with evidence. It wasn't "healthy" to talk about the murders. White men also were being killed. Witnesses left the Osage; some vanished suddenly into Mexico. Fearful Osages strung electric lights around their country homes. At night the " 'fraid lights" cast an eerie glow over a bountiful land once so peaceful.

In desperation, the Osages appealed to the Great White Father in Washington. When would tall men come riding?

CHAPTER ONE

For several days the dogs had been dying in Fairfax, Oklahoma, a friendly Indian town of 2,000 in southwestern Osage County. There seemed to be a pattern to the cruelty, concentrated in a particular part of town on the hilly west side. Angry Osages and whites alike, who fancied bird dogs, wolf hounds, and dogs in general, voiced their outrage and blamed some mind-twisted crank, complaining that rarely were dog poisoners ever caught.

It was early March, 1923. A young spring was moving into the rounded hills and bluestem cattle ranges, a welcome change to uneasy tribesmen. It was a relief from the hard winter, from last February when full-blood Henry Roan was found murdered northwest of Fairfax in Sol Smith's pasture, head-shot, sprawled in his car. And dead before Roan, hardly a year ago in his Fairfax home, had been Osage Bill Stepson, apparently of poisoned whisky, and in May, 1921, Osage Anna Brown was found shot northeast of Fairfax in a lonely ravine. Fairfax was getting to be a town with the furtive smell of death.

On the evening of March 9th, William E. Smith, a middle-aged white man married to an Osage woman, stopped at the home of a friend, Fred DeNoya, also a member of the tribe. Smith seemed deeply troubled and depressed.

"Now that we've moved into town from Gray Horse, maybe they'll let us alone," he said as the two men sat in the shadows of the front porch. "Reta's scared."

"You say *they*. Know who they are?"

Smith hesitated, reluctant. "Not sure."

"What've they done?"

"Sometimes, late at night, they'd slip around the ranch and pound on the sides of the house. Sometimes we'd hear 'em howl like coyotes down by the creek, or scream like a panther. Reta thinks it means she's gonna die before long. You know how superstitious some full-bloods are."

DeNoya made an impatient sound. "If it's that serious, why don't you pack a gun?"

Smith was slow answering. A peaceable, inoffensive man, he had no reputation for violent ways. As an Osage squawman, he was thought more careful of his wife's money than most, not given to the excesses generally indulged in by white men marrying Osage women for meal tickets. "No," Smith replied, "I wouldn't want to take the law in my own hands. Maybe this will blow over."

"You never took the matter to the sheriff?" DeNoya persisted.

"Yes, I went to Pawhuska. Was told that unless I had some names, there was nothing they could do."

DeNoya let it rest, but plainly persecution had driven the Smiths to town for greater safety. A hell of a note and another sign of the general lawlessness around Fairfax, in fact, the whole county.

Smith left on a happier note, telling DeNoya about a new electric range he planned to purchase for Reta at the Big Hill Trading Company.

His friend's troubles lingered in DeNoya's mind when he retired.

A cool, blustery wind set in as the night advanced. Traffic died, and the streets fell silent. At three o'clock in the morning, Saturday, a rumbling shook the sleeping town. It seemed the night would never stop trembling.

Fred DeNoya came awake with a sudden upward fling of his head, then froze, thinking the door of the newly installed coal-burning furnace in the basement had blown open. He dashed the thought at once. This blast was much too powerful.

He ran to the front door and looked north toward the Smith house, about a block and a half away. Something seemed to be missing in the reddish glow. The house, he realized with a sudden sinking sensation, was no longer there. He could see small flames. Now he could hear Bill Smith whooping for help.

DeNoya started running, his sense of lateness growing as he ran. By this time more citizens were rushing outside their homes, firing rifles and handguns to alert others. Something terrible and awesome had just happened to their town. Was it a bomb? Or had a nitro truck gone off? They dreaded to know.

DeNoya, dimly aware of other rushing figures, ran over to where a modern, eight-room bungalow had stood against the limestone hill that rose above the town. All he saw was burning, smoking wreckage. Now more men came up, shouting, pulling uncertainly at the heaped rubble, or just standing, dazed, appalled at the destruction.

Someone was groaning under the tangle of timbers. As firemen played water on the site, DeNoya heard Bill Smith's muffled, revived voice. But he couldn't see him. Smith was buried under the débris.

"I'm all right!" the trapped man suddenly called, his voice coming stronger, surprisingly clear. "But Reta's dead. . . ."

"What happened, Bill?" a fireman called.

"Nitro . . . I guess." Smith's voice trailed off. Then he said: "Mollie and the kids are here somewhere."

Mollie — Ernest Burkhart's wife — was Reta's sister. Frantic rescuers worked faster. Smith, they determined, lay beneath the gables of the house. He said: "I can move a little . . . but I can't crawl out."

He would have to be freed. There was a scramble to get heavy jacks. Using Smith's voice as a guide, firemen started burrowing, scooting the jacks under the gables. Slowly, while the slow clicking went on, the wreckage began to creak and lift.

Smith called out again, sharply, in great pain. Firemen underneath saw why. The smoldering mattress on which Smith lay with his dead wife was afire, fanned by a draft created as the jacks raised the timbers. Firemen worked faster. Smith, unable to roll free, endured the searing pain until searchers reached him and dragged him out.

DeNoya and Dr. J.G. Shoun carried Smith, groaning, toward the doctor's car. All at once he began protesting, pleading with DeNoya: "If you've got a pistol on you, for God's sake shoot me! I won't live! Go ahead . . . nobody need know!"

DeNoya tried to comfort him. "Bill, you're gonna be all right."

"I'm burned from my hips down. I can't make it."

"I won't let you suffer," Shoun said. "I promise you."

Smith moaned. "I don't want to live. Reta's gone. I'm no good this way."

Grimly they took him on, groaning. Examination at the hospital showed Smith was horribly burned from the waist down. Hardly had rescuers carried him inside when city officials set up lights outside the building and posted guards, in case the murderers tried to finish Smith before daylight.

Other volunteers, digging under débris on the north side of the shattered house, stood back in shock at the torn body of Mrs. Nettie Brookshire, the Smiths' seventeen-year-old white housekeeper, left armless, legless. But Mollie Burkhart and the kids? Bill Smith had said they were in the house. Frantic searchers could find no more bodies. Where were they? Could they have been blown away?

A hurried check at Mollie's home in Fairfax provided the missing family. Yes, Mollie said tearfully, she and her two small children had gone to spend the night with Bill and Reta. But early in the morning one of the kids got sick, and Mollie, Indian-like, didn't wait for light. She'd bundled them up and hurried home — at 2 A.M., an hour before the explosion.

Daylight came. Body parts, clothing, and bedding hung on telephone lines and trees for blocks around. Heavily damaged nearby houses resembled pincushions. As the milling curious, stepping gingerly, tramped around the house, angry and horrified residents tried to reason why.

Bill and Reta were friendly and well-liked.

Reta, a sister of the murdered Anna Brown, was considered a "good mixer." Before their marriage, Bill was the husband of Minnie, Reta's older sister, who had died of natural causes in 1918. Why would anyone murder them? And Nettie Brookshire, no more than a girl? Was she merely an accidental victim? And the waste. The Smiths had bought $3,000 worth of furniture from the Big Hill Trading Company for their new home, just purchased from Dr. Shoun. Also destroyed was a Studebaker, parked in the basement garage.

Rumors multiplied in shocked Fairfax, gripped in the town's greatest excitement and no little fear. Did Bill Smith know too much about Anna Brown's murder? Both he and Reta had been outspoken that Bryan and Ernest Burkhart were involved. The brothers were nephews of W.K. Hale, the most prominent man in town, also the biggest cowman in a county of many big ranchers, a power in Democratic politics, and frequently referred to in the state press as "King of the Osage Hills." Bill Hale had posted bond for the two and made light of the charges, dismissed for lack of evidence. Evidently witnesses were reluctant to testify against kin of Bill Hale amid rumors of threats.

One fact stood out: grieving Mollie Burkhart was the last of the four unlucky daughters of Lizzie Q, also known as Lizzie

Kile. Now, if Bill Smith died, Mollie would inherit the family's fortune of shares, or headrights, from the tribe's common pool of revenue from the booming oil fields. If Mollie died, husband Ernest would get the whole treasure trove, augmented with quarterly payments. An ugly question persisted. Did Ernest know Mollie and the kids would spend the night with Bill and Reta? And where was Ernest that night?

Had Hale played a hand in this? He and Smith were known to be at odds over money Hale reportedly owed Smith. But Hale was taking in the Fort Worth Fat Stock Show with colorful Henry Grammer, widely known as a champion roper and more currently as the county's kingpin bootlegger, both in the making and distribution of whisky. Lou Oller, a crony of Hale's, had wired Hale the morning after the explosion, but, strangely, no record was kept of the telegram's contents by the M.K.&T. agent.

Another thing. When backtracking residents recalled the extraordinary number of dog poisonings, sudden meaning took hold. Those dogs had all died in the immediate neighborhood of Bill Smith's place. Thus, when the killer or killers slipped up to the house, there wasn't a single watchdog within blocks. Now both Indians and whites could ask who was next?

Outraged city officials notified county officers, who came, saw, asked questions around, and departed. They were still working on the Henry Roan murder.

Authorities convened a coroner's jury and called in a chemist from Oklahoma A&M College. After examining the wreckage, he reported that nitroglycerine, commonly used in the Osage oil fields for shooting wells to loosen oil-bearing formations, had caused the explosion. Further conclusive proof was discovery of a charge wire leading from the basement garage to a safe distance higher up the hill. There, officials reasoned, a portable firing battery was employed.

For local consumption came a shuddering afterthought, when the explosives expert said that had the nitro been placed higher up in the house, the surrounding neighborhood might have suffered loss of lives. Fortunately the basement walls helped contain the blast, which tore a hole six feet wide and three feet deep in the center of the six-inch concrete floor. Poor Nettie Brookshire, sleeping directly over the garage, had taken the main force of the charge, while the Smiths, in a bedroom toward the front of the house, were spared some of the shock, although Reta had died instantly.

Meanwhile, Bill Smith lingered on hopelessly at the hospital, moaning: "I don't want to live. They'll get me anyway."

They? Did he mean Hale and the Burkharts?

17

About dark the evening after the explosion, another rumor took flight. Bill had regained consciousness. Maybe he'd talk now. Maybe he'd name the killers. Fairfax remained nervously quiet, filled with whispered alarm. Later that night edgy residents, driving the street, saw eerie proof that Bill Smith somehow still clung to life. Floodlights stayed focused on the rear and front entrances of the hospital. Armed men stood guard. More weird, more frightening for the spreading fear it cast, was the town itself, which seemed all aglow. Not only Indian homes, but whites' alike.

A drive east of town across Salt Creek to the little Indian village of Gray Horse, that edged into the Blackjack Hills, disclosed the same terrified alertness. In the wide, empty yards the " 'fraid lights" ringed the houses, dogs barked. All rather pathetic precautions, some said, in view of the raw, contemptuous display of murderous violence at the Smith house. Somehow the night passed without change.

On Sunday, Reta Smith — "badly burned and her skull crushed from behind, though her face did not show but one small bruise," reported the *Osage Chief*, the town's weekly newspaper — was taken along the dusty road to the old Indian cemetery just beyond Gray Horse, where Henry Roan lay in a quiet woodland of wind-sighing blackjacks and costly Italian marble mingled with simple granite headstones and the softly hewn faces of stone angels looking down, as if grieving while watching over the once-troubled.

Nettie Brookshire, her body torn beyond recognition, was buried in City Cemetery. "The little child of Mrs. Brookshire is said to be living with her grandparents in Cushing," said the *Chief*. The editor had no progress to report on the investigation of the murders. "The deed was so completely covered by the perpetrators that it has been impossible to gain any information that would lead to arrests."

On Tuesday, Bill Smith was reported "rational" by physicians. On Wednesday, Smith seemed stronger. He ate a breakfast of hotcakes and coffee, then asked to see his old friend, Fred DeNoya.

Shortly after, the turning point came. Smith was in convulsions, dying, when DeNoya hurried to the hospital. By 1:30 P.M. Smith was dead. But for the draft fanning the smoldering mattress under his trapped body, he would have survived to seek out his wife's killers. Speculation quickened. Had Bill Smith talked? Named anyone?

"Efforts to get him to talk were to no avail," reported the *Chief*. "If he knew, or had an idea, of the persons responsible, he never mentioned their names, according to those in attendance."

Others said differently, whispering that

Smith had named names. Local names. Big names. But he gave DeNoya no names.

Fairfax was a sounding board of rumors. H.E. Wilson, the local coroner, issued a statement next day, denying the jury had evidence implicating local people.

Yet violence continued to erupt in Fairfax following the triple murders. During the night of March 22nd an explosion shook the town, a rattling boom, but not of the magnitude of the Smith blast. Shaky citizens feared another Osage home had gone up and its occupants murdered. Instead, officers said, an attempt had been made to blow open the grave of Helen Tallchief, seven, daughter of Mr. and Mrs. Alex Tallchief, buried in City Cemetery.

"A charge of explosive had been placed in the ground and shot, but did not penetrate a steel vault placed in concrete," the harried editor of the *Chief* reported. "Robbery was believed the motive." That figured. Osages often buried jewelry with their dead. In the same issue, notice was carried of the death of William U. Bennett, "for many years a resident of Fairfax and Osage County, who died unexpectedly at University Hospital in Oklahoma City. Mr. Bennett, 45 years old, suffered a fall when he stumbled and fell down a stairway."

Stumbled or pushed? Friends said he had spoken in public of possessing information about the Indian murders. Bennett, part Osage, a respected citizen and well-known stockman, left a widow and six children.

Fairfax found a surprising disclosure in the March 30th edition of their newspaper. Instead of just one heir to the estimated $300,000 estate of W.E. and Reta Smith, as generally assumed, that being Mollie Burkhart, there were two claimants: Smith's father, Thomas Smith, address not known locally, and Mrs. Ella Rogers, living in Arkansas. She was Smith's daughter before he married Minnie, Reta's deceased older sister. A joint will of the Smiths provided that the survivor of the two would acquire the estate of the first to die. Since Smith had survived his wife by four days, the estate passed to him and his heirs. Had the whims of fate intervened in somebody's brutal calculations?

Who was next? The question seemed to be on everyone's lips. George Bigheart, 46, strapping son of the last hereditary chief of the Osages, fell ill of a puzzling ailment at his home near Gray Horse and asked to be taken to the University Hospital in Oklahoma City. His condition turned critical. Sensing death, he had a call put in to his trusted friend and attorney, W.W. Vaughn, in Pawhuska, to come at once.

Friends believed Bigheart made a deathbed statement to Vaughn. Bigheart died June 29th. Hospital records, which the *Daily Okla-*

homan carried June 30th, did not state the cause of death.

Late that Friday night Vaughn, in company with several attorney friends, boarded the M.K.&T. for home. In the baggage car lay the body of Bigheart. When the train stopped at Hominy, a Fairfax ambulance would meet it. Vaughn, a weary man, said good night to friends and retired to his berth.

Toward morning, still dark, as the train approached the small Osage town of Pershing, where Pawhuska passengers disembarked, a porter called Vaughn. When there was no response after several calls, the porter looked inside. Vaughn's berth was empty — the window raised. His clothing lay in place.

Friends started a frantic search of the train. Vaughn was not aboard. Train and police officials all along the line back to Oklahoma City were notified. Saturday passed without a trace.

"Mystery still surrounds the disappearance of W.W. Vaughn, Pawhuska attorney, who was missed from the M.K.&T. train Saturday morning when it arrived in Pershing," the Pawhuska *Journal-Capital* reported Sunday. Not until 36 hours after his disappearance was Vaughn's underclothes-clad body discovered, on the right-of-way three miles from Tryon, Lincoln County, his neck broken, his head crushed. Officialdom ruled his death an "accident," deciding that Vaughn had mistaken a Pullman door for the restroom and fallen off the train. Nothing was said about the raised window in Vaughn's berth nor Vaughn's possession of a dying Indian's statement, since none of his papers was found, having gone out the window with him or having been taken.

"Mr. Vaughn," the Pawhuska daily recorded in regretful tones, "leaves eight sons and two daughters, besides Mrs. Vaughn, to mourn the loss of a devoted father and husband. He was 53 years old."

Osages shuddered. Now prominent white citizens were being murdered in this bloodiest year of all. A general outbreak of lawlessness intensified during the spring and summer. County officers hit the western county boom towns. "Hundreds of hijackers, bandits, bootleggers, vagrants, dance-hall loungers, gamblers, immoral women, murderers, and thieves fled in motor cars upon word of the approach of the raiders," the Hominy *News* reported. "The raiding squad began work at Whizbang and took in Cooper, Shidler, Webb City and other places. Fourteen people were arrested. Narcotics and liquor seized was valued at several thousand dollars."

The *Chief* noted with indignation the invasion of its town when three "pistol-toters" robbed the Fairfax National Bank in bold daylight. "The trio took $2,279 and escaped in a Hudson Super-Six."

Other towns took bold hits during the bank-robbing spree, and Barnsdall, in eastern Osage County, could claim the dubious record of being robbed twice in two weeks. Keeping up with the times, the *Chief*, describing the second robbery, wrote: "After locking the men in the vault, the three robbers departed in a leisurely manner, passing one customer. Getting into a Stutz sedan, they drove into the country."

Bandits looted an M.K.&T. passenger train at Okesa. In June, county raiders closed five gambling houses in Wynona, between Hominy and Pawhuska. Alva McDonald, U.S. marshal, led a posse that killed bank robber Al Spencer, known as "The Phantom of the Osage Hills," whose trademark was audacious getaways in high-speed cars.

By now it was obvious that officers were more proficient at raiding and catching bootleggers and gamblers and other minor criminals than bringing suspects to trial in the sensational Fairfax murders and in the other mounting unsolved Indian murders over the county. Assailed by a deepening futility and an awakening that a far more powerful agency was required, the Osage Tribal Council passed a resolution requesting the federal government's aid in halting and solving the baffling murders. Looking in all directions for help, the Council also went to the Indian Rights Association, and, when its secretary came before the Council, the spokesman told him: "If this murder ring is not put out of business soon, the Osage country hardly will be a safe place to live for any of us. You can help to have it cleaned up. For God's sake, get busy!"

"At first such a declaration seemed to be extreme," the secretary wrote in his report. "But it was soon found that a reign of terror existed in the town of Fairfax and vicinity, and most Osages were afraid to venture out after dark. The local judge who held the inquests was so affected by the atmosphere of the place that, before talking to his visitor, he took him to a back room and fastened the door, seeing to it that the windows were closed. The interest of U.S. Senator Charles S. Curtis of Kansas, a member of the Kaw tribe, was enlisted in the matter, and through his courtesy our facts were put directly to the Attorney General."

Help was in the offing, but when? The federal government never moved swiftly in Indian affairs. Now, who was next?

CHAPTER TWO

Roy Bunch left the Big Hill Trading Company where he was employed as a meat cutter and headed down the street for a late lunch at the Silver Moon Café, which served the best chili in town. A well-built man in his late twenties, Bunch wore his blond hair cut short and had a quiet, friendly air. But today he could feel the increasing pressure more than ever as people stared at him, then looked away. It had been like that since Henry Roan's murder. He'd call Mary tonight and tell her he'd better not see her for a while. Maybe this would blow over. Yet maybe not. He might be charged with Roan's murder. He realized he was an obvious suspect.

It had begun as a gradual affair, this pretty Indian woman coming often to the butcher shop. Indians always bought a lot of meat. Too much for their own good. Mary Roan, pretty and lonely. It was known around Fairfax that Henry was a drunkard. Gone from home for days. Sometimes for a week or two. No children. Mary Roan had warm, appealing dark eyes and a nice smile. He had felt an instant attraction.

One day she had happened to mention that

her husband was gone again, or was she trying to tell him something without being bold about it? On daring impulse, he'd asked if he might come to her house that evening. She smiled and said yes. He didn't sneak around about it. He parked his car in front. She met him at the door and invited him in.

"Please sit down," she had said, gracious about it.

An embarrassed silence had followed. He hardly knew what to say, feeling uneasy in another man's home. Then she had said: "Henry's been gone a week. I heard he was gettin' whisky from John Ramsey." Her voice had trailed off. "He could end up like Anna Brown."

"Can't you talk to him?"

"I've tried . . . again and again. He won't listen. I'm just his wife. The whisky's got him."

"Too bad."

She had looked down. "It will end up bad, I know. I feel it. An Indian can't take the white man's whisky road and live."

"How long has this been going on?"

"Long time."

Her concern became suddenly evident. Tears filled her eyes. Feeling for her, he leaned across and touched her arm, sensing that she needed someone to talk to and listen.

"I'd better go," he had said. "Me comin'

here will be all over town by morning."

She had shrugged. "Nothin' new. What people don't know, they make up. Been a heap of talk because Henry's gone so much. Last week, after I drove to the Agency on business, word got around I was goin' with a guy there." She had laughed, shaking her head.

He had hesitated. "Would it be all right if I see you again?"

"Don't see why not. I'd like to get out a little."

"Could you call me at the store?"

"All right."

He had stood up and hesitated again. "People will talk."

"They'll talk anyway."

"Guess that's right." They had kept looking at each other, something left hanging between them. He had said it all at once: "Maybe we could go riding some evening."

An instant look of pleasure had risen to her high-boned face. "I'd like that. I need to get out more. Tired of stayin' in so much." She had held out her hand. "I'll call you."

So it had begun, and flourished. Sometimes he would pick her up, and sometimes she would pick him up after work or at his rooming house. Before long, inevitably, they became lovers. Of course, eyes followed them. Henry Roan found out. Once he came to the butcher shop and hit Bunch with a club. Bunch did not strike back. Somebody broke it up before they could fight. Once Bunch ran into a pool hall and hid when Roan was looking for him.

In his heart, Roy Bunch knew that he loved Mary Roan and that she loved him. He was going to marry her, but now was not the time. It just wouldn't look right. As he walked on, hurrying a little, he saw Bill Hale in his red Buick driving in the same direction. Hale spotted him, and swung over to the curb at once. Bunch groaned to himself, wishing Hale had gone by. Hale waved and motioned him over. Reluctantly Bunch went to the car.

Hale was smiling. Genial Bill Hale. He always showed a friendly face to the public. *The Indian's friend. Like hell!* Bunch thought. Hale lived off Indians. One way or another. He had cheated Henry, Mary said.

"Howdy, Roy." Hale greeted Bunch as if he were an old friend. "Wanted to tell you something. That five hundred I offered you? Well, I've doubled it, if you need it, and it shore looks like you will."

Bunch said nothing, just turned his back in disgust and walked away, thinking: *The scheming son-of-a-bitch. He's still trying to involve me.* His mind flashed back to the night Roan's body was brought to the undertaker's, when Hale had sought him out.

"If I were you, Roy," Hale had said, "I'd

29

hightail it outta town mighty fast. Head for Mexico."

"I'm broke," Bunch had replied uneasily, realizing he was on the spot. "Besides, I didn't do it."

"People will think you did. They know you've been goin' with Mary, stayin' at her house sometimes. You and Henry have fought. Shore looks bad for you. I've got five hundred dollars on me. You can have it. I'm doin' this as a friend."

"Why should I run, when I didn't do it?"

"Don't matter. People think you did. They've seen you with her. Think about it. Let me know if you need it."

But why would Hale offer him five hundred dollars to leave town? He wasn't a friend. Bunch had never met him, only knew who he was. Everybody in Fairfax knew who Bill Hale was. Big rancher. Biggest man in town. Had an interest in the bank and the gold mine called the Big Hill Trading Company. Hale had been a pallbearer at Roan's funeral. Self-appointed, Mary had said. She hadn't asked him.

Still uneasy after Roan's death and Hale's offer of money, Bunch had asked the advice of a trusted old friend, who flatly told him: "If you run, they'll hang it on you for sure. Don't do it! The worst thing you could do . . . same as an admission of guilt. If you run, they'll bring you back and convict you."

★ ★ ★

Bill Hale watched Roy Bunch until he entered the café. Then he backed out and drove away. At least he had Bunch thinking. A thousand dollars was a lot of money to a man on a modest salary who blew it all on a good-looking Indian woman whose husband had been murdered. *Better think about it, Roy. You're already the prime suspect. Everybody knows about you and Mary. You'll get stuck sure as hell if the county attorney charges you.*

He drove rapidly north to Henry Grammer's ranch. Not that Grammer ran many cattle there; he didn't. It was his "whisky ranch," an outlet for whisky hauled in from Kansas City and his still in the western part of the county.

Hale got out of the car, shut the door, and stretched, a stocky, erect, self-confident man with a broad face and straight black hair, as usual wearing a business suit, bow tie, and a fine gray Stetson. He was vain about his hat, and his boots, hand-made in Fort Worth, always shined. Peering through thick glasses, he gazed all around, always the cowman. Grass looked mighty good. You couldn't beat the Osage range country.

The place was stone-still, not even a horse in the corral. It occurred to him that Grammer should keep at least one horse to make it look like a ranch in case some deputy came by. Grammer had made a com-

31

plete change from the early days as the cowman and top roper he used to be. Now he rode a Cadillac. Always drove like a bat out of hell.

Grammer came to the door, grinning in a slack way. He was drinking, Hale noticed right off.

"I see you're lookin' over my place," Grammer said. "Want to buy it?"

"Hell, I can't take care of what I've got. Too hard to find people who want to work."

"Ain't like it used to be, is it, Bill?" Grammer said in a mocking voice. "Ain't, because a man wants to make a livin' now. Damned if I'd ride for twenty-five dollars a month again."

"Been a long time since you did." Hale laughed. "You married an Osage."

"An' she's still livin' on the old home place. Aw, come on in. Have a drink."

"Too early for me, but I'll come in."

Hale went in, found a chair in the cluttered, untidy room, and got down to business without delay, feeling nervous today. "I thought John Ramsey would be here."

"He went to Gray Horse. John shore enjoys drivin' that new Chevy and showin' it off."

Hale scowled. "Be better if he didn't and stayed put here or at his home in Ripley. Can't you find some carpentry work for him?"

"I have . . . but not much to do."

"Then make up something to keep him busy. I don't want him flashin' around in that car."

"Hard to disguise that. Besides, he has to make a livin'. He's not like you and me . . . livin' off Indians. With that big family of his, he has to hit the grit."

"You forget that I am a *very* successful rancher. If he needs money, tell him to see me."

"He knows that."

Hale wasn't satisfied. "Believe I will have that drink," he said.

Grammer set out a murky glass and a fruit jar of light-colored whisky. Hale got up to pour his own, sat down again, sipped, and grimaced.

"It's better if you age it." Grammer laughed.

"Then why don't you?"

"Hell, they buy it so fast. There's five gallons lined up behind the house right now . . . all I've got on hand. I've quit buryin' it in the corral."

"That's a dangerous thing to do," Hale lectured him. "Some deputy come snoopin' around and see that, you'd be in trouble again."

Grammer shrugged. "Only caught me one time, and got outta that."

An impressive cowboy-looking man, rangy, keen-eyed, sharp features, that devilish grin, Henry Grammer made no pretenses. He feared no man. He was what he was — reckless, tough, always seeming on the edge of danger. He'd won the World Championship Roping Contest in New York's Madison Square Garden. He'd toured Europe with the famed 101 Ranch Wild West Show and performed before the crowned heads of Europe and flashed his arena smile. He hadn't roped much in recent years, too busy bootlegging and getting rich. He also was fast with a gun. Officers avoided tangling with him if possible. He drove the tuned Cadillac sedan like a racing car, passing everything on the narrow, dusty roads. Better get the hell out of Grammer's way.

Too reckless for his own good, Hale mused.

Henry Grammer also knew more about Hale's numerous deals than any other man, even squawman Ernest Burkhart, who obeyed his strong-willed uncle's every whim like a puppet on a string. Grammer had no use for Burkhart. No guts.

Finishing his drink, Hale shuddered and said: "Have you paid Ace Kirby?"

"Every cent," Grammer said, and frowned.

"Something wrong? Did he complain?"

"Not Ace. Why should he? That was a lot of money." But a questioning expression jumped to Grammer's face. "He talks too much when he gets to drinkin' an' feels flush, which he shore is now."

"You talk when you're drinkin'."

"Nobody'd ever get anything outta me in court."

Hale started to say that every man has his breaking point but, knowing Grammer's touchy anger, said nothing.

Grammer eyed him. "You've got a lot of irons in the fire, Bill. You need to be more careful of the birds you pick. I happen to know that Ace's been drunk ever since I paid him." Grammer took a sip from the fruit jar. "Don't think you know it, but he's got a rep for braggin' when he's drunk."

"Long as he don't blab to the law."

"Don't figger he'd do that," Grammer said, still in the cautioning tone. "It's his braggin' around how much money he's made that might reach the county attorney from other sources."

"Maybe I'd better talk to Ace. Where would I find him now?"

"Drunk, at his boarding house in Shidler. If not there, anywhere."

"I'll give him a little visit in a few days."

"Good idea. You know, I don't think you should've paid him all of it at once. Space it out."

Hale felt a ruffle of anger. "Hindsight offers damn' poor satisfaction. Like the farmer who knows he shouldn't have left the barn door open. Point is, Henry, Ace wouldn't do it for less, and had to have it all at once. That was the deal."

"Well, it was a good job."

"It was. Complete." Hale got up, feeling heavy on his feet today. "When Ramsey comes in, tell him what I said about the car. Don't look good, showin' it off. People will wonder where he got the money to buy it."

Grammer broke into uproarious laughter. "Why, he got it doin' carpentry work!"

Hale had to grin. Nothing worried Henry. He didn't care whether school kept or not. Really didn't give a damn. Driving off, Hale felt his nervousness return, and he thought: *I need to take the wife and slip off to Florida for a vacation. Or maybe wait till Willie is out of school at Kidd Key College in Texas.* The thought passed as quickly as it had come. He couldn't afford to take the time. Like Henry said, he had too many irons in the fire. It was getting harder to find reliable men with a steady nerve, like in the early days. There was too much easy money floating around in the oil fields and because of the Osages, who threw it around like chicken feed. Another thing: a man needed to cover his back trail. That thought stayed with him the rest of the day and kept growing, and he awoke to it several times.

Next morning Bill Hale left early and took the road to Pawhuska. He knew exactly what he was going to do, after playing it back and forth in his mind during the night. He wondered why he hadn't thought of this earlier.

Ace Kirby would do anything for money. Along the way Hale returned the waves of passing motorists. It was a source of satisfaction for him to know that he was one of the best-known men in the county, if not *the* best-known. When he stopped for coffee in town, several men and an Indian spoke to him. He took the time to stop and visit briefly with each. He'd signed a note last year for one of the white men, and it sat in his mind that, if the time ever came that he needed friends and public support, these fellows would remember that genial Bill Hale, "King of the Osage Hills," had chatted with them that day in the City Café and had been the first to offer his hand.

From Pawhuska he drove eastward some miles and presently came to a store and filling station at a crossroads. He pulled up at the one gas pump, turned off the motor, and idled a moment. He'd stopped here a few times over the years but didn't know the proprietor, assuming the same person still owned it. Didn't matter, it would still work out. This place was just right. Off by itself in the country. No neighboring houses. Like a bird nest on the ground.

As he stepped out of the car and waited, a heavy-set, graying old man wearing an apron came out of the store.

"Might as well fill it up," Hale said genially.

"You bet."

"Nice day."

"Cool for this time of year. Had a little shower last night."

The old man had gray eyes set in a strong, broad face. He kept looking at Hale. He said: "Aren't you Bill Hale?"

Smiling, and pleased, Hale said: "That's what they call me." He offered his hand; they shook.

"I believe you've stopped here before. My name's Mason . . . Alva Mason."

"Been a few years back. Was with friends. We stopped for cold drinks. I remember you. That's why I drove over today."

The gray eyes widened. "Oh?"

Hale lowered his voice, wanting it to sound important. "Tell you about it inside."

Mason topped off the tank, and they went inside. After Hale paid, he said: "Don't want to alarm you, Mister Mason, but I heard something and thought I should pass it on to you as a friend."

Mason stood quite still. "What is it?"

"My business interests take me over much of the country. As a result, I get wind of things. There's a lot of rough stuff goin' on now . . . home robberies, folks gettin' hi-jacked on the road." He paused. "But reason I'm here today is to tell you there may be a move on to rob you. It's in the wind. Have you had any trouble?"

Surprised, Mason shook his head. "Been here for years and nothin' more than a few

38

minor thefts . . . kids stealin' watermelons stacked on the porch . . . somebody drivin' off without payin' for a gallon of gas. I keep the pump locked at night. Just country folks, mainly."

"That's all I've heard. But don't think you should ignore it."

"I keep a pistol under the counter. A shotgun in my bedroom."

"Good."

"Any suggestions, Mister Hale?"

"Just keep 'em handy. Stay alert. Particularly at night."

"I'll do that. I'm sure much obliged to you."

"You're mighty welcome. I just came by as a friend. Hope there's no trouble and it's no more than wind."

Driving fast, he had a late lunch at Pawhuska, then headed west for Shidler. Before long, in the rolling distance, he saw an emerging forest of derricks, and soon among them he heard the *clank-clunk* of drilling tools, and on the prairie wind he caught the smell of sulphur. Trucks labored by.

A young Osage, behind the wheel of a red Dodge roadster with the top down, passed him like a shot and left Hale cursing and choking in a cloud of gritty dust.

Damn them, he thought. *This is all theirs, and they've never worked a day for it and never will.* Although he always pretended to be friendly, he actually despised the Osages, all

Indians, in fact, and among his cronies spoke of Osage women as squaws. He was still in the contemptuous frame of mind when he tore into town.

He knew the location of the boarding house, which served the dual purpose of a front and a base for Ace Kirby's far-ranging criminal pursuits. It was a long, one-story wooden building with a central hallway running its length. The dining room and kitchen occupied the rear portion. Preparations for the evening meal were already under way, judging by the appetizing smells. Oil field workers had two principal needs: plenty of solid food and a place to sleep at all hours, day and night, as they came off shifts. Here they had both in the same location. And if one slipped a girl into his room, no questions were asked. Just don't disturb other sleepers.

John Mayo, a stoical, fleshy-faced individual recently released from the Kansas State Penitentiary, was in the office.

"Is Ace around?" Hale asked.

Mayo hooked a thumb. "Back there. Takin' a nap."

What Mayo meant was that Kirby was sleeping off a drunk. The room smelled of whisky. Kirby sat up at Hale's knock, looking surprised. "What're you doin' here?"

"Got a tip for you. But you'll have to sober up."

"Reckon you're talkin' money?"

"That's all I talk. You know that."

Kirby got up, considered for a moment an open bottle of whisky on the dresser; instead, he poured a glass of water and drank it all, then sat down and looked at Hale. Kirby could get down to business when he had to. A brawny, black-haired, cold-eyed man in his late thirties, Ace Kirby was a jack-of-all-trades in the rough oil fields: roustabout, tool dresser, driller, rig builder, and could handle the tricky, dangerous nitro used to break open oil formations. Seemed to have no nerves. Henry Grammer, nervy himself, had said he'd never seen his like. His only weakness was his loose tongue when drinking, and he drank constantly when flush, a weakness that could not be chanced with the way matters were shaping up at the Tribal Council, pushing to bring in federal officers.

"What d'you have for me, Bill?" Kirby asked in a vague way.

"There's a little country store southeast of Pawhuska that's like a bird nest on the ground."

"Yeah?" Kirby's hangover was a throbbing drumbeat. "Don't sound like much . . . a little store."

"Wait till you hear."

Kirby belched loudly. "I'm takin' it easy right now. Better pass it on to one of the Whizbang bunch."

"I stay with my friends."

"You got plenty connections. Why just me?"

"That was an extra good job you did. I'm returning a favor."

"I always do a good job. Better count me out this time."

"Like I said, wait'll you hear. I'm not talkin' about a fruit stand, Ace."

Kirby's response was a yawn.

"An old man runs the store by himself. Keeps considerable cash."

"Y'mean in the cash register?" Kirby mocked. "To make change, when somebody comes in for a soda pop?"

"Kind of a queer old duck. Don't trust banks. Lost his stake once in a bank failure back in Missouri. Pays cash for all he buys."

"Just how d'you know all this?"

"I've known the old man for years. His name is Alva Mason. Lived in Fairfax some years ago. In fact, I made him a loan one time. He never forgot it. . . . I stopped there last week on the way to Avant. He brought me up to date."

"I dunno," Kirby muttered. "It'd have to be big."

"It is . . . the old man also keeps diamonds. Figgers that's sure money any old time, if a bank folds."

Kirby picked up. "Diamonds? How many?"

"Hell, I didn't ask him that. He was just talkin' to me as between old friends. But he didn't say diamond . . . he said *diamonds*."

Kirby sat up. "Where does he keep all this stuff?"

"He did mention that . . . in a portable safe in his bedroom closet at the back of the store."

After a moment, Kirby asked: "Where is this store?"

Hale told him in detail, down to the mileage, and went to the door and looked back. "Just thought I'd pass it on."

Kirby had a swig from the bottle before he answered. "I'll think about it."

Think about it, hell, Hale thought as he walked to his car. *You're gonna do it.* He knew Ace Kirby would do anything for money. The stage was set.

He gauged the brassy sun. Still time to make that second stop, instead of driving back in the morning. He jerked the Buick around and burned rubber for Whizbang.

In his experienced judgment Whizbang was the toughest of all the rawhide oil boom towns. It materialized as a treeless sprawl of frame houses and shacks and rutted streets and mounds of stacked pipe and rig timbers and heavy equipment. The principal street crawled like an ant hill of men and cars and trucks and big, fine-looking teams of draft horses, often matched pairs, pulling timbers and boilers. The raw smell of oil rode the wind, and there was the endless rhythm of drilling tools.

Whizbang was Henry Grammer's town, with connections all the way to the Kansas City underworld. It was common knowledge that, if you wanted a job done, you could find the right man in Whizbang, for a price, of course.

He parked at the A-1 Garage, where Grammer had his cars tuned, and went in the garage entrance. He'd been there twice with Grammer. A boy was pounding on the rumpled fender of a Hudson touring car in an apparently losing effort to straighten it. On the other side of the garage a mechanic peered under the hood of a Pierce-Arrow. Closing the hood, he noticed Hale and waved.

Hale knew him as Jess Reed, a runty, squint-eyed man endowed with an unusual savvy about motors and, to the contrary, a totally disgruntled outlook on life. He wiped his hands on a bundle of rags and strolled over, seeming glad to stop work.

"Howdy, Mister Reed," Hale said. "I'm Bill Hale." When you wanted a man to pull a job for you, your first move was to show respect, as he'd just done.

"I remember you."

"Was goin' by, thought I might find Grammer in with his car."

"He's due any day. Oughta be on the tracks, way he drives."

"How're things goin' with you here?"

Reed shook his head. "We get more wrecks to work on than anything else. And the pay is slow. These Osages run up a bill, then tell me to collect through the Agency. If I get me a stake ahead, I'm gonna head back to Detroit."

Hale moved in a step closer. The boy was still banging away. "How would you like to make some easy money? Enough for a good stake?"

"You're talkin' to the man. I'm wore out with this place."

"Where can we talk?"

"Follow me," Reed said, and led off into a back room cluttered with parts.

It took less time than Bill Hale had figured. Money talked. Always. Long ago he had learned it was wise to carry enough to swing the deal on the spot. All a man saw was that wad of cash, his eyes getting bigger and bigger. Never mind what he would do later.

Driving south, Hale felt his uneasiness lessen. A man had to cover his back trail. Today he had done that.

CHAPTER THREE

Henry Grammer liked jovial company when on a spree. Gunning into Shidler in his Cadillac touring car, tuned up just this morning in Whizbang, he suddenly thought of ex-con John Mayo, who could hold his whisky as well as his tongue. Never mind that cold fish, Ace Kirby. It was like drinking with a ghoul. Mayo and his wife lived next to Kirby's boarding house in a tarpaper shack.

Mayo met him at the door and invited him in for a drink.

"Let me bring in a bottle," Grammer offered, and went back to the car. He looked around first, then dug a quart from a side pocket. The town marshal had arrested him once for possession. Grammer had paid a fine and was immediately released. No more than a nuisance, but still a nuisance.

Mary Mayo had a drink with the men, and the Mayos agreed it was extra good stuff.

"From my still east of Kaw City," Grammer said, pleased. "Made with spring water." He laughed. "Gettin' hard to keep up with the demand." After another round, Grammer said: "On my way to a little business appointment at Webb City . . . man has

46

to take care of his customers, you know." They all grinned at that. "Could you-all come along? I'll have you back before dark."

"Why not?" Mayo readily agreed. "I'm just waitin' around."

Mary Mayo, a plain, cheerful little woman with tired, loyal, brown eyes, slanted her husky husband a look. "They say there's plenty of work. New wells coming in every day."

He avoided her eyes. "I've promised Ace I'd help him on a job. After that, we'll see."

Her weary expression said she doubted he would. But she said no more.

Mayo stuck a revolver in his waistband, and they all trailed out to the Cadillac. Grammer packed a .45 in a shoulder holster under his calfskin vest. He took off with a roar.

The road to Webb City was deep with ruts from heavy travel. But Grammer straddled the ruts, avoiding the high centers, traveling fast. Before many minutes they reached town, weaving through a noisy tangle of trucks and cars and loaded freight wagons and shouting drivers. The place seemed to vibrate with life, a sense of urgency. The smell of oil and smoke and dust emitted a reckless air. Grammer squeezed into parking near the Goodtime Billiards, then led the way through the pool hall, empty except for the smiling old black man in charge and two laughing Indian boys playing snooker.

Through a swinging door at the rear, and down a short hallway, they entered another world of voices beating like surf against the walls of green lumber and, crowding the plank bar, men from the oil fields in grease-stained clothes, a few curious cowboys and local business types and a swarm of drifters. Tobacco smoke hung like morning fog.

Grammer took the Mayos to the only opening near one end of the bar and waved a bartender over. Mary Mayo had beer, the men whisky.

Grammer was drawing eyes. As a walking picture of the old-time cowboy and championship roper, he stood tall and straight, had a bold look, and wore the big Stetson as if it were daily attire.

Following another drink with Mayo, he worked around through the constantly shifting crowd to a door beyond the bar and went in without knocking. After some minutes, he rejoined the Mayos, nodded, and they made their way out to the hallway.

Suddenly two men blocked their passage with drawn revolvers, the nearest a hard-featured character with yellow skin and a black patch over one eye. His burly companion was nervously waggling his gun.

"Well, if it ain't One-Eyed Tex," Grammer said, showing total disdain. "I thought you's in jail up in Kansas."

"I broke out."

"Plumb daring stuff, huh? Daylight or dark?"

"Cut out the talk. Hand over that bankroll!" He was snarling through broken teeth. "You always carry one."

"Oh . . . well. . . ." As if complying, Grammer reached under the calfskin vest, swiftly drew the .45, and crashed the barrel across the skull of One-Eyed Tex. Blood flew. He went down like a pole-axed steer, his revolver flopping to the floor. Mary Mayo screamed once. Almost as fast as Grammer, her husband grabbed the other man's gun arm, and, as the weapon fired into the ceiling, Mayo seized it and smashed the barrel of his own revolver twice against the other's head.

All at once it was over, both gunmen down.

"Let's get outta here," Grammer said. "The town marshal will try to hold us."

Too proud to run, Grammer led out at a deliberate walk, and, when a snooker player yelled — "What happened?" — Grammer only shrugged.

Apparently a gunshot was not unusual in Webb City, because no man with a star came running into the pool hall . . . yet.

"You drive," Grammer told Mayo. "I'll keep an eye out."

Grammer winced as Mayo, rough with clutch and gear shift, backed out, shifted twice, and virtually bulled his way into outgoing traffic amid curses and shouts and fist wavings.

Once clear of town, Grammer said: "Let this thing run. Just had it tuned up."

Except for a truck or car now and then, the rutted road soon became theirs. The miles fell behind as Mayo kept a heavy foot. Maybe it was the whisky. Mayo nodded off for a second, and the Cadillac slipped into the ruts.

At the same instant, Grammer shouted: "Look out . . . that big rock in the rut!"

Mayo stomped the brakes and tried to wrest the car out of the ruts. Something audibly snapped.

"It won't steer!" Mayo yelled.

By now it was too late. Mary Mayo screamed as they smashed into the rock.

Osage County was shocked at the news. The Pawhuska *Journal-Capital* ran a page-one banner headline: **Henry Grammer Killed In Auto Smashup**. Not invincible Henry Grammer? Champion roper and featured star with the 101 Ranch Wild West Show in Europe, performing before kings and queens? Rancher and alleged bootleg king of the Osage? Yes. Grammer had died at the scene of a broken neck, pinned under the wreck, with $10,000 in currency on his body. John Mayo was driving. Neither Mayo nor his wife

Mary was seriously injured. County officers said the group was headed for Shidler, after fleeing Webb City, where Grammer and Mayo had allegedly beat up two men in a fight.

In further investigation, authorities said the steering gear of the Cadillac touring car showed signs of having been sawed nearly through, causing it to break and making the car unmanageable.

Two men drove up to the country store and talked a while before getting out. Alva Mason didn't like the looks of this pair. He told himself he'd been around the Osage long enough to spot suspicious characters when he saw them. As they approached the store, they seemed to look all around in detail.

Mason posted himself behind the cash register and mentally checked the .45 under the counter.

"Mighty hot out . . . got any pop?" the first man asked, sauntering in. There was a hard cast to his face, and he had the coldest eyes Mason had ever seen.

"Sorry, I ran out yesterday," Mason said, "and my delivery man is late." He felt certain now that he was being cased for a robbery, seeing the second man gazing about, front to back.

They left at that, taking the Pawhuska road.

"How does the lay-out look to you, John?" Ace Kirby asked.

"Wouldn't be hard to break in. Question is . . . where does he keep the stuff?"

"In a portable safe in his bedroom closet in the back of the store."

"Cash and diamonds?"

"That's what Hale told me. He knows the old man."

"How much cash, you reckon?"

"He don't trust banks . . . keeps his bank-roll there."

"Now you're talkin'. Where you figure to fence the diamonds?"

"Now that Henry's gone, Wichita or Kansas City."

"When do you want to do it?"

"What's wrong with tonight?"

"Nothin'. Let's do it."

"Maybe we'd better pick up another guy or two."

"All right."

After the two drove away, Mason loaded his 12-gauge shotgun and kept it handy. A flurry of business kept him occupied until evening. He closed a bit early, ate supper, and stationed himself in the front part of the store to wait. Instinct told him they would come that night.

It was after midnight, and he was about to go to bed when he heard a noise out front.

Light steps on gravel. Of course, they'd parked off a way and walked up.

Now he could see a figure at the door. He thought: *Be simple to break the glass, reach in, and unlock and open the door.* When the door rattled, he fired the shotgun. As he reloaded, he heard the man cry out and fall and saw figures running up. He held his fire, waiting. Then he heard them carrying him off, and, presently, he heard a car start up and take the Pawhuska road, going fast.

"Asa 'Ace' Kirby, of Shidler, died Friday night in the Pawhuska hospital from the effects of a gunshot wound inflicted by the keeper of a country store east of here, which it is alleged Kirby and three associates had attempted to rob." So the local daily reported.

Now there was no back trail. All signs had been rubbed out so as to leave no trace, as if it had never existed. Old-timers would remember Henry as one helluva steer roper and horseman and showman, Bill Hale thought. He'd got drunk with Henry many times and whored around with him at Fort Worth while taking in the Fat Stock Show, whoopin' it up together. He felt a short-lived twinge of conscience. But a man has to cover his back trail. As for Ace Kirby, who was he? Just another oil-field worker on the rough side who'd made the wrong move.

CHAPTER FOUR

A towering, well-built man wearing a Western hat and speaking in the soft accents of a native Texan entered Department of Justice headquarters in Washington, D.C., and went to the offices of J. Edgar Hoover, director of the U.S. Bureau of Investigation. Calling was Thomas B. White, Sr., agent-in-charge of the Houston, Texas office and Acting Inspector of the South and West. He was a powerful man of 46, standing nearly six feet four, not looking his solid 250 pounds, with light blue eyes, a calm, unfailingly courteous manner, and a habit of listening. He gave the impression of not becoming easily excited. In a short time he was renewing a friendship that went back to when Hoover had come to the Bureau as a young clerk while still in law school.

Talk then shifted to the Osage Indian murders in Oklahoma, and Tom White began to understand his instructions to hurry here for an important conference. He had read and heard about the many savage, unsolved murders in Osage's bloody hunting ground, and had wondered as to the cause of their frequency.

"The Osage investigation is being reopened,"

Hoover said. "Senator Curtis of Kansas, himself of Kaw Indian descent and very much interested in protecting the rights of Indians everywhere, has requested action from the Attorney General's office." Hoover said he was greatly distressed over the Bureau's failure in the initial investigation, starting in 1923. Some 24 adult Osages had died in recent years. Few of the deaths could be called from "natural causes." "The situation," Hoover went on gravely, "is fast becoming one of the blackest episodes in the white man's dealings with the American Indian. The Osage Tribal Council is pleading again for help."

One Blackie Thompson, Hoover said, a witness paroled from the Oklahoma state prison to assist federal agents, had wrecked the investigation. When an agent failed to keep him under surveillance, Thompson had escaped and joined in a bank robbery in which an officer was killed. Now, he said, the loose-herded bandit was back in the Oklahoma prison, serving a second life sentence, and the investigation had ground to a halt.

After reviewing other phases of the case, Hoover looked directly at White and said: "I want you to take over the Oklahoma City office as the new agent-in-charge and direct the investigation. I'll assign as many agents as you need. You know the Southwest, so I want you to pick the men."

White nodded. "I know the men." He felt like smiling a little, but didn't. Hoover hadn't given him one inkling as to why he had been summoned to Washington. This was Hoover's way, direct and to the point. Why not? This case already had moss on it.

Next morning Tom White was on his way back to the Southwest. If possible, he preferred to work up his own cases, a style learned from his late father, a Texas sheriff, and followed by Tom as a Texas Ranger and special investigator for the Santa Fé and Southern Pacific railroads, and since becoming a special agent in the Bureau. As a Department of Justice trouble-shooter, he had probed reports of graft, smuggling, and incompetence at the federal prison in Atlanta, Georgia, which led to the warden's conviction. But he realized the Osage investigation was a bigger challenge than any case of his experience. It wasn't just one murder. It was many murders against a background of wide and violent scope — the wildcat oil-boom towns, magnets for a variety of criminals and drifters, the towns tougher than any frontier settlement he'd known as a Texas Ranger, chasing bank robbers on horseback. He did some research on the Osages to familiarize himself. The tribe had been removed from Kansas to Indian Territory in the 1870s. Their new reservation wasn't suitable for extensive farming, only grazing, which pleased the old men, who had said, in effect: "This is good. Now the white men won't want it as they did our Kansas land."

But eventually oil was discovered, plenty of it, so that now in the 1920s the Osages had become the richest nation in the world per capita, paid quarterly, and they were being robbed and murdered for what they had. The year 1923 had been the bloodiest, and the little town of Fairfax appeared to be a well-spring of killings. So far federal agents had been unable to build a case. A new approach was needed: men familiar with all aspects of life in the Southwest and able to handle themselves in tough situations.

He selected four particular agents he knew well — Alex Street, Gene Parker, Charlie Davis, and John Wren — all former Texas and New Mexico sheriffs and Texas Rangers. It was now July, 1925. One by one, the four started drifting into the Osage country as undercover agents.

Street, a former Tucumcari, New Mexico sheriff, arrived first, driving to Fairfax and putting up at the only hotel in his rôle as a Fort Worth cattle buyer. He attracted no particular attention; buyers were no oddity in cow country. There seemed nothing unusual about a quiet man of 45, standing five feet ten, a lean 160 pounds. He was gray-eyed with iron-gray hair. He spoke in a calm voice, seemed somewhat reserved, and made a favorable impression. He was in charge of the undercover group.

Parker, Street's assistant, arrived soon after, also posing as a cattle buyer from Brownsville, Texas. Besides Ranger duty and riding for cow outfits in Texas and New Mexico, he had been in the U.S. Customs Service along the border before becoming a federal agent. A stocky man, he had strong-looking features, was gray-eyed and blond. Perhaps most important at this early stage was his talent as an entertaining mimic who could also spin an amusing story, which eased his entry among strangers. It was easy to like Gene Parker.

Third man in was Charlie Davis, a contrast in Western types among the agents. Here was another Texan, from Lockhart, a businessman whose background embraced experience as a county clerk and insurance agent. Although a town man, he knew cattlemen and could talk about range and market problems. He was older than his fellow operatives, near 50, soft-spoken, efficient, and obliging. His first move was to rent an office in downtown Fairfax and start selling bona-fide life insurance policies. His story wasn't unlike that of many other newcomers to the fabulous Osage area: he'd come to oil-boom country to make money. And, he confided wryly, considering the short life expectancy around here of late,

58

life insurance might be a good thing to have, especially for family men. His rôle as an agent was to observe the town, get acquainted, mix, and listen.

While Street and Parker worked the ranches and cow camps, and Davis inserted himself into the business life of the town, including joining the Chamber of Commerce, Agent Wren began to circulate among the Osages. He assumed the rôle of an Indian medicine man from New Mexico, searching for relatives who had moved to Oklahoma years ago. A physically impressive six-foot, 190-pounder, bearing a prominent nose and wide-boned features, he looked part Indian and with pride said he had Mexican-Indian blood. The elderly Osages, themselves large of physique and erect, liked the sight of a large, powerful man. Wren also spoke excellent Spanish, as did Parker. Before coming to the Bureau in 1916, he had been an agent for Mexican revolutionary leaders in the U.S. Wren's dossier credited him "with an exceptional memory for details, taking seemingly unrelated bits of information and linking them into an unbroken chain of evidence."

Gradually, as Osages saw that this friendly man with twinkling black eyes and the thick, proud mustache had no desires on their possessions, and had nothing to sell them at fantastic prices, he was invited into Indian homes over the county and to Indian dances at Gray Horse, Pawhuska, and Hominy. In his amiable way, he made "medicine" of sweetened water. The Osages liked him, confided in him, and he began to pick up bits of information about the murders formerly withheld in fear from men they had known as federal agents in the first investigation.

Also now working closely with Tom White as an assistant was Frank Smith, of Fort Worth. A gray, heavy-set man of middle age, he had a firm, dogged jaw and resolute features, and behind him twenty years of law enforcement from city to the county level. "One glance at Frank Smith and you knew he was the law," Tom said.

Henceforth they would work as a team, Smith's voice blunt and impatient, Tom's soft-spoken and unhurried, a difference of tone that might prove effective when questioning suspects. Agent John Burger, active in the original investigation, was stationed in Oklahoma City because he was known in the Osage area as a federal officer.

Aware that their lives were at risk, the four undercover agents met late at night in remote places, including a railway trestle not far from Fairfax. Reports were mailed from neighboring towns, never Fairfax. Ralston, just across the Arkansas River to the south, was the nearest; even so, it was still mighty close to the hub of the probe, and letters addressed to the federal building in Oklahoma

City could well attract enemy eyes. Therefore, Street often drove to Hominy, some 25 miles southwest, or to Pawhuska. He felt phone calls were risky; it was too easy to listen in. At a rendezvous, they would decide where to meet next time, but never the same location twice running. Sometimes agents drove to Oklahoma City or Guthrie.

As the agents met and talked, they rehashed Indian murders that had preceded the Smith atrocity, and out of the puzzling array of contradictions the name of W.K. Hale kept bobbing up here and there. Hale was a big cattleman, known as the most generous man in Fairfax and the most popular, a "great friend" of the Osages.

"I understand," Street said at a meeting in the hills east of Gray Horse, "that when a full-blood dies, particularly around Fairfax, Hale soon appears with a claim against the estate. Since he helped a lot of guardians get their fat jobs, you can figure the claim will be paid. Easy to see why he's known as King of the Osage Hills."

"Hale is a man of vast influence all over the country," Charlie Davis stressed. "When his nephews, the Burkhart boys, were charged in Anna Brown's murder, Hale posted their bond, and they never went to trial. And it's damn' well known that both were with Anna Brown that night . . . obviously, nobody wanted to testify. Maybe word was passed not to."

"I've heard around Fairfax that Henry Roan was shot during a robbery," Gene Parker put in. "A robbery, hell! A man he knew and trusted shot him. He was shot from behind, just back of the left ear. I'd say it was a bootlegger. No reason for Roan to be out there in the country, northwest of Fairfax, except to buy whisky."

"And Hale claims Roy Bunch, who was goin' with Roan's wife, killed Roan," Davis said. "Sounds good at first glance, but Bunch hasn't been charged. Now what the hell is Hale's hand in this? I ask you, boys?"

"Easy," Parker said. "There's money somewhere . . . and money trails to Hale, somewhere."

"Indians are deathly afraid of being seen talking to a strange white man," John Wren said, and chuckled. "Of course, I don't count. I have stayed overnight a few times at their invitation. It's an eerie feeling when the 'fraid lights come on, and they turn out the guard dogs. A few Osage boys in the war who brought back German shepherds from Germany are glad they did." He paused. "The old Osages feel there's a mysterious force at work, killing their people . . . and not just around Fairfax . . . that their oil riches have only brought them the white man's whisky and death and a fear that never goes away."

"Another character who keeps popping up

is this Kelsey Morrison," Street said. "Around Fairfax, he's called a dope-head. A sort of ladies' man . . . has manners, at first. Some people think he gave Osage Bill Stepson the poisoned whisky that killed him back in February of 'Twenty-Two. Morrison married Stepson's widow. She didn't live long, and Morrison got the estate." Street rolled a cigarette, then added: "He was with the Burkhart boys the night Anna Brown was shot . . . but prove it."

Davis, the town's new low-pressure insurance salesman, was getting acquainted as he started selling policies, and in doing so gained entrance to the homes of leading citizens. He made it a point to meet Hale and was invited to the Hale home. His host was a friendly man, although overbearing at times. He liked to talk about his cattle deals and boyhood days in Texas, relating with pride how he'd run off from home to become a cowboy. Already that year, he confided to Davis, he'd banked $75,000. Hale, Davis learned, had the local reputation of "holding himself high" and being "money mad." Still, the town's leading citizen seemed nervous. He spoke of making a long trip and complained to Davis of "stomach trouble" and having difficulty sleeping.

"I'm too slick and keen to catch cold," the cowman stated irritably to others in the presence of Davis. "I'm tired of two-bit crooks riding the public on my reputation."

Locally Hale was regarded as generous. "For example, if a ranch family was burned out and a collection was being taken up in town," Davis told his fellow agents, "Hale would give fifty dollars where another man might give five. And he'd do it publicly, so others would know. . . . One time Hale was moving a little bunch of cattle from one pasture to another. Happened a boy was riding his bicycle on the narrow road. The cattle came upon him suddenly. The boy had to leave his bike and run to the fence. The cattle trampled his bike. Next day, in town, Hale bought the boy a new bike, and you bet the boy spread the word. You have to give a man credit for being generous. But it seems to me that W.K. Hale, through public favors, has been conducting a vigorous campaign for years to win as many friends as possible. He's uneasy about something. I gathered that."

Meanwhile, Tom White was informed, Street and Parker talked about buying cattle for their ranches in Texas. Both became acquainted with Hale, who welcomed them warmly as fellow Texans. At Hale's Gray Horse Ranch they mixed with Hale's friends and cowhands, some ex-convicts who unknowingly dropped bits of fact into the widening pool of information about the murders in and around Fairfax. To the two Texans,

Hale's ranch was what they knew as a "tough lay," an outfit that hired badmen or gunmen.

Further, Street and Parker made the deadfalls in the nail-hard towns of Whizbang, Burbank, Shidler, and Webb City. Toughs, they said, used the little oil-boom towns as retreats after committing crimes over the county and along the Oklahoma–Kansas border. Bootleggers thrived. Rotgut whisky sold for $10 a quart.

At a rendezvous, Street reported following up on Henry Grammer's death two years ago and the rumor about the steering gear on Grammer's car being "worked on." "In Whizbang we found out that the mechanic who usually tuned Grammer's Cadillac disappeared the day after Grammer died. Figure that. Looks like Grammer was set up, but why? What do you think, Charlie?"

"Grammer was Hale's closest friend, or seemed to be. They were together at the Fort Worth Fat Stock Show when the Smith house was blown up. Grammer could have known too much."

"And the Fat Stock Show was an ironclad alibi for Hale in the Smith murders," Street said. "Why did he need an alibi, if he wasn't involved in the case? I understand he hasn't been to the Fat Stock Show since the bombing."

No one spoke for a while. Wren broke the silence with: "I can give one good reason for needing an alibi. Hale owed Smith six thousand dollars and wouldn't pay it . . . so Homer High Eagle told me just the other evening. It was a debt that went back several years. Reta was mad about it, upset with her husband for making the loan. She didn't like Hale . . . never trusted him, High Eagle said."

"Why didn't Smith sue Hale?" Davis asked.

"Maybe he was afraid to. Smith was also letting drop around town that he was gathering evidence in Anna Brown's murder. If Hale had a hand in that, it was another reason to kill Smith."

Instructed to check out the Roy Bunch angle in Henry Roan's murder, agents reported that Bunch was in the clear. "And why," Street reasoned, "did Hale offer Bunch money to leave the country? Bunch said Hale was no friend. We found that out, too. Hale had a twenty-five-thousand-dollar life insurance policy on Roan. Hale was covering again. Did he have Roan murdered? In all the Fairfax murders, everything swings back to Bill Hale as the mastermind pulling the strings. . . . Take the Lizzie Q family. From all indications the plan was to kill off Lizzie, who had died under mysterious circumstances, and daughters Anna and Reta so their headrights would go to Mollie Burkhart, in control of husband Ernest. The only time they slipped up was when Bill Smith outlived

Reta and their estate went to his white daughter."

Street said that in October, following Roan's murder in February of 1923, Hale had sought payment as beneficiary of the insurance policy. But Capitol Life refused to pay, contending fraud and misrepresentation. Hale had filed suit in federal court. Agents learned that Roan owed Hale $6,000 on a house in town, but there was no evidence of additional indebtedness approaching $25,000. But Capitol had stood its ground, and Hale was forced to settle out of court for only $2,000. As usual, agents found, Hale had run roughshod. It was extraordinary even in lawless Osage County for white men lending Indians money to take out large life insurance policies to cover far smaller loans. Also, a white man with a legitimate loan could collect on a restricted Indian through the Osage Agency.

Tom White soon saw that the general air of condoned avarice in Osage County hindered the investigation, the white man and his endless tricks, the schemes and rackets practiced behind the respectability of Main Street store fronts and frosted-pane office doors. Encouraged by bankers and merchants and car dealers, Osages were constantly borrowing at interest rates reaching as high as ten percent a quarter. But lenders said Osages were slow to pay, which accounted for the rates. In some stores like the Big Hill, where Hale had an interest, there were white and Indian prices. It required no flexing of the mind to see who paid more. Some 200 guardians held financial control over 500 Indians considered incompetent to handle their own affairs. Strangely many wards became deeper in debt while their so-called guardians prospered.

Other enemies of the tribe wore blue-serge suits, white shirts, and ties, sang in church, and were regarded as pillars of their communities. They had formed the Home Owners Organization, consisting mainly of bankers and guardians and businessmen. All had purchased surplus land on the reservation. They contended that the mineral rights under their holdings belonged to the surface owners, not the tribe. This came at the crucial time the Osages were asking Congress to extend their mineral trust period, which would expire in 1931. The well-heeled HOO employed prominent attorneys to appear at hearings in Pawhuska and Washington to oppose the extension.

"Hell," Frank Smith exclaimed to Tom, "it was just an open attempt to steal the tribe's heritage."

"They didn't get very far," Tom explained. "The Tribal Council adopted a resolution to withdraw all tribal funds from any bank whose officers or directors were active HOO members, fighting the Osages' extension.

Copies went out to guardians and the seven banks in the county with Osage funds on deposit. The Secretary of the Interior and the Commissioner of Indian Affairs were asked to remove any guardian using his influence to prevent the extension. Money talks, as the saying goes. Bankers and guardians said they wouldn't fight the extension, and the Home Owners Organization ceased to function. But if nothing else, the attempted big steal exposed people who up to then had pretended to be friends of the tribe. Instead, the Osages knew they had spoken with a forked tongue. Trouble is these people are still around. You can bet the Bureau will get no co-operation from them."

Hale's dealings with Indians continued to reach agents. One indicated Hale seemed to practice his handwriting expertise with highly profitable results. This instance had come from City Marshal Bob Parker, whom Street and Parker considered a good officer, although handicapped by local apathy and Hale's power in the town. Parker knew Ernest Burkhart, who sometimes confided in the marshal. To Parker, Burkhart was a "good-natured person dominated from early youth by his strong-willed uncle." Burkhart told Parker that Hale had held a $150 note signed by George Bigheart. After Bigheart's death in Oklahoma City, Hale had changed it to $6,150. "Uncle Bill practiced his handwriting until he got it just right," Burkhart had told Parker.

It seemed that the "King of the Osage Hills" could get in touch with outlaws whenever he chose. There was the late, notorious Al Spencer, whose specialty was robbing banks along the Oklahoma-Kansas border, then escaping in fast cars into the hills of the northeastern Osage area. Agents learned that Hale had met the outlaw and tried to hire him "to kill some Fairfax Indians," which fit Henry Roan and Reta Smith. Spencer had refused, saying he didn't mind robbing a bank or train and shooting individuals who tried to stop him. "But damned if I'll murder helpless people for money." Then Hale propositioned other criminals. One was reckless Dick Gregg, now in the Kansas state prison, who likewise had passed up the offer.

But who had blown up the Smith house with such deadly efficiency? Obviously it had required specialized knowledge, a man accustomed to handling the tricky nitro, used in shooting oil wells. No trail pointed to a particular suspect, as in the other murders. Hale had covered his tracks well. Despite the intense work of four veteran agents, the Bureau still lacked evidence for a single murder indictment.

Tom realized the investigation was headed down the same blank road of frustration as before, unless someone talked for the record.

Individuals with possibly important information had "gone up Salt Creek," a euphemism in Fairfax for found dead or missing; others had vanished, reportedly in Mexico.

A change of direction that had been growing in Tom's mind suddenly locked into place: perhaps the break they'd been searching for lay beyond Fairfax and the tough oil-field towns, in the Oklahoma state prison at McAlester, among the band of criminals sent there from Osage County. Time was pressing. The investigation was stalled. It was late December, 1925.

CHAPTER FIVE

Not all the bits of rumor reaching Bureau headquarters were more smoke trails on the wind from the cat-footing, tight-lipped Indian country. One concerned Governor M.E. Trapp who was supposedly considering a parole for Blackie Thompson, the veteran con who had slipped away while in federal custody and taken part in a bank robbery and had brought the first Osage investigation to the brink of scandal. The parole hinged on whether Thompson provided vital information on the murders. Thompson was known as a small-time criminal with Osage County connections. His alibi to state officers after the bank hold-up had been the usual howl of innocence. His pals, of course, had threatened to kill him if he didn't go along.

An established way of operation followed in the Texas Rangers held true here. You stayed on a trail to its very end, no matter how faint or where it led.

"We'll go to McAlester and talk to Thompson," Tom decided. "But, first, we'd better see the governor, hear what he intends to do, or if it's just another rumor."

"I'm for it," Frank agreed. "I'm plumb

wore out with office work and waitin' around for something to break."

Governor Trapp was both cordial and blunt. There could be no clemency for Thompson, the murderer of two men. "He's lucky to get off with his neck and a life sentence." Trapp shook his head. "I don't know where this parole rumor got started. It didn't come from here."

Tom smiled. "We get 'em all the time. But we feel we have to track each one down, if there's a chance it might lead to something."

As the agents left Trapp's office and started out, Parker LaMoore, a former newspaperman and the governor's executive secretary, came over. He grinned at them in such a way that said he knew what the governor had said.

"Wait a minute," he remarked. "We've been getting information from a prisoner at McAlester who claims to know a great deal about the Osage murders. His name is Bert Lawson. Might be a good idea to talk to him when you go down there."

"We'll do that," Tom assured him. "We're much obliged to you."

Next day, in a room off the warden's office at McAlester, the agents waited for Blackie Thompson. Not to sweat a statement from the bandit, but rather to inform him how his chances stood for a parole, always a prime talking point for a beginning.

Thompson entered, a tall, balding, dark, flat-nosed man, with a hard cast to his lean face. His manner was bold, showing utter contempt for the agents. He took a chair, lighted a cigarette, looked Tom in the eye, and snapped: "Well, what do *you* want to know?"

Tom said — "We just came from the governor's office . . . talked to him about your case." — and waited.

Thompson's set features altered a trifle. When a few moments passed and Tom did not elaborate, the outlaw demanded: "Well . . . what did he say?" His tone held a hint of hope.

"We're federal agents," Tom said, "and I'm going to tell you word for word what the governor told us. He said he'd do nothing in the way of a parole for you. Not after that bank robbery and killing. He said you're lucky you didn't get the chair."

Thompson didn't appear concerned as he looked off and took another drag on his cigarette.

"If you don't believe me," Tom said, "get in touch with your wife. We know she's pleaded your case with the governor."

Thompson said nothing.

"The thing for you to do," Tom kept on, "the only thing . . . is to tell the truth and all you know about the Osage murders. Then you'll have something to offer in exchange for clemency. Think that over."

Evidently Thompson was not impressed. He got up and just stood there, looking at the agents without expression.

"We'll run out any leads you give us," Tom said. "If the men involved are convicted, you could ask for consideration with some hope."

Thompson continued to stare, giving no sign.

"Otherwise," Tom said, "in keeping valuable information to yourself, your case is hopeless."

"I'll think about it," Thompson said after a pause. "I'll let you know." He turned and left the room, as bold and cocky as when he had entered.

"A hard one," Frank said. "I bet he could put the finger on the whole Hale outfit."

Tom nodded, thinking ahead, sensing they would be seeing Blackie Thompson again. He was close to what was going on in and around Fairfax. He'd had dealings with Ernest Burkhart. It was believed that he had taken the rap for Burkhart in a stolen car case.

Bert Lawson came in, a middle-aged man, sorry-looking, long hair and low brow, acquitted of murder by a district court jury at Pawhuska in 1923. Whereas Thompson had been close-mouthed, suspicious, and hard, Lawson was grinning friendliness and cooperation. He seemed almost too eager as Tom invited him to sit and talk.

"You bet," Lawson obliged, quickly seating himself and leaning forward, ready for the first question.

"We understand from the governor's office you have information on the Osage murders," Tom began.

Lawson beamed. "I shore do, an' I aim to make a clean breast of ever'thing, I do. Right now . . . here . . . if you say so." He grinned anew. "Say, who are you fellers, anyway?"

"Federal agents."

"Hot feds, huh?" That appeared to please him more than ever.

Tom sat back, studying Lawson. Even Frank, who was seldom surprised by any turn of events, looked remotely at a loss as to how to assess this willing informant.

"Like I been writin' the gov," Lawson said, brimming with enthusiasm, "I want to tell all I know about the case."

"Case?" Frank questioned gruffly. "What case, Lawson? Been more than one Osage murdered up there."

"Why, that house we blowed up in Fairfax. Back there in March of 'Twenty-Three, an' killed them three folks. The Bill Smith house."

"All right," Tom said, his doubt of Lawson's credibility growing. "Tell us the truth, all you know about it. You understand, of course, this can be used against you?"

Lawson's instant jerk of his head said he did. "I shore do, but I don't care. Hit's been preyin' on my mind. Can't sleep nights no more. Guilty conscience, I reckon."

While Tom asked questions and Frank took down the confession, Lawson, who kept referring to the agents as "hot feds," recited a rambling, disconnected story. He told them of being held in the Osage County jail at Pawhuska, charged with murdering a fisherman near Hominy. One night, he said, a deputy sheriff came to his cell and led him to the office where a man waited. "Go with that man," Lawson said the deputy had ordered, and the man was Bill Hale. They left Pawhuska in Hale's curtained car. Lawson claimed Hale made him a proposition: set off the bomb in the Smith house, then Lawson's confession, in the county attorney's office, would be destroyed and Lawson acquitted. All neat and tidy, it seemed.

Lawson said he had agreed to the deal, lighted the fuse that exploded the bomb, and was returned to the jail at 3 A.M. And, he went on, his confession was stolen and the charge against him quashed. The man who had stolen the confession was murdered soon after that. He claimed that Ernest Burkhart's home in Fairfax was used as the base of operations, and, he said, Hale had provided the nitro.

"How much did Hale pay you?" Tom asked.

"Oh, Hale promised plenty. He shore did. Five thousand dollars." But later Hale beat him out of his "wage," which was another reason why he was talking to the hot feds, to get back at Hale. "That's how she happened," Lawson concluded cheerfully, after signing his confession. "I feel better gittin' it off my chest to you hot feds. I shore do, now."

Both agents were extremely thoughtful after Lawson, still chirping his willingness to cooperate with hot feds, was returned to his cell.

Tom saw at least three glaring weaknesses in Lawson's purported confession. First, Lawson wasn't capable of handling the dangerous nitro, which was known to go off when jarred. Sometimes light trucks, although especially fitted to transport the stuff, blew up in the oil fields on the rough roads. Neither was Hale capable. Also, it would have been out of character for Hale, whose style of operation was to get others to do his dirty work. His hands were always ostensibly clean. The Smith job had required an experienced well shooter. Second, the house was blown up at 3 A.M., the hour when Lawson said Hale drove him back to the Osage County jail. Last, Lawson was an ignorant, shiftless sort who had bummed around the Osage towns and ranches, hardly the loose-mouthed type Hale would hire to carry out a killing.

Nevertheless, for the first time, the Bureau had a confession sworn to and signed. Moreover, it was all the team of agents had to go on, and time was a factor.

"Never saw a man so eager to go to the electric chair," Frank said skeptically. "What do you think?"

"I doubt at least part of his story, but it's a start."

Still weighing Lawson's astonishing account, they started driving back to Oklahoma City.

After a while, Tom remarked: "Lawson reminds me of a hog thief who wants out of jail."

"Maybe he knows we can't prove anything on him," Frank said. "Maybe he's just repeating what he's heard other inmates say. Or took his cue from Blackie Thompson, when Thompson was paroled the first time. But I'm convinced of one thing. There's a regular pipeline of information running straight from Osage County to the state pen."

They drove on a distance, not speaking, wrapped in thought, until Frank Smith said in his direct way: "Tom, what do you figure on doing with that confession?"

"File on Lawson, Hale, and Burkhart . . . for murder."

CHAPTER SIX

January 4, 1926. For years the "King of the Osage Hills" had operated as he pleased, building an empire of land and cattle, playing politics, cheating Indians, seeking out hirelings among the county's criminal element, increasing his business interests around Fairfax and elsewhere, strewing his charitable acts for many to witness first-hand, or to be grateful recipients, or to hear about and to remember and talk about later.

On this day Bill Hale was in busy downtown Pawhuska, chatting with George V. Labadie, a young Osage attorney, when the afternoon edition of the Tulsa *Tribune* reached the streets. There was a whir of excitement, voices, bystanders staring in the direction of the county's best-known citizen.

Hale bought a paper, and his eyes jerked to a black-bannered story carrying a Pawhuska dateline: "Information charging W.K. Hale, of Fairfax, 'King of the Osage Hills,' Ernest Burkhart, W.A. Boyd, former Osage County deputy sheriff, and Bert Lawson, prisoner at McAlester, with the slaying of W.E. Smith, March 10, 1923, was filed by the attorney general's office here today. The four defendants were accused of having 'joined together to murder Smith, his wife, and a hired girl'." Boyd, believed to be living in Oklahoma City, was the former deputy Lawson alleged had released him from the Osage County jail to blow up the Smith house.

Tom White and Frank Smith had not delayed after returning to Oklahoma City from the state penitentiary. Presenting Lawson's confession and other suspicious information to Roy St. Lewis, newly named U.S. attorney for the western district, they were authorized to file complaints with the U.S. commissioner at Guthrie. Warrants went out to Osage County. Agents Parker and Davis and three deputy U.S. marshals left Tulsa with more than one hundred subpoenas for Indians and whites in Osage County. Roy Bunch was taken into custody for further questioning.

Hale appeared unshaken at the afternoon news. "Guess I'd better see what this is all about," he remarked to Labadie, stepped to his car, and drove up the hill to the county courthouse. Still showing no outward concern, he walked boldly into the office of Sheriff H.M. Freas and nodded all around. "Understand I'm wanted . . . thought I'd save you the trouble."

Freas offered his hand before passing Hale the warrant, a wise political protocol in case Hale went free. After thoughtfully reading the warrant, Hale said: "I was expecting this."

Federal and state officers had left Pawhuska earlier to arrest Hale and Burkhart, but the cowman had evaded them. A man of vast pride, Hale had got wind of his approaching comedown and ducked out of town and drove to Pawhuska. It looked better for a man of his standing to give himself up than to be arrested like a common criminal.

Hale asked that his Pawhuska attorneys be summoned, then he was arraigned before County Judge J.A. Justus and ordered held without bond. As Hale was leaving the courtroom, U.S. marshals entered with Burkhart, arrested in Fairfax by City Marshal Bob Parker and Deputy Sheriff Smith Leahy. The search for Burkhart had been uneventful and brief. Officers found him in McInroy's Pool Hall, which Parker called "that breeding place."

There was no let-up. That night, under heavy guard, Hale and Burkhart were transported in cars to Guthrie and jailed. Such swift action cost Agent Charlie Davis a sale. He was close to selling Hale a life insurance policy when Hale was arrested for murder.

What's this? Bill Hale arrested for murder, in jail at Guthrie? Astonished Osage County residents found it hard to believe their newspapers. Those who had benefited in gifts and other favors angrily voiced their loyalty in cow-country language. Just what the hell was goin' on? What did the god-damned federal guv'mint mean comin' in here, placin' Bill Hale under arrest for the Smith murders? Wasn't he the biggest-hearted man in the Osage? Wasn't he good to old folks and young alike? Everybody knew that. By God, Osage County could handle its own affairs without any interference from Washington. Well, Bill Hale is a mighty big man. I've knowed him for years. He'll come clear. You can bet on that!

Squawman Ernest Burkhart was accorded few such laments. He wasn't as well liked in Fairfax as his genial, publicly generous uncle, far from it. He ran with a whisky-drinking crowd of bad reputation. If he wasn't wheeling around in Mollie's big car, he was loafing at McInroy's. He made no pretense of working, hadn't since driving a taxi before he married Mollie, and picked his teeth with a gold toothpick. If Bill Hale was really in trouble, it must be because he'd tried to help his two worthless nephews, Ernest and Bryan, Hale sympathizers said.

With the case looming like a sensational trial, the Tulsa *Tribune* sent a reporter to Fairfax to feel the public pulse.

"Why, Bill Hale stood right here," said Homer Huffaker, president of the First National Bank, "and gave five hundred dollars to the Baptist Church when they came around with their list. And he's always been for law and order, a mighty good man who loves his family and home."

Another big splash for others to see and hear about said residents who asked to remain anonymous. Be hard to convict Hale in Osage County, they pointed out. It only took one to hang a jury.

"It looks a whole lot like Hale was mixed up in it," Roy Jennes, a special federal enforcement officer whose main pursuit was to catch bootleggers, told the *Tribune*. "None of the rest of the bunch had enough sense to plan the thing."

Other Fairfax citizens were of the opinion that "hophead" Kelsey Morrison, not Lawson, had planted the explosive or bomb.

Another man said: "Hale was this way . . . he was well liked by his friends and hated by his enemies, and he had plenty of both."

A neighbor of Hale's played it safe. "I don't know a thing. I'm ignorant of the whole business."

To persons who had reason to fear Hale — and Agent Charles Davis while spreading the benefits of life insurance during such dangerous times had discovered a rather surprising number — Hale's arrest came as a big surprise. Bill Hale had run roughshod for years. Nobody bucked him in Fairfax. After the first feeling of elation that justice had finally come to the crime-ridden Osage, a reminding caution followed. Hale, with his money, would hire the sharpest legal minds in Oklahoma. Therefore, it wasn't wise to come out in the open yet. If you testified against him and the charge didn't stick . . . well, a man's life might be in danger.

Agents had heard of Hale's brag to Ernest Burkhart — "I've got everybody fixed from a road supervisor to the governor." — and Burkhart had grinned and passed the remark on to Marshal Bob Parker. Hale and Henry Grammer had attended as invited guests Governor Jack Walton's inaugural barbecue, the biggest ever staged in Oklahoma.

Agent John Wren reported that Osages were astonished at Hale's arrest, particularly the old tribesmen. To these generous people, friendship had special importance; they admired generosity in others. On occasions when the tribe had welcomed home a young man from the Great War, Hale would contribute a fat beef for the ensuing feast and was regarded as a great friend of the tribe.

But not to old Newalla, who happened to be talking to a friend downtown when Hale drove by. "Son-o'-bitch, my friend, I don't like Bill Hale," the old Osage complained.

"But he's a friend to us Indians. Why don't you like him?"

"Three times he steal my cow. Three times me buy cow back. Son-o'-bitch, my friend, I don't like Bill Hale." Then old Newalla took a cautious look around. "But don't you tol' him!"

"Don't you tol' him!" became a grimly humorous byword in Fairfax.

Ever in the public eye, Hale was known to shower handfuls of silver on groups of children. Agents heard a young woman say that as a child: "There was nobody I'd rather see comin' down the street than Bill Hale."

At Henry Roan's funeral, Hale had been one of the two leaders who walked ahead of the pallbearers. After the services, he shook hands all around, and the Osages, reminded of the generous days of old, had loaded Hale's Buick with bright, beautiful blankets and other gifts. However, some Indians said his place of honor was self-appointed, that Mary Roan had not asked him to be a leader, but, they agreed, it would have been embarrassing to cause a fuss at a funeral and deny him the honor. So he got away with it.

It wasn't known that anyone beyond his hometown had ever taken a shot at Hale or confronted him physically. If he packed a gun, he didn't show it. Apparently few men had the nerve to go against him. An exception was Norris Watkins, Pawhuska rancher. He swore out a warrant charging Hale with the theft of two heifer calves marked with Watkins's brand. The case got no further than the first spittoon court. G.W. Hargis, Pawhuska justice of the peace, released Hale from the charge following a preliminary hearing and dismissed the matter.

"Hargis," the Pawhuska *Journal-Capital* reported September 8, 1921, "held that while Watkins may have lost the calves in question, there was no evidence to indicate Hale had taken them."

Hale had said nothing.

Agents Street and Parker, making the rounds of the cow camps and ranches as prospective cattle buyers, while doing more listening than talking, picked up the trail of another range shenanigan, reporting: Hale insured a 30,000-acre tract for one dollar an acre, then one night had his cowboys set fire to the grass. Records of the northern U.S. District Court, Tulsa, showed that *William K. Hale vs. Hartford Insurance Company* was "dismissed with prejudice," meaning the case could not be refiled.

Agents dug into Hale's background, looking for leads that might throw additional light on the man whose dominating shadow lay across the town. What was his story, his rise from a Texas cowboy to the most powerful man in Osage County?

William King Hale was born in the country near Greenville, Texas, December 24, 1874. He left home at sixteen to become a West Texas cowboy. Apparently he made friends easily. At eighteen he drifted north to southwestern Oklahoma and rode for a big outfit running cattle on the Kiowa-Comanche Reservation. After a year, he went back to Texas where he made his first real money, handling cattle at age twenty-three.

Trailing north again, he spent two years in the Kiowa-Comanche country. There he learned valuable insights into Indian nature, such as the love of ceremony and how to go about leasing Indian grazing land, business experience that would prepare him for his venture into the Osage. In 1902 he made arrangements to handle 2,000 head of cattle on the reservation. While in Texas, he married Myrtle Fry, a pretty schoolteacher.

For one year in the Osage they boarded with a ranch family, then returned to Texas to spend the winter while Hale fed cattle. Next spring the Hales returned to the Osage and lived in a tent during the grazing season. That year he found himself $10,000 in debt after selling a home in Texas to help meet obligations.

He began to lease land, first taking up 600 acres east of Gray Horse. During the fall of 1905 he was hired as superintendent and manager of a large ranch. Two more years and Hale was on his own. When the surface rights of Osage land were put up for sale, he entered into a partnership with two prominent bankers. Hale, the story went, never had a written contract with his partners. Those were times when a man's word was contract enough, satisfactory as long as all parties hewed to the marrow of honesty, one in which a white man could fend for himself better than a trusting Osage, uninformed about figures and values and the white man's slick methods.

"I never pretended to keep any set of books on my business," Hale once testified proudly. "Most of it was carried in my head, or sometimes I'd make a little memorandum."

Bill Hale rode late. He was often away from home on deals. He worked when less successful, resourceful men slept or played. He swapped with the shrewdness of a traveling horse trader. It was said he took his losses with a laugh, but he didn't take many. He followed the cattle business and farmed on a small scale. It was not unusual, in the early days, to see him at night, horseback, or driving his Buick. He always drove Buicks, usually a roadster. A rancher signing up leases had to keep odd hours.

By January, 1926, W.K. Hale stood on the highest peak of his career financially, popularly, politically. By means of leases he controlled some 45,000 acres of select pasture and had acquired 5,000 acres outright of beautiful, rolling blue-stem grassland considered by many cowmen to be the finest for cattle-grazing in the nation. In addition, agents learned, Hale had built up a fortune of $200,000 or more in cash reserves. He also had an interest in the First National

Bank of Fairfax and the Big Hill Trading Company, the town's largest general store, and the Big Hill Funeral Parlor.

Hale had sound reason to feel confident about himself. As the U.S. Bureau of Investigation of the Department of Justice was about to learn, he had many staunch and powerful friends. He was a Scottish Rite Mason, a member of the Guthrie Temple, the Fairfax Blue Lodge, an Elk, and a Shriner, holding membership in Akdar Temple, Tulsa. He was a leading Democrat in a section of the state where Republicans were nearly as scarce as buffalo. It was said that he ran Fairfax and that, as long as he did, Negroes never lived within the city limits. Mrs. Hale and their daughter, Willie, were members of the First Baptist Church. Myrtle Hale was regarded as a fine woman. Pretty Willie was popular with many friends.

Hale owned a ranch near Gray Horse and a modest home in Fairfax. Neighbors would notice that he had the habit of precaution by immediately drawing the blinds when he entered the house. After Hale was charged, townsmen recalled, he would stand without turning his back to the door when talking to someone in a store. Agents saw him as a transitional figure between the vanishing frontier and Oklahoma in the 1920s, turned hell-bent and slam-bang by the booming oil fields. To his old-time rancher friends he represented their ideals and stood as an example of the Western tradition of helping your neighbor.

One summer drought had burned the Osage ranges. Water holes and tanks dried up. Creeks fell low. A neighbor of Hale's was in poor shape for grass and water. Hale, in a more fortunate situation, told the rancher to turn his stock into one of Hale's pastures along Salt Creek. He refused to be reimbursed for the large favor.

"I've got more water than I can use right now," he had said.

There came a season when the circumstances were reversed. Hale, heavily stocked, needed pasture. His neighbor, in turn, insisted on making his grass and water available to Hale, who accepted. When he moved his cattle out later, he rode over to settle up his range bill.

"Believe it's the other way around," the rancher had told him. "I still owe you, Bill. I turned more cattle in on you that time."

Hale had shaken his head. "You don't owe me a dime."

Long ago he had sensed that a man he relied on might not stand hitched under pressure, and he could find himself in court someday. Would his many well-known acts of generosity, which had given him much power and prestige over the years and placed many individuals under obligation to him, be an unbreakable shield against his accusers? He knew Westerners were a loyal breed, slow to turn on one of their own, particularly a generous man, and further favorable to him were the have-nots, who worked for the big cow outfits or rented small places or scraped out a living farming along the lower reaches of the Arkansas River, or held modest jobs in town. People far down the economic scale resented the rich Osages and their extravagance, and by some hangover of frontier thinking a dead Indian did not seem as important as a dead white man. *It took only one to hang a jury.*

CHAPTER SEVEN

Hale and Burkhart were in federal custody, whisked out of Hale's bailiwick, but the pressure of proof came now in increasing force against Tom White as agent-in-charge and the investigating team as the scene shifted to Guthrie. Immediately after Burkhart arrived, Tom decided to start questioning him for stronger evidence. Shaky as Bert Lawson's account was of the Smith house explosion, it seemed to contain elements of truth. Of the two suspects, Tom and Frank Smith agreed that only Burkhart might talk. Hale's decidedly strong character and bold front indicated the cowman would make a full denial, regardless of the evidence.

Just before Burkhart was escorted in from the Guthrie city jail, Frank broached the question of whether Lawson's confession should be disclosed to the Osage squawman. "I'm afraid," he said, scowling, "Burkhart will say Lawson's tale is all jailhouse blow and that Burkhart can prove it."

"Maybe so," Tom said, "but it's still all we have to go on."

Then there was Hale's iron-clad alibi that he was out of town, in Fort Worth, attending the Fat Stock Show with Henry Grammer at the time of the explosion. It was known around town that Lou Oller, Hale's crony, had sent a telegram next day to Hale at Campbell, Texas. Now Lawson's story hung by a thread. Why had Oller sent the telegram? It was such a terrible tragedy, he said, exhibiting a long face, he thought his friend Bill Hale should be informed as the town's leading citizen.

Another report, unverified, was that Oller had wired Hale the day before the explosion. Did that mean he had known in advance what was coming? And why, Tom and Frank reasoned, had Hale gone to the Fat Stock Show, which he had not attended since, to establish an alibi? Suddenly the answer seemed to jump out at them: *because Hale knew the house would be blown up that particular night on March 10th, when he was out of town.*

Burkhart was jumpy, his movements nervous, quick, jerky, when he entered the room. He struck Tom as a small-town dandy, well-dressed in a Western way, expensive cowboy boots, loud shirt, flashy tie, and an expensive-looking tailored suit. Ernest Burkhart was thirty-four years old, round-faced and blond, with a heavy jaw, a fairly good-looking, sturdily proportioned man of medium build. Tom gained a deeper impression of him right away. Burkhart was a weak sister, which helped account for Hale's domination of his nephew.

Tom opened the questioning: "We want to talk to you about the murder of Bill Smith's family and Anna Brown."

"Hell, I don't know a thing about it!" Burkhart shot back.

"We've talked to Bert Lawson, in the pen at McAlester. He says you know a great deal about both cases."

"I don't know this Bert Lawson. Never heard of him."

"He says you were the contact man in setting up the Smith house explosion." Another loose bit Lawson had asserted in his rambling account.

"He's lying!"

"He says your home was used as the base of operations."

Burkhart also denied that.

"My advice to you is to tell it all . . . tell the truth."

"There's nothing to tell."

The examination continued as both agents questioned Burkhart, following the Bureau's rule of no threats or use of force. Burkhart firmly denied any connection in the case, politely turning aside all implications, explicitly refuting Lawson at every turn. Tom offered Burkhart no inducements, no immunity.

It was early morning when Tom broke off the interrogation and sent Burkhart back to his cell. Before that the agents had become aware that Lawson's confession, particularly his asserted rôle of being freed from jail to blow up the Smith house, was pure fabrication, evidently given in hope of gaining temporary release from prison. He'd heard just enough at "Big Mac," tuned in to what Frank Smith called a "pipeline of information" from the Osage, to make up a story that, on the surface, appeared to contain factual evidence.

Meanwhile, Bill Hale had entered the Logan County jail in amused and lordly fashion, the two agents heard, joking over the absurdity of charging him with murdering Bill and Reta Smith and that hired girl, and expressing his opinion of how dumb these federal birds are. An enterprising reporter from the Guthrie *Leader* described the cowman as "obviously unnerved by the events of the day, although he tried desperately to cover up his uneasiness."

Hale told the reporter he had no statement to make, did not want to "try my case in the newspapers."

"How old are you?"

"I'm fifty-one years of age."

"How long have you been in Oklahoma?"

"Twenty-five years, more or less."

"Have a large number of friends?"

"I think so."

"Wouldn't they like to have a statement

from you, even though you merely say . . . 'I'm innocent'?"

"I'll try my case in the courts, not in the newspapers. Cold night, isn't it?"

"Hale paced before the fire," the reporter wrote. "He nervously rubbed his hands. His ruddy face was aglow with cold and excitement. There is nothing to denote Hale as a cattleman. The sombrero, roweled spurs, boots, etc., that one might expect of the 'King of the Osage Hills' give way to a neatly pressed suit, nicely shined shoes, a brown and fashionably plaid overcoat, a neat felt hat and horn-rimmed spectacles. A diamond-studded lodge pin adorns his lapel and is the only show of wealth he is alleged to possess."

As for Hale's being "obviously unnerved," and trying "desperately to cover up his uneasiness," the press would not catch him in that unready state again as Oklahoma's most sensational murder case began to unfold. Thereafter, reporters would comment on his "iron nerve" and confident bearing.

For the time being, Hale was left to reflect on what evidence the federal government might have against him. He knew that he had covered his back trail well. He took satisfaction in that.

Tom did not think Hale would talk now. Better to let the pressure build. Give him time to think about the charge against him.

Let him stew a while. But Burkhart's silence was stalling the investigation. To break the stalemate, Tom saw Governor Trapp the following day.

"We need to have Blackie Thompson brought to Guthrie," Tom explained. "See if he can persuade Burkhart to loosen up. It is our understanding that Thompson took the rap one time for Burkhart over a stolen car."

The governor agreed to have Thompson rushed to Guthrie under heavy guard.

Meanwhile, Bert Lawson was visibly enjoying his rôle as an informant and treating himself at government expense. Three times daily he was dining on steak, French fries, having double helpings of pie and ice cream, and entertaining agents with his comical, bumpkin ways, which steadily diluted confidence in his eager confession.

Some 160 persons, served subpoenas in Oklahoma's northern district, were filling Guthrie's hotels preparatory to appearing before the federal grand jury being empanelled. Seventy came from Fairfax alone, a cross-section of Osage Indians, ranchmen, bankers, clerks, Fairfax and county officers.

State newspapers watched closely. The Tulsa *World* noted: "There are Indian squaws in their blankets, old braves in their robes and with their braided hair, young braves dressed like American sheiks, and gentle Indian girls who have learned the art of using paint, powder, and lipstick."

Tempers in Osage County, already touchy over the investigation, flared again when the Tulsa *Tribune* editorialized: ". . . in the final analysis, the people of Osage County get the kind of government they stand for . . . and in some of the years just passed they haven't demanded a very high quality. Osage County has to be cleaned up. In its wild and woolly state, it is a disgrace to the State of Oklahoma and a menace to Tulsa. No Tulsa oil or business firms want to try lawsuits there. It isn't because the judges are crooked, because they are not. It is because of the temper of the people themselves. Many of the men who go to Pawhuska and other court towns in that vast county to serve on juries do not see eye to eye with most reasonable people in the matter of law enforcement and justice. What has been a crime everywhere else has been passed over in the Osage." The *Tribune* called for Osage County's "better element" to assert itself.

Angry Pawhuska city commissioners passed a resolution condemning the editorial as false. Pawhuska was also the site of the Osage Agency and a mecca for shady lawyers feeding off Indian affairs. Fairfax was too excited over what might happen to its leading citizen and Ernest Burkhart to make public refutations.

A tense air of impending action pervaded

Guthrie, once Oklahoma's capital. Strangers thronged the streets and smoky hotel lobbies. Men clustered in small groups or sat silently apart. An Indian woman sat in the lobby of the Hotel Ione and pointed out relatives of more than twenty Osages who had been murdered or had died of mysterious causes. Rumors fueled the tension. Agents heard Indian witnesses were being fed rotgut whisky. Other witnesses were threatened, warned to "talk right." Loud-talking, booted men not on the subpoena list stalked the crowded lobbies, openly proclaimed themselves friends of Bill Hale, and boasted of running all government men plumb out of Oklahoma.

One persistent voice was that of rancher Lou Oller, who had sent the "alibi telegram" to Hale in Texas. Oller liked to brag in public of his exploits as a gunslinger on the old frontier. Agents had wondered whether the telegram, besides proving Hale was out of town, knowing in advance when the Smith house would be blown up, was just a matter-of-fact confirmation that the horrific deed had been carried out. Reports of what Oller intended to do to certain agents, which would be calamity aplenty, kept reaching the Texans, and Tom White had difficulty restraining his men.

"Let Hale's friends shoot the air," Tom said. "Don't engage in any public row. It's obvious that he's sent word out for 'em to come in here and throw fear into grand jury witnesses."

Agent Alex Street bristled under the threats, stood them, and tried to avoid a confrontation and did until entering the lobby of the Ione where he heard a loud voice mouthing familiar reprisals. It was Oller again, talking big and tough, around him a knot of avid listeners. They turned watchful as Street paused. Oller's voice grew louder, and he laid a hard stare on Street as if to frighten him.

All at once Street's control snapped. He wheeled, pitching his .45 automatic on a sofa, and strode across to Oller, his boot heels striking deliberate taps. He said — "Lou, I understand you've been talking about us . . . now let's see how salty you are." — and caught Oller's nose, twisted hard, and stepped back, waiting.

Oller's face was crimson. He wiped at his smarting nose.

"Let's go to the alley," Street challenged, his voice crowding Oller for action. "Come on!"

"You're all wrong," Oller said. "I wasn't talkin' about you boys."

Street hopefully watched the face of Hale's man for a stretched-out moment. When Oller said nothing more and made no move, Street closed in, searched Oller, and found a loaded six-shooter. He unloaded the gun and returned it. No more was said. The crowd faded away. Oller never threatened the agents again. Hereafter, the threats would be hurled in court by Hale's formidable array of high-priced attorneys.

State officers had Blackie Thompson in Guthrie the evening after Tom's morning conference with Governor Trapp. Tom was waiting. He and Frank Smith decided to question Burkhart again that night. Thompson, with two life sentences against him, had agreed at McAlester to assist if Burkhart balked again.

Once more the two agents waited in the room where they had questioned Burkhart the previous night, the jury room on the third floor of the federal building. To Tom it was not unlike rehearsing an old act when the suspect came in, his same flashy clothes looking slept in, his fleshy features bearing the same innocent look of inquiry.

"We're not satisfied with the answers you gave us," Tom began. "We believe there's a good deal you didn't tell us."

Burkhart was very polite, still nervous. "All I know is what's common talk in Fairfax. I told you the rumor somebody was after the Smiths' diamonds."

Tom fixed him a look. "Blow up the house to get the diamonds? When they could've been robbed? Come on. Get down to the truth."

"Yes," Frank followed up, "tell us about your uncle hiring the job done and the men who did it."

Burkhart looked uneasy, but his reply was calm. "You're liable to hear anything in Fairfax. Everybody seems to have a different idea who did it."

"We didn't hear about Bill Hale in Fairfax. Bert Lawson told us."

"That Lawson's full of bull."

They talked on, Burkhart continuing the polite front of total ignorance, insisting he possessed no information relative to the Smith murders. An hour or more passed. The agents didn't gain a single new lead. Burkhart, it was evident, had no intention of spilling anything except generalities that could be heard six days a week at McInroy's Pool Hall.

Stumped, the agents left Burkhart under guard while they went to where Thompson was being held.

"We're not getting anywhere with Burkhart," Tom informed the convict. "Think you can talk him into telling us the truth about the Smith murders?"

Thompson's black eyes glittered with anticipation. "Listen, just give me three minutes with that guy . . . alone . . . and I'll make him tell it all!"

Tom checked him. "We won't let you third-degree him or beat it out of him. You understand that?" A pause followed. "You clear on that?" Tom insisted.

One corner of the dark, flat-nosed man's mouth curled. He seemed amused that the agents would show concern for a suspect's welfare. Then he said: "Don't worry. I'll just talk it out of him."

But not yet. Before Thompson was allowed to see Burkhart, armed agents and state officers were posted at vantage points. One man took position on the roof where he could look into the jury room. Besides seeing that Burkhart was not mistreated, there was the necessity of maximum security for Thompson, a slippery escape artist.

Thompson's manner was confident when he stepped into the room. Agents left the door ajar to observe the pair from the hall, to protect Burkhart and to watch Thompson's movements.

Thompson started talking, his tone positive. Burkhart's voice was lower, and neither voice was distinct enough to be understood in the hall. Agents caught a sudden gush of talk — Thompson's voice — then silence on Burkhart's part, as if he pondered something. Now their voices rose and fell, no let-up, both men speaking directly to each other, not unlike friends. Certainly they knew each other well, Tom thought. The agent's hopes rose.

Thompson said his piece in a short time,

looking toward the doorway when he had finished. Two agents escorted him out.

Tom and Frank resumed the questioning, feeling hopeful. But Burkhart hadn't broken. "I don't know a thing you want," he shot back. Still, Tom thought, he was beginning to show signs of worry, more than before.

Now Tom, then Frank, persisted with the old, worn questions. Bill Hale. What was Burkhart's rôle in the explosion? Hale? Hale? Why did he want the Smiths murdered? Was it because Hale owed Bill Smith money and refused to pay? Had an oil field worker named Ace Kirby, now dead, played a hand in this? Had he handled the nitro? Kirby's name had surfaced just lately, thanks to Alex Street and Gene Parker making the oil boom towns.

Hale? Hale? Wasn't he the mastermind behind all the Osage murders around Fairfax? Tell us and clear your conscience, Ernest. You don't have to share your uncle's blame. Frank's queries were gruff, nettling to Burkhart. Tom's were as persistent, but soft-spoken. Burkhart kept parrying, pleading lack of knowing anything, stiffening up whenever his uncle was mentioned, showing a mixture of fear and dread.

Around midnight Tom and Frank left several agents with Burkhart and retired to their hotel rooms for a few hours of needed sleep, Tom feeling a heavy discouragement. He had counted on hardened Blackie Thompson to unlock Burkhart's tongue, but Thompson had failed. Maybe he'd been too tough. They had all failed on this frustrating night. Burkhart was afraid to talk, deathly afraid of his domineering uncle. Tom figured it had been that way for many years.

Tom had no more than dozed off when the ringing telephone routed him out of bed.

An agent spoke rapidly, urgently: "Burkhart's ready to tell his story. But he won't give it to us. Says it's got to be you."

CHAPTER EIGHT

Tom saw the backbone, the pose of innocence, had gone out of Burkhart entirely. His
somewhat fleshy, good-looking face was slack,
his shoulders slumped, his head down. He
glanced up when Tom and Frank entered, a
resigned look, yet one of release. He had lost
some of his nervousness and fear. Actually he
seemed glad to see the agents.

"I want to tell the whole story to you," he
said, speaking to Tom without hesitation.
"Get it over with."

Painstakingly, as if searching his mind for
the exact beginning, Burkhart began by
bringing in Ace Kirby's name.

That was too much for Frank. He heaved
to his feet, snorted. "Now he's gonna tell us
all about dead men." He stalked out, dis-
gusted, leaving Tom alone with the prisoner.

Tom settled down to an unhurried visit,
just chatting, letting Burkhart take his time,
gather his thoughts, and choose his own
starting point.

Frank glanced in presently and returned to
the table. Tom nodded at him, knowing his
partner wasn't about to miss this.

Directly Burkhart found his voice again.

While Tom asked a question now and then, Frank wrote. Burkhart talked steadily. But it wasn't about dead Osages. He talked in a reminiscent vein of his boyhood in Texas, spent in the vicinity of Greenville, living there until he was twenty years old, when he moved to the Osage. Hale, his uncle by blood, being a brother to Burkhart's mother, often had been around the Burkhart home in Texas. A closer association was formed between uncle and nephew in Indian country. He became Hale's constant companion and a great admirer of Hale, then a small rancher stealing cattle and defrauding Indians in various ways, Burkhart said, while denying that he had participated in any of the deals.

"I relied on Uncle Bill's judgment in everything," Burkhart said, his speech coming faster. "About a year before the Smith house blow-up, he started to abuse and ride Bill Smith hard. Smith was after Uncle Bill to pay him a six-thousand-dollar debt. Smith hounded him about it, besides accusin' him of responsibility in Anna Brown's death. It got worse between them, and Uncle Bill told me he was gonna have Bill Smith killed. Blow up his house."

An argument developed, Burkhart said, between him and his uncle when Burkhart pointed out an explosion that powerful would kill Reta and others in the Smith household. Hale, Burkhart continued, had said: "What do you care? Mollie, your wife, will fall heir to Reta's fortune."

"Bill and Reta have already made a will. Their estate would go to somebody else."

"Hell, we'll break the will," Hale had assured him, "and you needn't feel uneasy. You and Mollie will get the money."

Burkhart went on, saying his uncle had masterminded the plot and persuaded him to approach Curly Johnson, bootlegger and Whizbang gambler, and Blackie Thompson to blow up the house. Both refused. After that, Hale proposed the killings to outlaws Al Spencer, Dick Gregg, and John Mayo. Each turned down the proposition for the same reason. "They said it wasn't their style, and there were too many complications. Gregg said he'd rather shoot it out with a man, that explosives 'ain't my tools'."

Tom knew from reports by Street and Parker that Johnson had died mysteriously after the triple murders in March, 1923, presumably of poisoned whisky. A posse had gunned down Spencer, Osage County's front-page bandit, in September the same year, conveniently silencing another person privy to the plot. Gregg and Mayo were tucked away in Kansas state prison. It was wryly interesting to Tom that Hale would contact outlaws at his pleasure. He had been obsessed with murdering the Smiths.

Hale, his nephew related, finally secured

Ace Kirby, a nitro expert, for the job and hired Ramsey to assist Kirby. Questioned about his own rôle, Burkhart said his consisted only of driving Bill Hale's red Buick roadster from Fairfax to Ripley to tell John Ramsey to tell Ace Kirby to do the job, that Uncle Bill, who was at a Fort Worth cattlemen's convention with Henry Grammer, wanted the job done while he was out of town.

As the story took shape, an awareness traveled through Tom's mind, growing clearer by the minute: garrulous, steak-eating Bert Lawson's self-important version was pure fiction. Lawson hadn't even named Kirby or Ramsey, the latter the number two man on the Smith job. Another fact stood out the longer Burkhart talked. It was evident in the uneasy eyes, in the jerky tone of the defeated voice when he mentioned Uncle Bill. Ernest Burkhart was deathly afraid of Bill Hale, afraid for his life now, although he continued to go on with his case-breaking confession.

Burkhart's voice pinched off after a while. A rather odd and knowing expression worked along his mouth, ending in a twisted smile that really wasn't a smile.

"Now you don't believe me," he said to Tom, "because Ace Kirby's dead and Henry Grammer's dead, do you?"

"Why should we?"

"For one thing, you've got another inno-

cent man in jail besides Bert Lawson. I mean
Roy Bunch. If you'll get John Ramsey in
here, he can tell you who killed Henry Roan
. . . because he done it for Uncle Bill."

Tom and Frank traded swift looks.

"Tell us all about it, Ernest," Tom said.

Early in 1923, Burkhart said, he and Hale
had driven to Grammer's ranch, and there
Burkhart had seen Grammer and Hale
talking aside to Ramsey. Driving off later,
Hale had nodded in Ramsey's direction and
commented: "There's a man who's all right,
and you can depend on him. He'll do anything for money. Took a fall for Grammer
some time years back in a cattle-stealing
case."

Burkhart said he understood Grammer had
paid Ramsey $1,000 to serve a term for him
in the Oklahoma penitentiary. There was no
let-up now as Burkhart seemed eager to
spill it all and free himself of the past.
Hale, he said, had taken out a $25,000 life
insurance policy on Roan, with Hale the
beneficiary. Uncle Bill had expressed worry
that Roan, a heavy drinker having family
trouble, might commit suicide before the
policy was a year old, nullifying the payoff.

Ramsey showed up in Fairfax not many
days after the meeting at Grammer's ranch.
He had confided to Burkhart — "I'm gonna
kill an Osage for Bill Hale." — who had
promised him a new Ford automobile and

$500 for the murder. Sometime in February, Burkhart said, Ramsey had told him in Fairfax that he had done the killing.

Hale, too, confirmed that Ramsey had carried out the Roan murder, then asked his nephew if he knew Ramsey's whereabouts.

"Went home to Ripley," Burkhart had told him.

Hale had frowned at that, disapproving. Burkhart had said: "Wrong thing to do. Somebody might suspect him of the killing."

In the eyes of his nephew, however, Hale never worried. He was always confident. "I've got the state and federal authorities fixed," he'd brag, although he never got down to specifics. Burkhart said he'd heard his uncle make those statements, and Burkhart had believed him, for Bill Hale had run the Osage for a long time.

That wasn't all. Burkhart went on. Hale, a supposed friend of Roan's, was a pallbearer at the funeral. Ramsey was also there, pretending to be deeply moved. Hale had leased Roan's grazing land for a song, loaned him money at usurious interest rates, a common practice in the Osage. Commission of the W.E. Smith crime had cost his uncle $2,000. Ramsey had since moved from Ripley to a farm near Fairfax.

Most of the night had slipped away when Burkhart's confession ran out, made voluntarily and without force. After signing it,

Burkhart loosened up even more and implicated Kelsey Morrison, now a prisoner at McAlester, in the murder of Anna Brown, found May 27, 1921, north of Gray Horse in Three-Mile Cañon. This, Tom figured, was information Ernest had from his brother, Bryan, who had been thick with Morrison and the murdered woman.

After Burkhart was escorted back to the city jail, Tom and Frank reviewed the confession and new developments. Suddenly the investigation was breaking wide open, lapping over into the Roan and Brown murders. After two thwarting years, the federal government had the pegs on which to hang not one but three cases. Burkhart's confession, given despite obvious fear of his uncle, definitely named Hale as the mastermind; it involved John Ramsey for the first time, and it could explain why Curly Johnson and Ace Kirby and Henry Grammer no longer lived.

It came to the agents once again that the Bureau's policy of running out all leads, no matter how unpromising they might appear at the start, had paid off. The suggestion of Parker LaMoore, Governor Trapp's executive secretary, that agents question Bert Lawson, had helped break the case. Following up on Lawson's claims, wild as they seemed, then taking the principals into custody, had led to Burkhart and, at last, to firm ground.

"Burkhart surprised me," Frank said a bit

thoughtfully. "He did find some live ones to talk about, after all."

Tom said: "He could have let us take the wrong case to court and let it backfire. All he had to do was sit by while we stayed on the wrong track. But he wanted to tell the truth in face of the fact that he can be murdered for testifying against Bill Hale. I believe him, Frank."

"But will he say it in court?"

Just what had impelled Burkhart to confess? Yes, he'd said he wanted to tell the whole story. But it struck Tom there was yet a stronger force: the desire to get out from under the grinding iron will of his domineering uncle, reaching back to the days of his boyhood. Burkhart was weary of everything, that was evident. He wanted to tell the truth. Now he faced the threat of Uncle Bill's wrath when he learned that his always-compliant nephew up to now had told it all. Also uppermost in Burkhart's mind had to be the logical fear that, if he served time, prison walls might not be adequate protection against his uncle's vengeance. Bill Hale had many connections in the Oklahoma underworld.

At three o'clock in the morning, Tom placed a telephone call to Agent John Wren, the wandering "Indian medicine man" in Fairfax. Their conversation was brief and to the point.

"There's a suspect up there named John Ramsey. Take him into custody right away and bring him down here."

"I've heard of the man you want," Wren said, after a short pause. "Believe I know where to find him."

Just what had passed between Blackie Thompson and Burkhart? Had he persuaded Burkhart to confess? Agents learned this, in brief, occurred:

"Ernie, you better tell the feds all you know, if you expect any consideration or clemency."

"Why talk," Burkhart had retorted, "when they're off on a false story? Bert Lawson don't know anything."

"Just the same, it could convict you, Ernie. I'm serving a life term and have no reason to do you harm. Now, don't you get in for life. Tell the truth."

Thompson had finished on that reminder. He had used the same reasoning on Burkhart that agents had used on Thompson.

Burkhart's confession also resulted in the release of Roy Bunch, whom Hale had openly accused in Fairfax of being Roan's killer.

CHAPTER NINE

Agent Wren's sharp memory proved a timesaver in a fast-moving game. He had John Ramsey in Guthrie before noon, and within minutes Tom and Frank prepared to question him. As Ramsey was brought in, Tom could not help but feel some regret for the suspect's situation from the standpoint of family. Here was a man with a wife and six children, a respected family and a struggling one. While Hale had everything — wealth, prestige, power — Ramsey was a poor man who had always found the economic going rough. Despite the family's status, one daughter had become a well-regarded schoolteacher. Ramsey's boys worked hard, had law-abiding reputations. Only a year ago Ramsey had moved from Ripley to a farm west of Fairfax. He lived quietly, farmed some, did carpentry work, and also sold Henry Grammer's whisky to Indians. His arrest came as a surprise in Fairfax.

Tom saw a lank, black-haired, sharp-featured man of forty-six years. On March 10, 1910, state prison records showed, Ramsey had started serving a sentence of one year and a day after pleading guilty to receiving stolen cattle in Osage County. He had listed his occupation as cattleman. This was the case, Burkhart had said, where Ramsey had been paid $1,000 to go to prison for Grammer.

Like Burkhart, Ramsey was visibly uncomfortable in the alien atmosphere of the bare jurors' room. Suddenly whisking the two men out of the familiar Osage, away from Hale's dominating support and friends, had shaken their nerve. If Ramsey didn't confess, the plan was to confront him with Burkhart.

"We're going to talk to you about the murder of Henry Roan, done at the order of Bill Hale," Tom led off, after introducing himself and Frank as federal agents.

"You're barkin' up the wrong tree," Ramsey said, deftly rolling a brown-paper cigarette.

"We have Ernest Burkhart's statement to that effect," Tom replied, and displayed the written sheets. "All about how Hale hired you and how you did it. Here it is in my hand."

"I don't believe it."

Ramsey made no particular assertion of innocence, not one denial. However, he looked troubled and nervous. For the next several minutes he just smoked and indicated no willingness to talk.

Frank took up the questioning, speaking bluntly. "Here, Bill Hale was getting an easy twenty-five thousand dollars from Henry Roan's insurance . . . and paying you a

117

cheap five hundred and a car to do the killing."

Ramsey blew smoke.

"Hale was using you as a cheap tool to do his dirty work," Frank hammered.

"How do you figure that?" Ramsey asked.

"Why, letting you take the chances and the blame . . . that's how. And Henry Grammer . . . Hale's friend . . . paid you a thousand bucks to ruin your reputation and serve a sentence for him in the state pen, didn't he?"

"I served a short term, sure," Ramsey admitted, and no more.

The agents noticed Ramsey reacted most when Bill Hale's name figured in the interrogation. Like Burkhart, he shied from discussing the cowman, appearing more concerned what Hale, rather than the United States government, might do to him. The hour was late now.

"I want you to hear some of Burkhart's statement," Tom broke in as the stalemate continued, and he read Burkhart's account of driving his uncle to Grammer's ranch and seeing Hale, talking to Ramsey. Continuing, he read where Burkhart told of seeing Ramsey later in Fairfax.

The lank man on the other side of the table turned quite still, his eyes fixed on the sheet of paper as Tom read distinctly: " 'John Ramsey said he was gonna kill an Osage for Bill Hale.' "

Ramsey made an abrupt, silencing motion, and Tom read no more. Ramsey shifted uneasily in his chair, looking at neither agent, shaken. In a low-pitched voice he said: "Let me talk to Ernie Burkhart."

Burkhart was close at hand. Frank went to the door and motioned for him to be brought in. When Burkhart entered, Frank asked him: "Did you tell the government about the case?"

"I did," Burkhart replied, nodding, his gaze moving from Frank to Ramsey.

Ramsey spoke up. "Let me talk to Ernie alone."

Tom and Frank withdrew, leaving the door ajar. They watched the two converse for some minutes, then came back inside.

"John," Frank said, "are you satisfied that Ernest told the truth?"

Ramsey looked glum. "Yes, he spilled the beans. He told it all. I guess it's on my neck now. Get your pencils."

Another break in the case!

Burkhart was taken out, and Edwin K. Brown, the assistant U.S. attorney general, joined the agents. Warned, as Burkhart had been, that any statement he made might be used against him, Ramsey began to talk in a steady way while Frank rapidly took it all down.

"Sometime in the early part of Nineteen

Twenty-Three, the date I don't recall, Bill Hale came to Henry Grammer's ranch, where I was working for Grammer selling whisky. I was in the bunkhouse, and Grammer called me. I went out and saw him and Hale standing together. I walked over to them, and the three of us walked out several hundred yards to a road and stopped. Henry Grammer turned to me and said Hale had a little job he wanted done and asked me if I would like to do it.

"I said . . . 'It depends on what the job is.' Grammer said he wanted an Indian bumped off. I said . . . 'That's different.' Hale, Grammer, and I then talked the matter over for a few minutes. I don't recall just what was said, but I remarked that I would look it over, and I went back to the bunkhouse."

It was interesting to Tom that Grammer, married to an Osage woman, the mother of his three children, had not been averse to helping line up Ramsey to kill a member of his wife's tribe. Manifestly, killing an Indian was not the same as killing a white man.

In a few days, Ramsey said, Grammer had told him that Hale was getting anxious to have that job done. The next time Ramsey saw Hale was in Fairfax. "We had another talk about the Indian he wanted killed, and I told him I would do the job, but that I didn't have any way to get around. Hale said he would see me in a day or two."

Soon, thereafter, Ramsey said he had met Hale at Grammer's ranch, and Hale had told him he was going to buy him a car and gave him five hundred dollars. Something was said about where Ramsey would buy the car, and he had said Ponca City. Ramsey said Hale drove him to Pawnee, where he caught the train to Ponca City, bought a new Ford roadster, and drove back to Grammer's ranch. Later, in Fairfax, Hale pointed out to Ramsey the Indian he wanted killed.

"I don't remember Hale ever telling me the Indian's name. Several days after Hale pointed this Indian out to me, I met this Indian in a restaurant in Fairfax, and he sat down beside me. I smelled whisky on his breath, and we got into conversation about whisky, and I told him I could get him some. He said he wanted some, and I told him to meet me on the road running through Sol Smith's pasture about ten o'clock, and I would have the whisky for him. I left him and went to Grammer's and got some whisky and drove back to the road leading through Sol Smith's pasture and found the Indian sitting in his car, waiting at a point near Salt Creek. I drove up and got out of my car, and we took several drinks from a bottle I had. I then got in my car and drove back to Fairfax."

Several times later Ramsey said he had met this Indian and given him drinks of whisky.

"This went on for several days and I was trying to rib up a little more courage. Finally, one day, I decided to pull the job, everything being favorable, so I told the Indian to meet me on the road running through Sol Smith's pasture, that I would have some whisky for him. I told him about what point on the road I would meet him, so he went out on the road and I on another. . . . We met about the foot of the big hill near Salt Creek. I motioned him to go up on top of the hill, which he did and stopped. I drove up. I saw a car coming, and I told him to drive off under the hill, which he did. I got out of my car, and, when the car I'd seen had passed, I then walked down under the hill where I found him waiting for me. He got out of the car, and we sat on the running board of his car and drank what whisky I had. . . . The Indian then got in his car to leave, and I then shot him in the back of the head. I suppose I was within a foot or two of him when I shot him. I then went back to my car and drove to Fairfax."

After a few days Ramsey said he had seen Hale and had told him enough to understand that he had killed the Indian. There was very little said at the time. Some little time later, Ramsey again met Hale, and something was said about paying him the balance of five hundred, Hale insisting he would pay him a little later, as he would have more money then, and Ramsey had told him that was all right, that he didn't need it then.

Within a month or two, Ramsey said, Hale had paid him the balance of $500. "Some several days . . . I don't remember just how long . . . but something like ten days, this Indian's body that I killed was found, and I remember that was the first time I found out his name was Henry Roan." Ramsey was finished.

Frank looked up. "Want to read it now?"

"No," Ramsey said.

"I'll repeat it to you, then." Frank read the confession through and handed the pencil to Ramsey, who signed his name voluntarily. No one had threatened or abused him in any fashion.

"John, what kind of gun did you use?" Frank asked Ramsey.

Agents Davis and Wren had entered the room. Ramsey's eyes paused on Wren.

"Just like the one he's got on? That it?" Frank asked.

Wren was packing a .45 automatic.

Ramsey nodded affirmation, said he had used a weapon belonging to Henry Grammer.

Ramsey appeared vastly relieved and talked on, adding that Roan had the car in gear when Ramsey lifted the curtain on Roan's side and shot the Osage behind the left ear.

Roan loved whisky, Ramsey said. Ramsey

drank that day just to nerve himself up. Ramsey's attitude indicated that killing an Indian wasn't a particularly serious crime. In his defense, he said: "White people in Oklahoma think no more of killing an Indian now than they did in Seventeen Twenty-Four."

Officers learned later, through Burkhart, that Hale was about to fire Ramsey when he had delayed murdering Roan. If Ramsey failed to come through, the plan was for Grammer to hire a killer out of Kansas City, further showing the connection between that underworld and the rough-tough Osage. Ramsey's coming clean had taken hours, past midnight, an interval that federal officers were to have pounded at them accusingly in the looming court battles.

Obligingly Ramsey had another story to tell the following day. "Wanting the government to know everything, I now wish to tell all I know about the killing of Bill Smith and family. Before I was hired to kill Henry Roan, through talking with Henry Grammer, where I was selling whisky, I knew that Bill Hale wanted Bill Smith murdered, and I knew that Henry Grammer was helping Bill Hale arrange to have him killed. I can't remember right now the different conversations that I had with Grammer which convinced me that they were going to kill Bill Smith. I can't say for sure whether it was before I killed Roan or shortly after that Grammer told me he had a man to do the job, and that it was Ace Kirby.

"A little while after Grammer told me, Ace Kirby showed up at Grammer's. That was the first time I met him. Grammer was very drunk, and he, in the presence of Ace Kirby, told me that Kirby was all right, that he would do that job he wanted done, and told Kirby to talk to me and for me to help Kirby all I could. Kirby then talked to me and asked me what was the job Grammer wanted done. I told him that he wanted a squawman killed near Fairfax by the name of Bill Smith. Kirby then said . . . 'Well, I wasn't figuring on staying here long,' and wanted to know what there would be in it for him. I told him I did not know. He said . . . 'Well, I'll see Grammer and talk it over with him.'

"I don't remember now the other little details and conversations, but I do remember that the next thing was I took Kirby down near Gray Horse where Bill Smith was living on a ranch and pointed out Smith's house to Kirby. The next thing I remember is that in some way I heard Bill Smith had left the country and gone to Arkansas. In fact, Ernest Burkhart told me Smith had gone to Arkansas, but he did not think he would be gone long and for me to tell Ace Kirby. I told Kirby what Ernest Burkhart had told me. The next thing that followed, and I don't know how long after, Ernest Burkhart told me that Bill Smith had moved into town, and told me to tell Ace Kirby everything was ready and tell him as quick as I could. I told Ernest my wife was sick, and I could not get away. I'm not sure I went after Kirby that day or the next."

Ramsey went on that he had driven to a little oil town, where Kirby ran a rooming house, and met Kirby and told him everything was ready, and Ramsey would take him and show him the house. "Kirby and I drove to Fairfax, and I showed him the house that Ernest Burkhart said Bill Smith lived in. Kirby asked me if I knew where there was any soup, and I told him I did not. Then there was something said about there being plenty of soup stored in the oil fields, and there would be no trouble to get it, if he needed it, but that he wasn't sure whether he would blow Smith up or shoot him.

"Soon after, possibly the next night, Smith's house was blown up. At some stage of the game before the blow-up, I asked Kirby if he needed any help to do the job, and he had said no. Some few days after the blow-up, Kirby told me something about doing a good job. Grammer asked me if I had seen the blow-up, and he said it was a fair or a good job. Neither Hale nor Grammer paid me anything for the part I did

126

in this. I was supposed to be just helping out. But at different times since the blow-up Hale has given me a little money, and, when I needed a little money, I let Hale know, and he never failed to favor me. Henry Grammer told me he got Ace Kirby for the job, and I asked Ace if he got a settlement, and he said Grammer had come to pay him, but went on a drunk and spent a few hundred dollars, but later paid it all."

Ramsey told it with few pauses and no prodding. Now he paused again and, after a heavy silence that ran on for some moments, said: "I make this statement because it is the truth, and, before I got mixed up with Henry Grammer, I did not think it possible to do the things I did." Like Burkhart, he had not been touched or forced to talk.

Ramsey's confession revealed that Burkhart had played a constant and implicating rôle in the Smith murders. Besides driving Hale's red Buick to tell Ramsey to tell Kirby to do the job, Burkhart had kept Ramsey informed on the whereabouts of the Smiths and, finally, pointed out the doomed house in Fairfax to Ramsey.

Next there was a meeting with W.K. Hale. When the three Texans faced off, there was a fast sizing-up by all. Hale greeted the officers with a genial: "Howdy, men. Hope I'm not keeping you up too late." He was maintaining his public façade even now.

In that briefness, Tom understood a great deal more about this controversial, money-driven, gray-eyed man. Hale's voice was neither loud nor harsh, but even-toned, positive, forceful, persuasive. It went with the broad smile; it could sway people, bend them to his iron will, like the Burkhart boys, his nephews, particularly Ernest Burkhart, who had helped set up the Smith murders, including Reta Smith, Burkhart's sister-in-law.

Hale was not an extra large man, but he made a presence. He had a military bearing. He was not over five feet seven or eight inches, but he was strongly cast, well-preserved at fifty-one, the shoulders compact, the neck thick, the ruddy face broad, the black hair combed straight back. He wore thick glasses, which gave him a benign, friendly look. In contrast to Burkhart and Ramsey, he affected a complete self-confidence. Neatly dressed, he held his head high, chest out. There was a strut to his walk.

Tom identified Frank and himself as federal agents and, without further preliminaries, said: "We have unquestioned signed statements implicating you as the principal in the Henry Roan and Smith family murders. We have the evidence to convict you."

Tom waited for Hale to speak, but Hale seemed content, in his total confidence, to let the agents show their cards, in effect, before he played his hand. Tom had no intention then of revealing who had confessed.

"We believe you're a man who loves his family," Tom said. "We don't think you want to expose them to a long trial and all this sordid testimony, the shame and embarrassment. You can avoid this by telling us your story and pleading guilty. Furthermore, with the high-powered staff of lawyers you have, you'll be drained to your last dollar and your family left in strained circumstances."

"I'll fight it out to the finish!" Hale all but shouted, his head high, breathing defiance and assurance. "Because I'm not guilty!"

Tom had expected that answer, for it was Hale's character to dominate, to rule, never to bow. His denial ended the interrogation.

With Hale returned to the Logan County jail, Tom and Frank took the signed statements of Burkhart and Ramsey to Roy St. Lewis, the U.S. district attorney, and T.J. Leahy, veteran Pawhuska attorney, just appointed as a special prosecutor to assist the government. They, in turn, had Federal District Judge John H. Cotteral call a special session of the grand jury to hear the agents present the confessions and describe the procedure in securing them.

Ramsey was promptly billed for slaying Henry Roan, while Hale was dealt a double blow. In addition to the federal indictment of complicity in Roan's murder, specifically that

129

he had hired Ramsey, a state case filed at Pawhuska in district court alleged that he had conspired to cause the death of W.E. Smith. It was January 9, 1926.

Hale heard the bad news that night. When a U.S. marshal entered his cell to read the warrant declaring him under indictment for the murder of Roan, the cowman was stretched out on his bunk, wrapped in a blanket, napping. Awakened, he sat up and smoothed his straight black hair with unshaking hands while the indictment was read. He said nothing; he showed nothing. Wasn't he W.K. Hale, "King of the Osage Hills"?

No less silent was Ramsey when led into a corridor. As the marshal finished reading, Ramsey turned on his heel and sauntered off to his cell, apparently unconcerned. Was he already having second thoughts? Was he thinking Bill Hale's lawyers would get him out of this and prove his confession had been forced?

Tom White and Frank Smith and the other agents had corralled the principals they believed guilty beyond any doubt. But would Ernest Burkhart overcome his fear and testify against Uncle Bill? Would Ramsey, who also feared Hale? Tom knew the battle had just begun.

CHAPTER TEN

Bill Hale was indeed prepared to fight it to the finish. Agents learned from sources around Fairfax that he was not surprised to have his long reign of one-man rule finally challenged, not by county or state authorities, whom he disdained, but by the United States government. A man of means, he immediately surrounded himself with a shield of veteran trial lawyers: S.P. Freeling, former Oklahoma attorney general; J.I. Howard, prominent Oklahoma City attorney; and W.S. Hamilton, a seasoned campaigner in Osage County courtroom clashes.

J.M. Springer, a rough-and-tumble defense lawyer from Stillwater, represented Ramsey. Tom White heard that Hale had paid Springer $10,000. Springer could be expected to come on the attack, hurling charges, mouthing insults, with hinted threats to follow outside the courtroom.

The prosecution wheeled up big guns as well. In the line-up with St. Lewis and Leahy were Edwin K. Brown, special assistant to the U.S. attorney general; O.R. Luhring, chief of the criminal division of the U.S. attorney general's office; George Short, Oklahoma attorney general; and Edwin Dabney, assistant state attorney general. Leahy, regarded as dean of Pawhuska attorneys, had been a member of the State Constitutional Convention and was prominent in Osage tribal affairs. St. Lewis was known as an aggressive prosecutor. Among Brown's assignments was giving legal advice to agents.

As news of Hale's arrest and indictment spread like a March prairie fire, Osage County became riveted on the case, while the state watched from the sidelines. "Never in the history of Oklahoma has such an array of convicted criminals been assembled for a court session," the *Oklahoman* noted. On hand were Dick Gregg, former member of Al Spencer's bank-robbing gang, and John Mayo, a companion of Henry Grammer when the bootleg king died in a car wreck possibly caused when the partially sawed steering gear became unmanageable. Mayo had been with hardcase Ace Kirby when a storekeeper, alerted by his "friend," Bill Hale, greeted the nitro expert with a shotgun blast in a robbery attempt. Gregg and Mayo, brought in to testify before the grand jury, were serving time in the Kansas state prison for bank robbery. Gregg, slim and youthful, still with a wild and reckless look, drew warm greetings from former Osage County acquaintances when seen on the street in chains.

On the other side, Bill Hale was pulling on the strings of old friendships, obviously for public effect and possibly to influence some juror. Three well-known Oklahomans from the early days suddenly appeared in Guthrie: Major Gordon W. Lillie, known as "Pawnee Bill," and Colonel Zack Mulhall, pioneer rancher, and Frank Canton, former U.S. marshal. "All are friends of Hale," the *Oklahoman* reported, "and said they merely came to pay their respects to the federal officials. All expressed their confidence in Hale's innocence." It was as if they were saying that true Westerners didn't walk away from old friends without knowing the whole story. The newspapers didn't say whether the three visited Hale in his cell.

Meanwhile, the grand jury had a look at the bullet-riddled skull of Anna Brown. Witnesses from the Osage made a steady, nervous procession in and out of the jury room. Both Indians and whites seemed reluctant, even fearful, to testify, observers said.

When the grand jury recessed until February 12th, newspapers began writing about the Osage's violent past, of "an alleged conspiracy to destroy an entire Osage family with a fortune of $2,000,000."

"Nothing as far-reaching in murders has ever been revealed," said Special Assistant Brown. Some Indian witnesses were being passed whisky, he told reporters, in an effort to discredit or influence their testimony.

Newsmen, digging deeper, wrote of "dope doctors" and rich Osages drugged and rushed to another state and married to white whores; of white men with social diseases marrying Indian women and their deaths being hastened through doctor conspirators; of businessmen lending Indians money, sinking them in debt, then having the Indians take out large life insurance policies as security and naming the businessmen as beneficiaries. Three mysterious deaths of Osages which had occurred in Oklahoma City three years earlier drew fresh attention, those of George Bigheart, Henry Bennett, and a man named Gibson.

On the legal front both sides sparred. Firebrand attorney Springer hotly denied that Ramsey admitted shooting Henry Roan, and government officials declined to state publicly whether Ramsey had confessed. *Let the defense sweat.*

By now, prosecutors said, the point of law was clear. Roan's body was found on the U.S. government allotment of Rose Little Star, an Osage Indian. Therefore, Roan's death on restricted Indian land gave the federal government jurisdiction to prosecute a murder charge, an authority that appeared bolstered when State Attorney General Short, after a conference with St. Lewis, dismissed State charges in the W.E. Smith case against

Hale, still held in the Logan County jail as a government prisoner. Knowing Hale stood a much stronger chance of acquittal in state courts, defense attorneys went before Judge John H. Cotteral of the federal district court to contest federal jurisdiction, contending Roan wasn't a government ward and the alleged murder wasn't committed on restricted land.

Ever on the prod, ever accusing, the volatile Springer was waving affidavits, loudly claiming Department of Justice agents had used "third-degree" methods in securing Ramsey's confession. Ramsey now denied all, Springer said. Tom White and Frank Smith almost felt amused, knowing this was just the opening barrage of accusations agents would face.

A State charge against Ernest Burkhart of complicity in the Smith murders was dropped January 19th, leaving him free to go where he pleased. But he didn't return to Fairfax and his Osage wife Mollie and two children, as agents expected. Instead, he dallied for a day in Guthrie, sticking close to agents. Next morning, seeming to act on impulse, he hastened alone to Oklahoma City and searched out Tom White in the federal building, agitated and apprehensive. He started talking at once, holding himself very carefully. "It's impossible for me to stay in Oklahoma or go back to the Osage," he said. "If I do, I'll be killed. I want to know what protection you can give me until the trial starts."

Once again Tom saw Burkhart's fear of his uncle demonstrated. Tom didn't doubt that, unless Burkhart hid out or agents guarded him day and night, Hale would find a way to eliminate him. "I understand your concern, and I'll give you all the protection the government can afford," Tom assured him. "Whatever is necessary for your safety."

"That's what I want to hear. Get me out of Oklahoma!"

"Maybe we won't have to," Tom said. "If you'd rather be near your family, with safety, we can put agents with you at all times? Or we can take you back into custody, protect you in jail?"

"No," — Burkhart was positive — "I want to get out . . . leave Oklahoma. I want my whereabouts kept secret from everybody. Even my family."

"We'll do that," Tom promised.

That same day he assigned Agents Street and Wren to guard Burkhart and see after him, now the prosecution's star witness since Ramsey claimed he'd confessed under duress.

"Burkhart is afraid for his life," Tom explained to the agents. "We can't afford to have him killed or come under the influence of Bill Hale and his gang and change his story through fear. If he goes back to the Osage, one of those two things will happen."

136

Right away the three took a train to San Antonio. Their itinerary called for travel into New Mexico, up to Tucumcari and Hot Springs, and down to El Paso and around, treading time until the trial opened. Burkhart's correspondence with wife Mollie was mailed to Tom, who had agents deliver the letters in Fairfax.

As expected, the defense camp erupted violently when Burkhart's disappearance was discovered. Freeling, Hale's attorney, now loudly claiming he also represented Burkhart, went into federal district court seeking a writ of *habeas corpus*. Freeling alleged Burkhart was being held under duress, and asserted: "His wife is in this courtroom. Her two children are ill, and she needs him."

St. Lewis was ready, saying: "He's in good hands. I talked to him the other day, when he gave me this letter," in which Burkhart denied Hale's attorneys represented him.

Hamilton, of the Hale staff, then told Judge Cotteral that he also represented Burkhart and repudiated the letter. Free-swinging Springer added his strident voice to the clamor.

When Judge Cotteral denied the writ, the defense turned to the state district court in Oklahoma City. "A diabolical scheme," was being perpetuated, the defense charged, by keeping Burkhart "away from his family and friends." Freeling demanded that the prosecution divulge the missing man's whereabouts or "go to jail for contempt."

For the first time Tom White's name appeared in the *Oklahoman*'s coverage. Subpoenaed with seven others to show cause why they should not produce Ernest Burkhart, Tom found himself in the center of the defense's attack during the morning session.

"Do you know where Ernest Burkhart is?" Howard demanded.

"He is not in my custody," Tom replied.

"Is he in Oklahoma?"

"He is not in my custody."

During the afternoon session, Freeling fired the same question.

"Burkhart is free to go home, if he wishes," Tom testified. "He is not restrained in his liberty. He is with a federal agent working under my direction. He asked of his own free will that we assign a man to protect him and to go with him wherever Burkhart wants to go."

But where that was, Tom refused to say and the court sustained him. Next, Tom produced a letter from Burkhart requesting protection in fear of his life. Burkhart also denied that Freeling or Hamilton represented him, as claimed earlier in federal court. When Howard asked if Burkhart had confessed, St. Lewis objected and was sustained.

"The only reason Burkhart put himself under my protection is because I'm a federal officer," Tom told the court. "He said he did not want the letter to get out, and he sought protection because he feared violence."

"Did you advise Missus Burkhart . . . 'Don't let Hale's attorneys kid you into doing anything that will locate Ernie or hurt him'?"

"I did."

Legal tempers clashed again when St. Lewis, on the stand, said he had refused to tell Mollie Burkhart where her husband was when she came to his office January 23rd. "The reason I did not," he told the court, "was because I didn't want certain information getting into the hands of unscrupulous lawyers who are attorneys for other parties." He denied that he was casting reflections on Freeling, Howard, or Hamilton. But, newsmen asked, who else could he have meant?

After a day of bitter squabbling, District Judge Lucien Babcock held — "There is no showing that Ernest Burkhart is restrained of his liberty or is under restraint of any kind." — and denied the writ the defense sought in the name of Mrs. Burkhart.

About the same time the prosecution sharpened its case in the Roan murder by filing a new indictment that was more specific as to the location of the alleged crime on the Rose Little Star allotment. Newspapers reported federal authorities threw "a veil of secrecy" around operations of the reconvened grand jury, with increased precautions taken "in the interest of safety for the witnesses." At the previous session reports had circulated "of threats made against some who were believed to have testified."

Fairfax heard of one threat in particular. Rancher Sol Smith, in whose pasture leased on the Rose Little Star allotment the body of Roan was found, was reported to have had "a pistol shoved in his belly" before he went into the jury room. Who made the threat? Fairfax heard it was J.M. Springer, Ramsey's attorney. Did Sol Smith know too much? What did he know, if anything?

The story circulating in edgy Fairfax, and verified to agents by Marshal Bob Parker, was that Smith and a cowboy named Newton were working cattle in the pasture. They topped a hill and looked down and saw Roan and Ramsey drinking whisky while seated on the running board of Roan's car.

"I'd like to go down there and make 'em give me a drink," Newton said in a light way.

But there was work to do, and they rode on. Not long afterward Roan's body was found at that location. Newton was willing to swear in court what they had seen. But Smith, not unlike many others, was afraid to chance testifying against Hale or Hale's connections. When Smith wouldn't back him up, Newton refused to testify. So the story ran.

Sometime after that Smith reportedly drowned while attempting to cross rain-swollen Salt Creek on horseback, or, as the rumor flew, had he been knocked in the head? Marshal Parker, a fair-minded man with an objective view of matters while living in a town seething with almost daily wild reports, looked further into Smith's death and told agents: "He was riding a goosey horse and wearing a slicker," a combination of circumstances fraught with danger — horse spooks, throwing rider, tangled in long, cowboy slicker, and then the horse kicks or tramples the thrown rider unconscious. Evidently Smith had told the grand jury nothing, and his subsequent death threw another shadow across the many-faceted Osage investigation. So much had happened around Fairfax that, when a person died who was even remotely connected to any of the cases, rumors of foul play rose at once.

In Guthrie, heated dueling went on over the key issue of jurisdiction, building toward the awaited opinion of Judge Cotteral. Cotteral ruled the federal government had no jurisdiction in the Roan case, that opinions of the State Supreme Court determine that the allotment of Rose Little Star was not held in trust by the United States, and it was not Indian country at the time of the alleged offense, but the jurisdiction had been succeeded to by the State. With the indictment set aside, it appeared that Bill Hale's lawyers — just as his friends predicted —

141

had clipped the federal government's tail feathers good. St. Lewis quickly sued for a writ of error in federal court, and Judge Cotteral allowed the appeal to the U.S. Supreme Court.

Would the State try to hold Hale by filing new charges? It had dismissed a murder complaint against him January 18th in the W.E. Smith case following the federal grand jury indictment. No one would say, yet. But there was a feeling of imminent action around the U.S. district attorney's office. Edwin K. Brown was rumored conferring in Pawhuska with C.K. Templeton, Osage County attorney. That was the tip-off.

It happened immediately after Hale and Ramsey, neatly dressed, confident, and smiling, in federal court March 2nd, heard themselves freed on $25,000 bond each, pending disposition of the government's appeal. Unnoticed until now, Osage County Sheriff H.M. Freas stepped up to Hale. "Bill, I have a warrant for your arrest."

Hale looked startled. He glanced sharply at his expensive attorneys. As expected, Freas shook hands with Hale before placing him under arrest. He then turned to Ramsey, whose lean face had gone blank, and shook hands with him. Sworn out in Osage County district court, the surprise warrants charged the two with murdering W.E. Smith, his wife, Reta, and Nettie Brookshire, the servant girl

— bold action that state and U.S. authorities had taken to hold Hale and Ramsey in custody until the U.S. Supreme Court appeal could be processed. A dangerous move as well, because the prosecution would be battling the "King of the Osage Hills" on his own stomping ground. It took only one to hang a jury.

CHAPTER ELEVEN

On the eve of the defendants' preliminary hearing in the Pawhuska courthouse before County Judge L.A. Justus, agents caught wind of fresh threats, more intimidation. Again, Hale was drawing on old connections, this time the criminal element. One "Boots" Dolan, formerly a lieutenant in Al Spencer's band of roving bank robbers, now reputedly hauling whisky out of Wichita, Kansas, into the Osage, had just arrived on the scene. Bristles up, back arched, pawing the sod in a menacing manner, so to speak, he was passing the warning, promising to make every federal man hump out of town. Tom White and Frank Smith soon heard, as it was intended for them to hear. Both were tired of having to hold back and avoid action.

"We'd better head this off," Tom said.

"I'm in favor of paying the gentleman a call," Frank agreed. "Right now."

With .45 automatics in their gun belts, they located the frothy badman at a friend's house. Sure of himself, Dolan came out on the porch, a hard-featured, stocky man with a bullet-shaped head and pale, ruthless eyes. He fancied a bright purple shirt, a huge silver belt buckle that pushed against his paunch, and fancy black cowboy boots with white steer heads. He showed no gun.

Dolan blinked, his expression changing to surprise at sight of the two men confronting him. One towering, the other heavy-set and strong-jawed, both ready for business.

"We're federal agents, and we hear that you've threatened to run us out of town," Tom came to the point. "If that's true, grab a gun and we'll fight it out right here. We're calling your bluff right now."

Dolan wet his lips. "Don't know where you heard that. I sure didn't say it."

"We heard it . . . just like you figured we'd hear it," Frank corrected. "Not once, but several times. It's going around town."

"Must be a mistake. Me . . . I'm an old friend of Bill Hale's. Just happened to be in town. I ain't here to do any harm."

"That's just dandy," Frank said cynically. "Maybe you won't be sticking around town much longer?"

"Figured I'd drift on tomorrow."

"That's better." Frank looked at Tom, who said: "If you're not out of town by noon tomorrow, there'll be a warrant charging you with threatening federal officers. Understand?"

Dolan nodded, and went inside.

He kept his word, *after* telling Hale's attorneys, who complained loudly around town. The incident set the tone of the Hale fac-

145

tion's line of attack during the preliminary, that all federal men were outsiders, here trampling on local rights and ordering the good citizens of Osage County around. Not mentioned in the defense's public outcry was that the friend of Bill Hale's just run out of town had been a member of the disbanded Spencer gang, thus covering Hale's outlaw connections.

Tom interpreted the defense's complaints as an attempt to influence prospective jurors in Hale's favor. It was a smart strategy, since it was doubtful that Hale could be convicted in Osage County.

With the preliminary looming, fearful Ernest Burkhart asked for a secret meeting away from the Osage with T.J. Leahy, the respected Pawhuska attorney serving as a special prosecutor on the government's side. In Arkansas City, Kansas, Burkhart retold his story.

In another move, State officers brought a sullen Kelsey Morrison to Guthrie, where Tom and Frank questioned him, hoping to shed light on Anna Brown's murder. Morrison, serving time in the state penitentiary for robbing a federal Prohibition officer, refused to talk. Agents offered him no clemency.

March 12th. Long before Hale and Ramsey arrived for their preliminary hearing and were shifted to the district courtroom to handle the overflowing crowd, Hale's followers, loud and confident, and curious, silent Indians and reporters for the press services and the Tulsa newspapers filled the legal arena. Fairfax had the largest contingent. Tom White, seated at the prosecution table, sensed a hostile attitude at once. The pro-Hale crowd had gathered to back its generous champion and hurl abuse on the opposition.

A giant stir went over the room as the neatly attired defendants entered, Hale preferring a dark business suit, white shirt and hard collar, and black bow tie. He waved his customary, encompassing, genial greeting, smiling broadly, at ease, erect, assured, now on familiar footing. In response, the crowd was murmuring, cordial. To many Fairfax people it was as if seeing Bill Hale again in front of the Big Hill store, smiling, nodding, calling first names, grunting a little Osage with a jovial full-blood, joking, flashing his gold-toothed smile, tipping his hat and bowing, no man, no woman, no child a stranger. There was nobody like Bill Hale. How could the government charge such a man with anything?

Ramsey, equally smiling, made a ceremony of shaking hands with each member of the defense counsel: Freeling, Howard, Hamilton, Springer, and a fifth attorney just added, E.C. Gross of Pawhuska. Neither defendant appeared even slightly perturbed. They began chatting and joking with their attorneys. At Ramsey's side sat his wife, while Hale's wife and daughter, Willie, who had just arrived from a girl's school in Texas, were in the courtroom.

No sooner had the hearing opened than Hamilton, a thin, nervous man, jumped up accusingly: "Your Honor, I demand that T.B. White over there" — pointing hard — "head of the U.S. Bureau of Investigation in Oklahoma City, be searched for firearms and excluded from this courtroom!"

The Hale crowd ate it up. Tom heard a ripple of applause. He stood slowly, opening his coat to show he was not armed. "I will leave if the court orders it," he said to Judge Justus.

Justus, half smiling, denied both requests. Hale loyalists stamped to their feet, muttering at the decision. State officers, moving among them, quieted the outburst.

Hamilton was soon attacking from another quarter, telling the court very serious charges were going to be lodged in the near future against T.B. White and other federal agents. There were hoots of approval, quickly silenced again. But the open hostility persisted, heating up whenever the defense, not unlike school cheerleaders, agitated the home-country crowd.

Next, Dabney, the assistant state attorney general, requested a postponement for the

State to study testimony made available by the federal government, a maneuver designed to delay matters until the U.S. Supreme Court acted on the appeal from Cotteral's ruling. Dabney might have thrown a rock into a hornet's nest, so fast did the defense swarm the motion.

"The State has had plenty of time to examine its testimony," declared Springer, representing Ramsey, a thin, dark-skinned man, his courtroom manner combative, his eyes piercing. "These men have been incarcerated for nearly ten weeks, and the days of Russianism resorted to in denying them of their Constitutional rights, they ought to be given a hearing without delay."

Judge Justus sustained the objection.

A little later, Springer, with a small, anticipatory smile, reiterated Hamilton's threat of very serious charges to be preferred against Mr. White as the hearing was proceeding. Tom recognized the old tactic of fear and threatened reprisal unless a man knuckled under. It had effectively silenced Osage and white citizens alike for years and brought the first federal probe to a dead-end. He was getting it now, the full treatment, full force.

The hearing plodded on, the defense playing to the rowdy, partisan crowd, often having its way with the court, while the State presented evidence to show a premeditated explosion destroyed the W.E. Smith house in

Fairfax, and that Smith, his wife, and the servant girl died of blast effects. The defense sought to establish an accidental explosion, plus an old illness had led to Smith's death. Hadn't he suffered from a chronic stomach ailment?

It was true about the stomach ailment, said Dr. J.C. Shoun, who had attended Smith before his death, but Smith had actually died of internal poisoning resulting from burns. Approximately one-third of Smith's body was covered with burns, he testified.

Rebuffed, the defense fought to indicate something other than nitroglycerine had caused the explosion. Maybe the gas tank in the new Studebaker parked in the garage under the house exploded!

The next two witnesses for the State, including Fairfax Fire Chief Melvin "Boodge" Marion, told of finding a long piece of cord or a fuse leading from the outside into the garage. A veteran oil well shooter testified that nitroglycerine was used in the destruction of the Smith house.

Into the afternoon the hearing dragged as the crowd grew restless, the pace much slower after the rapid-fire exchanges of the morning. Hale conferred frequently with his chief counsel, Freeling, the former Oklahoma attorney general, a large, impressive man with slate-gray hair.

There was no notice of what was primed

to happen. But hell was about to pop, and it did when the courtroom door opened and suddenly Ernest Burkhart entered beside a deputy sheriff. Hamilton immediately leaped to his feet, shouting, pointing: "This man is my client! I've been kept from communicating with him! Not even members of his own family have known where he's been the past two months! I demand that he be asked if he doesn't wish to speak to me!"

What little decorum had existed earlier vanished in a noisy uproar of shouts and stampings, quieted momentarily when Burkhart was called to the witness stand.

Before Leahy could question him, Hamilton shouted: "I demand T.B. White's exclusion from this courtroom!"

Instead of settling Hamilton down, Judge Justus was allowing the defense free run of the proceedings. Tom withdrew voluntarily from the prosecution table without a ruling, hoping to speed introduction of Burkhart's testimony.

Hamilton was still blowing. "Let the court inform Ernest Burkhart of his Constitutional rights!" he shouted, waving his arms. "When he walks from this courtroom tonight, let not a federal officer lay hands on him!"

"Just a moment," retorted Leahy, "if the court please, this argument is a lot of hullabaloo about nothing. Burkhart is in custody of federal officers at his own request. I told him yesterday and federal officers told him, there was no charge against him, and that he could come and go as he pleases."

Hamilton, declaring federal officers were imposing on Burkhart, renewed demands for a private conference with Burkhart.

"Is Mister Hamilton your attorney?" Judge Justus questioned the witness.

Burkhart, flustered, looked around the packed courtroom and toward his uncle at the defense table and hesitated, saying: "He's not my attorney . . . but I'm willing to talk to him a little while."

Tom saw trouble coming fast. Burkhart was frightened. He was weakening under local pressures and fear of his uncle.

"The court will allow the witness five minutes to confer with Mister Hamilton," Judge Justus said.

Tom was taken aback at the extraordinary procedure: the defense being allowed to confer with the State's key witness, to leave the courtroom and go to the judge's chambers. With a knowing smirk, Hamilton closed the door. Tom felt a rush of anger and disgust. Justus had yielded his court to the bombast of Bill Hale's lawyers.

Five minutes passed, then more. The courtroom was quiet, down to mere shufflings. Tom's concern grew. Burkhart, through fear and bulldozing, might change his story or deny it.

Twenty minutes passed. The two had not returned. Hamilton was flaunting his total disregard for the court's instructions, knowing he could get away with it. Finally nettled, Judge Justus sent the bailiff.

Hamilton appeared, alone, demanding an extension of time. Leahy protested. Spectators left their seats and pushed to the front to get closer to the action.

Hamilton, who seemed to speak only in shouts, cried passionately: "This man disappeared the very day the federal grand jury was dismissed! Not a single member of his family has been allowed to see him since January Twentieth! He's been chased all over the United States! In the spirit of fairness, he should be allowed all the time he wants to confer with counsel!"

The debate boiled over into charges and counter charges. Burkhart had been held prisoner and forced to sign a confession. Burkhart had requested government protection in fear of his life, the State countered. No force had been used on him.

Freeling turned to the bench. "Your Honor, I'd like to ask the court to allow Mister Burkhart until tomorrow to confer with the defense, if he wishes."

Osage County Attorney C.K. Templeton objected vehemently, knowing that without Burkhart the State had no case against Hale and Ramsey.

"I'm going to permit the witness to do that, if he desires," Judge Justus ruled, and abruptly adjourned court, leaving Burkhart to act on his own.

At that Hale was on his feet, rushing into the chambers where Burkhart waited. After Hale came relatives and attorneys pouring into the room. The door was slammed and locked.

Tom listened grimly to calls and applause for Hale and observed the boisterous back-slapping and handshaking. He feared the worst. Now Ernest Burkhart would come under the virtual hypnotic control of his uncle again.

Hale came out presently, a big smile etching his broad, ruddy face. *En route* back to the county jail, he and Ramsey flashed triumphant grins at the huddled prosecution staff and federal men. The "King of the Osage Hills" was back on top again, riding roughshod as of old.

Burkhart, flanked by the defense team, appeared after some minutes. He averted his eyes, turned his head. He wouldn't look at Tom White or Frank Smith or T.J. Leahy and others as he went out with the exulting crowd to Fairfax. Tom, watching Burkhart get into a car, saw the exact turn of events that Department of Justice agents had worked to avoid since January. Again Burkhart was under his uncle's domination.

Nephew Ernest would be in the grip of old fears. He was afraid to testify, and the investigation was crumbling.

While the crowd still milled, Hamilton voiced a victorious prediction for the press: "When Burkhart goes on the stand, when he tells without fear of action from federal agents, the experiences he's had, it will astound the nation."

One thing was certain to Tom. Besides having the run of the county court, Hale's attorneys had won the day with bombast and wild accusations, and, in effect, had kidnapped Ernest Burkhart. Templeton was openly bitter. "Burkhart is afraid for his life. Ten minutes before he came into the courtroom, he told me he feared going on the witness stand . . . that they'd kill him. Burkhart asked for federal protection. He got it, but he's still afraid."

Would Burkhart, in Fairfax, surrounded and talked to by relatives and Hale's friends and attorneys, fail the prosecution a second time tomorrow?

March 13th, Saturday in the capital of the Osage Nation. In company of his wife Mollie and relatives, Ernest Burkhart arrived before nine o'clock, court session time. Something in his set manner warned members of the prosecution staff when they met in the county attorney's office.

Shortly, when court was called to order, a grim-faced County Attorney Templeton stood and announced: "Ernest Burkhart refuses to testify for the State."

The crowd was still buzzing when Templeton hurried outside. There he placed a warrant in the hands of Sheriff Freas, who found Burkhart.

Burkhart seemed dazed, bewildered, and uncomprehending at his arrest, now charged jointly with Hale and Ramsey in the W.E. Smith murders.

"Call the next witness."

"The prosecution will call Mister Frank Smith," said Leahy, also appointed a special prosecutor for the State.

Smith came forward, cool and determined, was sworn in, and took the stand. He identified a statement as made by John Ramsey, January 6th, at Guthrie, Oklahoma.

Leahy began reading: "Sometime in the early part of Nineteen Twenty-Three, the date I don't recall, Bill Hale came to Henry Grammer's ranch, where I was working for Grammer selling whisky. . . ."

Leahy paused suddenly. Somebody had slipped. Heads met at the prosecution table.

Leahy said: "The prosecution now moves the court for permission to withdraw this confession by John Ramsey, which was offered by mistake." Leahy had been handed Ramsey's confession of Henry Roan's murder, which had no bearing on the Smith case.

Seizing the moment, Hamilton leaped to his feet and objected to withdrawing this purported confession.

Judge Justus, following a wrangle, ruled it was too late to withdraw and ordered the document read into the record. The prosecution then produced the correct statement by Ramsey concerning the Fairfax explosion, and Smith said Ramsey had signed it.

Springer launched a tongue-lashing attack on Smith as the afternoon session began. "Isn't it true that you held this man a virtual prisoner from noon of one day until four A.M. the next morning . . . refused to let him leave the room . . . threatened him . . . told him you had evidence that would send him to the electric chair . . . that he had better tell the truth as you saw it?"

"We did keep Ramsey until late in the morning, but he wasn't threatened."

"Didn't you" — Springer was roaring and pointing — "shake your fist in John Ramsey's face and call him a liar when he refused to admit he had been implicated in the slayings? Didn't you?"

"Nothing of that sort happened. I did not shake my fist in Ramsey's face. We just talked to Ramsey, reasoning with him."

Smith left the stand after three hours, as unshaken as when the grilling began.

Over the weekend, court observers noted

certain developments and foresaw another. The snarling preliminary had taken on the aspects of a trial. The defense, quick to see an opening, had forced the State to show its hand when Ramsey's confession to shooting Henry Roan went into the record. Should the State fail to have Hale and Ramsey held to the district court, it was probable the Osage inquiry would be dropped.

Hardly noticed during the Sunday lull, several cars entered Pawhuska from the north, the direction of Kansas. They roared up the steep incline leading to the city's highest point, turned past the brownstone Osage Agency buildings, and drew up at the county jail.

Heavily armed U.S. marshals and Kansas state prison guards stepped out, shackled to two well-known actors on the Osage crime stage, outlaws Dick Gregg and John Mayo.

March 15th, Monday morning, State attorneys came out fighting.

"The Osage murder cases will be prosecuted to the limit," Edwin Dabney, assistant state attorney general, swore. "No matter what the decision in the present case."

Hale, well-dressed, presented a cheerful smile of confidence as he took a chair beside Freeling, his chief counsel.

The instant Dick Gregg's name was called as a State witness, Springer jackknifed up.

"We demand that T.B. White and all other federal agents and private detectives of the Capitol Life Insurance Company, sued by Mister Hale for the collection of twenty-five thousand dollars claimed due on a policy carried on the life of Henry Roan with Mister Hale as beneficiary, be excluded from the courtroom while this witness is on the stand."

Leahy intervened. "You would think the government committed the real crime in trying to ferret out the crime."

"Mister White and other federal officials may remain in the courtroom," Judge Justus ruled, "but I'll have to ask the insurance detectives to leave."

No names were called, however, and no one left.

Two men entered the courtroom, a uniformed prison guard and Dick Gregg, 24, boyish, handsome, slight, blue-eyed and fair-skinned, once a boon companion of dead outlaw, Al Spencer. Gregg was now serving from ten to twenty-one years in the Kansas state prison for robbing the Elgin, Kansas bank in 1922. Pale from imprisonment, Gregg showed a latent recklessness as he went to the witness chair. His guard stood close by.

"Are you acquainted with W.K. Hale, one of the defendants in this case?" Leahy asked.

Gregg smiled faintly. "I am."

"Tell the court the particulars."

Gregg said: "During the month of August, Nineteen Twenty-Two, I went to Ike Ogg's place near Okesa to meet Hale. Word had been brought to me by Rowe . . . Fred Rowe, a friend of Hale's . . . that Hale wanted to talk to us. When he came, he and Spencer went a short distance away and talked for some time. Then Hale left." Gregg was testifying with ease, in a conversational way. "The next time I saw Hale was in his pasture. He again sent for Spencer and me. With us at the time were Rowe and my father, John Gregg. Hale again talked for some time with Spencer. Five months later I met Hale on the Fairfax road, by agreement. With me were Lee Clingen and my father. Hale asked if I was ready to go ahead with that job. I asked him again what it was. He said it was bumping off a fellow named Smith, and that he would pay me three thousand dollars for the job. He said he didn't care how the job was done, as long as it was done, and suggested shooting or using nitro. He advised against explosives, however, saying Smith had a trunk of jewelry which might as well be gotten at the same time. With Hale then was a man I learned afterward was Ernie Burkhart. I told Hale I would think it over, and he suggested I visit the Smith house and look over the field. I said I would and drove out there."

The Smiths were then living in Gray Horse. Gregg said Smith invited him in, and he told Smith he was interested in buying his place. "I stayed there about an hour, but decided that I didn't want to do it. I had told Hale that Spencer didn't want to have anything to do with it."

Hale, Gregg said, had told him if he was going to do it, Hale wanted to be down in Texas so he would have an alibi. Gregg's father carried word to Hale when the young outlaw turned down Hale's offer, the witness said.

Making no attempt to refute the meeting between Hale and the bank-bandit gang, the defense asserted that Hale's conversations with Spencer had concerned the cattle business, and cited Spencer's former occupation as a cowboy and trick roper. Hale, also, was a well-known roper.

"Al never told me anything about Hale talking cattle," Gregg said, shaking his head.

For two hours Howard bombarded Gregg, but the youthful convict never varied his testimony of how Hale had tried to hire him.

Max Billingsley, former Okesa merchant and a witness before the federal grand jury, told of helping arrange the rendezvous between Hale and Spencer. "Fred Rowe and W.K. Hale came to my house in August of Nineteen Twenty-Two. Hale asked where Ike Ogg lived. The three of us went to Ogg's house . . . on the lease where Ogg was employed by an oil company and met Al Spencer and Dick Gregg there. Spencer and Hale went to one side for a private talk. I don't know what they talked about. Later, Ogg told me to tell Hale that, if the boys worked, Hale would have to leave some money. No money was left with me. I didn't want anything to do with it. I told Hale in Pawhuska what Ogg said."

There was a later meeting, the witness said, between Hale and the two outlaws on a remote Osage county road.

Ogg, a former member of the Spencer gang, testified that his home was used as a meeting place for the Spencer gang.

Tom White nodded to himself in a wry way. That explained how easy it was for Hale to meet the outlaws when he wished. Yet all through young Gregg's damaging testimony, the cowman appeared unconcerned. He showed no emotion whatever. He had an iron nerve. It settled in Tom's mind how relentless Hale had been in pursuing his obsession to hire someone to murder Bill Smith, how he'd kept looking until he'd found Ace Kirby, a man without a conscience, like himself.

Fairfax spectators listened intently when J.B. McNew, the town's Santa Fé agent, began testifying in a tight-lipped manner.

"Do you have a record of telegrams sent from the station during March, Nineteen

Twenty-Three?" Leahy asked.

"I do not."

"What happened to the telegrams?"

"They were destroyed."

It wasn't brought out at whose order the telegrams were destroyed, then Leahy asked: "Was a telegram sent to Bill Hale at Campbell, Texas, about the time the Smith house was blown up?"

"There was."

Leahy and Freeling tangled as the State sought to reveal the telegram's contents. Judge Justus ended the clash when he ruled the message was not admissible.

Checked there, the State brought in John "Pop" Gregg, a Nowata County farmer, who began repeating almost word for word the testimony of his son regarding various meetings with Hale.

"I'd left my farm and come down here," the elder Gregg said, "to talk to Dick. I wanted him to quit runnin' with outlaws. I remember Hale said once he wanted Smith bumped off that night, if possible, and the diamonds in the Smith house was worth four or five thousand dollars."

Of a sudden Hamilton loosed a violent objection against the defense's main target. "Your Honor . . . I object to the manner in which T.B. White over there keeps staring at the witnesses! They're afraid of him . . . they're shading their testimony in the State's favor!"

Leahy turned with a faint smile to the witness. "Mister Gregg, are you afraid of Tom White?"

"No," replied Gregg, the suggestion of a smile coming to his grizzled face.

"Has he ever threatened you?"

"Nope."

March 16th. Feeling that introduction of Ramsey's two confessions contained plenty of evidence to hold Bill Hale for district court trial, the prosecution continued to chip away at his heretofore impregnable public reputation built up over the years.

Florid-faced John Mayo entered, under close guard like Dick Gregg. He stood, scornful and cold-eyed while the oath was administered, a hardcase bank robber as old at the thicket game of outlaw as young Gregg was new, a companion of Ace Kirby's when the latter took a fatal dose of buckshot while attempting to rob a country store, and on location when Henry Grammer died in the wreck.

Until the grand jury investigation at Guthrie, Mayo said, he had known Ramsey only as "old John." "Kirby said he had a tough proposition," Mayo went on. "He told me John had a couple he wanted killed and that he was going to get two thousand dollars. I asked him who it was and he said . . . 'A blanket and her old man down the country.' I

164

told him I didn't think that was enough money. He said it didn't make much difference how they got killed, so it wouldn't be much trouble."

Hale and Ramsey leaned toward the witness, alert to each word, in surprise at Mayo's testimony. The easy smile on the cattle king's face had vanished. Now Ramsey sat erect, head thrown back, eyes fixed piercingly on the witness.

The courtroom became very quiet as Mayo continued about Kirby. "He said it would be best to blow up the house, as he'd probably have trouble getting in. He said John had showed him the house. Kirby asked me if I knew where he could get some grease, meaning nitro, but later said John was to show him where a magazine was located. When John came over, he drove off first, then Kirby. Later, he returned and put a five-gallon kerosene can in the kitchen. The next night . . . he came and got the can, wrapped it in a quilt and drove away. I didn't see Kirby until next morning. I asked him how things went, and he said the house was entirely dark and he figured he'd better wait a day. He left again the following night. That was the night of the explosion.

"Ramsey came two or three days later and told Kirby . . . 'That was a good job. Two of them are dead, and Smith will be dead in a day or two.' Later he came back and said Smith was dead and asked Kirby if he'd got all his money. Ace said no, but he would get it from Hank. I went with Ace to Grammer's place and saw Grammer hand him a large roll of bills."

Springer attacked, bringing out Mayo's hard-boiled background to discredit his testimony.

Mayo was not about to be buffaloed. Calmly he admitted being convicted of grand larceny as a youth and serving one year in the Oklahoma penitentiary. He said he had gambled, sold whisky, as if who hadn't, and run rooming houses in the oil fields.

"The State rests," Leahy announced as Mayo stepped down.

It was the prosecution's round, a big one.

The defense countered with Ernest Burkhart, Freeling examining.

"I didn't know any Ace Kirby," Burkhart said. Neither did he know Dick Gregg, who had testified to seeing Burkhart while talking over the Smith job with Hale on the Fairfax road.

A sing-song quality entered Burkhart's voice as he answered questions. "I deny any knowledge or connection with the deaths of W.E. Smith or Henry Roan. Frank Smith and T.B. White, Department of Justice agents, made me sign a statement implicating my uncle, W.K. Hale, and John Ramsey in the Osage murders. I wasn't allowed to read it until I'd signed it. White put a fountain pen in my hand, and Agent Smith held a gun at my left side and told me to sign. Then they let me read the statement."

Hearing that recited as if by rote, Tom White shook his head in disgust, seeing Burkhart turning to him in the jury room, relief in his face, pleading to tell his story, and, later, asking the government for protection, afraid to return to the Osage for fear his uncle would have him killed.

Confronted with his own grand jury testimony in the Smith case, as read bit by bit by Leahy, Burkhart haltingly identified it as his.

" 'If I go back there,' " Leahy quoted Burkhart at one point, " 'and Hale is out on bond and figures he's gonna get stuck, he would want to get me out of the country'."

"But," Burkhart told Leahy, "I didn't tell the truth to the grand jury. At that time I didn't mention the pistol the government agents used on me, because I'd agreed with Ramsey to wait until we both came to trial."

"I'll ask you once more," Leahy said wearily. "Is the testimony you gave the grand jury the truth?"

Before Burkhart could reply, Freeling shouted an objection, and with the case snarled on that point, Judge Justus adjourned court for the night.

March 17th. For the first time, Hale showed a break in composure. He was restless, tapping the table with a pencil and occasionally biting his fingernails. Ramsey took an attentive, listening attitude when Burkhart returned to the witness chair for the defense.

Burkhart spoke in the same rehearsed and denying voice of yesterday. Sitting far back in the chair, his eyes constantly roving the packed courtroom, he repudiated all previous statements made to federal officers and the grand jury, denied reported conversations with Leahy, and maintained he had no choice but go to Texas and New Mexico with federal agents.

"You came to Tom White's office and asked for protection," Leahy charged.

"I went because it was either that or go to jail on another murder charge," Burkhart replied, somewhat lamely, but he did not change his story.

"Didn't you tell me that Hale said to you . . . 'What do you care about bumping off Bill Smith, your wife is a sister and will fall heir to Reta's fortune . . . ,' and that you replied . . . 'I don't think she would because Bill and Reta made a joint will . . . ,' and that Hale then said . . . 'Hell, we'll break the will'."

"No, I said nothing of the kind."

But Leahy did make Burkhart admit that he had said and signed a statement to the effect that he left Oklahoma voluntarily and asked federal officers to guard him, away from Osage County, until the trial because he feared his uncle.

It was shortly after two o'clock when Freeling, striking a dramatic pose, faced the bench, and said: "Your Honor, although there are no legal grounds for holding my client, he has requested me to ask the court to have him bound over in order that his name be cleared of any stigma. He also requests the speediest trial possible."

Springer made the same surprise request for Ramsey.

"A very reasonable request," snapped County Attorney Templeton, at odds with Springer since the preliminary hearing began.

"I am taking this action," Springer said, "despite the fact there has been no evidence introduced on which Ramsey could possibly be held as a matter of law. The two alleged confessions of Ramsey implicating him and Hale in the Smith murders have been repudiated as having been made under duress and threats. The only attempt at corroboration the State has made is to introduce the testimony of John Mayo, a convict."

Whereupon Judge Justus ordered the defendants held for district court trial, thus closing one of the longest preliminaries on record in Oklahoma.

Immediately after adjournment came the very serious charges Hamilton and Springer had hinted at earlier. Hamilton, representing

Burkhart, filed suit for $250,000 in damages against Agents White, Wren, Street, and Smith, Edwin K. Brown, special assistant to the U.S. attorney general, and A.W. Comstock, Pawhuska attorney, assisting the prosecution.

To Tom White it was just another round in the old game of threats and intimidations. The defense's requests to go on trial were mere face-saving maneuvers, more Hale bravado, for in view of the evidence offered, there was no other course for Judge Justus to take but to hold Hale and Ramsey for trial. Yet, could the "King of the Osage Hills," widely acquainted and generally popular as a longtime cowman, be convicted on his own stomping ground? Another factor in his favor was Ernest Burkhart's switching sides, albeit in fear of his life. The odds favored Bill Hale.

CHAPTER TWELVE

On March 27th, Hale and Ramsey wanted out of jail and stood before District Judge Jesse L. Worten in a hearing. Hale admitted seeing Al Spencer, as witnesses had testified at the preliminary, but denied he approached the outlaw leader to commit murder.

"I met Max Billingsley for the purpose of buying a team," Hale said. "At that time Spencer and Gregg were introduced to me."

Ramsey said operatives of the Department of Justice "forced me to sign two confessions." He signed, he said, with the intention of later repudiating the statements.

Judge Worten denied both defendants bond.

During this lull the issue over the legal definition of "Indian country" stirred again when the solicitor general filed a brief in the U.S. Supreme Court, asserting federal authority to punish crimes committed on tribal Indian land. It was part of the appeal from Judge Cotteral's ruling, denying the jurisdiction of Oklahoma federal courts to try Hale and Ramsey for the murder of Henry Roan on allotted land. The defense fired back with bold denials.

Tom White, in Washington conferring with

J. Edgar Hoover, saw the solicitor's brief as a favorable sign. There would be a much stronger chance of convicting Hale and Ramsey in federal court in the Roan case than in Osage County for the Smith murders.

At the same time the county reached back into its oldest unsolved Indian murder. Moving with greatest secrecy, officers arrested Bryan Burkhart in Fairfax and took him to Pawhuska for arraignment in justice of peace court, charged with Anna Brown's murder. Bryan Burkhart, a younger brother of Ernest's, pleaded innocent and was ordered held without bond. This was his second arrest in the Brown case. On August 23, 1921 — three months after Anna's murder — he and Ernest had been charged in her death, but the cases were dismissed for lack of evidence. Uncle Bill Hale had gone their bond, making light all the while of the charge.

On May 14th, Bryan Burkhart's preliminary hearing portended another bristling fight of trial-like dimensions as the two sides lined up. The big guns of Hamilton, Howard, and Springer represented the defense. Freeling waited in the wings, if needed. Tom White and Frank Smith agreed that Hale was defending his flanks, and with good reason — Bryan led to Morrison and Morrison to Hale.

Heading the prosecution were County Attorney Templeton, Dabney of the state attorney general's office, and Leahy, the formidable special prosecutor. As if surprises were now the norm, Templeton also charged Morrison jointly with Burkhart in the Brown murder. Morrison was still in state prison.

Andy Smith of Fairfax testified to the gruesome discovery of the decomposed body of Anna Brown in Three-Mile Cañon, north of Gray Horse, while hunting, and Dr. J.G. Shoun explained the nature of the head wound discovered later that bared the murder.

The courtroom buzzed when Katherine Cole, Morrison's former wife, took the stand in another surprising turn. A pretty full-blood, somewhat dissipated-looking, she began testifying, fear and hesitation in her rich, halting voice. Yet, Tom thought, she was showing unusual courage considering the circumstances and the general unease among the Osages.

About a week before Anna Brown's body was found, she said, Bryan Burkhart and her husband drove up to her house in Fairfax. It was evening, and Anna was with them. Katherine joined them. Late that night, after much drinking, the party drove to a ranch house north of Gray Horse. The men went in, while she and Anna stayed in the car. Pretty soon the men returned. They drove

173

north to the head of Three-Mile Cañon.

She hesitated, then said: "Bryan and Kelsey took Anna out of the car. She was very drunk. When I started to go with them, Kelsey cussed me . . . told me to stay there." In a few minutes, she said, the men came back, explaining they had left Anna drinking with some other persons in the cañon. The three then drove back to Fairfax.

"Did you hear a shot at any time while you waited in the car?" Howard cross-examined.

"No."

"When did you first tell this story?"

"At Guthrie . . . to the grand jury."

"Why didn't you tell it earlier?"

"Because I was afraid . . . afraid I'd be killed," she replied resolutely, wide-eyed, a trace of that old fear rising to her voice.

There were no more questions.

The State followed with Matt W. Williams, a one-time Ralston saloonkeeper, now living in Denver. In May, 1921, Williams said, he and Shorty Wheeler had a room over the Ralston bank and Wheeler was bootlegging. On a Saturday night prior to the disappearance of Anna Brown, Bryan Burkhart and the Osage woman came to the room and Burkhart bought some whisky, then drove off. "Later that night Shorty said he had a delivery to make, and we drove to Three-Mile Cañon to wait for the customers. There was a car parked across the cañon when we drove up. We hadn't been there long when we heard a woman scream. She screamed four or five times. Then I heard a shot. The sounds seemed to come from the bottom of the cañon." Soon after that, Williams testified, Morrison and Bryan Burkhart appeared.

" 'What was that screaming?' " Williams said he asked.

" 'We had to lay out a woman,' " Williams said Morrison told him.

" 'There was a shot, too.' "

" 'Oh, my gun went off accidentally,' " Williams quoted Morrison.

The two men paid for the whisky, Williams continued, then went to the car parked across the cañon.

Despite Howard's severe cross-examination, Williams stuck to his account and reiterated hearing the screams and a shot.

"Do you know the present whereabouts of Shorty Wheeler?"

"I'm afraid he's gone up Salt Creek," Williams said. "In my opinion, Shorty was killed after he made a statement in the case. I know he disappeared from the county jail and ain't been seen since. The reason I never said anything back there in 'Twenty-One was because I didn't want to commit suicide."

Two other witnesses told of seeing Bryan Burkhart and the ill-fated Anna together late the Saturday night in question.

The State rested its case. Howard announced the defense would offer no testimony, and Justice of Peace W.T. Crozier ordered Burkhart held without bond for district court trial.

May 26th, Ernest Burkhart went on trial in district court for the W.E. Smith family murders. Mollie, wrapped in a pretty Indian blanket, sat somberly beside her obviously uneasy husband.

In the prosecution's opening statement, Dabney said: "We believe we will be able to establish that Ernest Burkhart sought out various individuals to have them kill W.E. Smith and his wife Reta. We believe we can further show that W.K. Hale approached various people to have them kill the Smiths. Testimony will show that on March Eighth, John Ramsey went to Ace Kirby and told him they wanted the work done that night. Also that Kirby had in his possession a roll of fuse one hundred feet long and a can of nitroglycerine, and on that night he took them to Fairfax to blow up the house. But the Smiths weren't there, so he waited until the following night, planted the bomb, lighted the fuse, the explosion following." As an additional motive, Dabney said, the State would show that Hale owed Smith $6,000, which Hale refused to pay.

On the second day Ernest Burkhart looked more at ease. Loyal Mollie, still next to her husband, wore a shawl of black silk tightly around a waist of dark purple, her garb a mixture of Indian and white. Her jewelry included several rings and a brooch. Many Indians crowded the courtroom.

Speaking deliberately, Tom White testified Burkhart had confessed how Hale had told him to find someone to blow up the Smith house. Next, Burkhart had admitted approaching Curly Johnson and Blackie Thompson.

Hamilton was waiting. "Were you armed, Mister White, when this statement was made?"

"No, sir, and I was not armed at the preliminary when you tried to disarm me. I seldom go armed. Burkhart volunteered the confession after being told anything he said could be used against him. He also said an innocent man was in jail in connection with the death of Henry Roan and that his testimony would clear the prisoner. This man, he said, was Roy Bunch. Later, Burkhart came to me and said he'd be killed if he came back to Osage County. He asked me to give him protection, which I did. I talked with him at San Antonio and Medina Lake, also at a hotel in Arkansas City. Mister Leahy and Mister Jeffrey were present. Burkhart repeated his confession after Mister Leahy said he'd have nothing to do with the case if Burkhart's statement wasn't true. Burkhart agreed to testify. He also made the confession, he said, because federal operatives had treated him well."

Tom's dispassionate testimony prompted a newsman to describe him as "the cool and sagacious chief for the federal government, the silent and all-powerful figure in the far-reaching Osage mysteries. He is the close-lipped, cool-eyed man the government put in charge of those it sent to ferret out the repeated tribal deaths."

The defense stuck to its strategy of duress in Burkhart's confession and claimed federal officers had hurried him out of state in order to keep him away from his attorneys.

On the contrary, Agent John Wren told the court: "Burkhart asked for protection. He and I made up the name of E.J. Ernest after we went to Texas. I wasn't with him all the time. He was alone several times."

On May 28th, Leahy testified about his going to Arkansas City, Kansas at Burkhart's request for a conference.

"I told Burkhart, if his statement wasn't true, I wanted nothing to do with it. He immediately replied that all he'd said was true. He told me his uncle, W.K. Hale, had asked him to get somebody to kill W.E. Smith, after Smith and Hale had trouble over a debt." Leahy then said Burkhart told of propositions to outlaws Dick Gregg and Al Spencer, and, finally, Ace Kirby was hired to destroy the Smith home while Hale was in Texas.

Tempers shortened as the court went into night session, and Howard charged: "The Oklahoma attorney general's office defrauded the Osage County district court when Ernest Burkhart was taken to Guthrie for questioning!"

Attorney General Short rose to answer.

Before he could speak, County Attorney Templeton shouted: "No man can say we practiced fraud on this district court, and, if the court permits me to say it, I'll meet the man who says so out in the court yard!"

When court was shortly adjourned, the two attorneys started for each other, but other counsel separated them before they could come to blows.

On May 29th, a Saturday, long arguments over admission of Burkhart's confession bored the crowd, which began to drift away. From the witness stand Burkhart denied everything, rambled, spoke with great positiveness, and often his testimony lacked connection or showed a constructive interpretation of events.

During the long questioning, with the jury excused, Leahy asked Burkhart about his employment.

"I don't work," he replied in contempt. "I married an Osage."

Burkhart said agents shocked him with electricity, that he never asked for protection, and Smith had "held a gun at my side, and made me sign a statement. I am not guilty and do not know of any facts in the Smith explosion or who did it."

But the day's leading attraction was just off stage. Word spread quickly that Bill Hale was going to testify. Soon spectators started filling the long seats, their anticipation comparable to waiting for a matinee idol to appear.

Judge Worten looked inquiringly at the defense. "What is the purpose of Mister Hale's testimony?"

"To corroborate Burkhart's testimony that his statements were not voluntary," Freeling said.

"Call the witness."

Sworn in after a nodding, smiling entrance, clad in a dark suit, white shirt, and conservative bow tie, Hale settled himself. He seemed as relaxed and genial as a man about to sit down for a visit with a neighbor. The jury was still out. Guided by Freeling, he began his story in the dead-quiet courtroom.

"Frank Smith kept shaking his finger in my face and edging closer and closer. He accused me of the W.E. Smith and other murders. John Wren stood behind him, and T.B. White sat nearby. I kept count on my fingers, and, as near as I can remember, they accused me of twenty-seven murders," Hale said wryly. "Smith asked me if I was ready to confess. I said . . . 'No' . . . and Smith said . . . 'Well, you will before midnight. We've made Burkhart and Ramsey confess, and we've got a way of making people if they don't want to.'" Hale said, hearing a pistol cocked behind him, he had looked, and "Frank Smith grabbed me by the shoulder and shoved a big gun in my face. He said . . . 'If you back up again, I'll beat your head off.'"

Hale, quite suddenly, snapped to his feet and leaped back and forth behind the witness stand, waving his arms, demonstrating.

"Next they asked me if I was ready to confess to the Smith murders, and I said I had nothing to confess." Motioning wildly again, shaking his fists, he strode forward and back beside the judge's bench, talking in a high, excited voice. "Smith sniffed the air and said . . . 'Don't you smell that human flesh burning? I've just electrocuted one of your pals, and I'm going to electrocute you.' They talked a while, then White said . . . 'Well, I hate to do it, Hale, but if you won't sign, we'll have to put you in a hot chair.' Then he pointed to a chair and said it was used to electrocute people."

If you're going to tell a lie, tell a whopper when your life is at stake and your past has caught up with you. Hale's theatrics held the courtroom entranced. Judge Worten hung on every word and followed every move of Hale's startling performance. Here was the county's best-known citizen making astounding accusations against Department of Justice agents. Calm once more, Hale returned to the stand. Then he claimed agents put a black cap over his head and shocked him several times "with a battery or something so I could feel it." Hale said he had been kept there for an hour.

Actually the confrontation at Guthrie between Hale and federal officers had been quite brief. Informed that they had evidence to convict him, Hale had denied it and said he would fight it to the finish.

Judge Worten ordered stricken from the record all of Hale's testimony except the reference to Burkhart's confession. "The court will rule later on admission of Burkhart's alleged statements," Worten said.

Tom White missed the day's big show. He and Edwin K. Brown were in Washington for another conference on strategy, unaware that Hale's remarkable dramatics were tied in with another forthcoming development in Washington that threatened the career of every agent in the Osage investigation. Hale's claims of third-degree treatment, while ridiculous in the eyes of the prosecution, nevertheless posed the question of duress. As Osage County's leading citizen — still to be tried and still to be found guilty — Hale's assertions, delivered in his clear, forceful voice, carried a certain degree of conviction to others in high places outside the investigative side of the Osage murders.

May 31st, Judge Worten excused the jury when court opened, marking the third day of exclusion. Voicing the old cry of duress, Hamilton clashed with Dabney over admission of Burkhart's statements to federal officers. "The question at issue," Dabney told the court, "is whether Ernest Burkhart or Frank Smith or Tom White told the truth. The burden of proof rests with the defense."

Worten broke the hard-fought wrangling when he announced that his written opinion was ready. Victory was indicated for the defense as he read:

"The court finds from testimony that the purported confession given by Ernest Burkhart to federal officers at Guthrie in the W.E. Smith case and his statement in the Henry Roan case were not voluntary. The court also condemns officers if they played the part they were alleged to have played in obtaining the confession."

The defense went into jubilant back-slapping and casting triumphant looks at the prosecution. However, the judge said, and defense faces began to change, the court was admitting testimony alleged to have been made by Burkhart to T.J. Leahy at Arkansas City and before a grand jury at Guthrie.

Now Dabney was jubilant. "Our case hasn't been hurt a bit," he told reporters, "because Burkhart repeated the same admissions to Leahy he had to Agents White and Smith."

June 1st, a forbidding gray overcast shut out the morning Osage sun, presaging high winds and slashing rain, another drawn-out day for trial followers, weary of endless legal arguments. But three events were to occur to make this a significant day for the often-maligned prosecution in the Osage probe, of such a sensational nature that the Ernest Burkhart trial, for the moment, was eclipsed in the wake of these rapid-fire happenings.

The first had been set in motion days earlier when Matt Williams, the former Ralston man who had testified in the Bryan Burkhart preliminary, hunted up Leahy and Agent J.R. Burger, to whom he had first revealed his experiences the night of Anna Brown's murder. Burger, familiar with the case from the first Osage investigation in 1924, had been shifted from the Oklahoma City office when the battlefront moved to Pawhuska.

"Now they're trying to bribe me," Williams complained. A black-haired man in his late forties, he seemed to have an unusual lack of fear for a State witness. He had come from as far as Denver to testify. On May 26th, he said, a man told him to go to the office of a local cattleman at 2 P.M. Williams did and told Leahy and Burger how the conversation went.

"Matt," the cattleman had said, "I have sworn lies for you and you have been raised with these boys, and I have told Hale and the rest I would see you and you would not go through with the play."

"I can't help you," Williams had said. "I'm already on record as a prosecution witness, and I won't betray the confidence of Leahy or Burger."

"I've been your friend for years, Matt. I'm surprised to see you taking the stand you are. *You'll have to suffer the consequences.* Now you think this over and come back and see me in my home or office at any time, day or night. I still believe in you, Matt, and I want to tell our friend, Bill Hale, that you won't be on the stand."

Williams had shaken his head. "I can't do it."

"Matt, if you'll come to my house, I'll give you two thousand dollars and a man will drive you to Brownsville, Texas. You'll go on to old Mexico. They won't extradite you. If you need money, write me. I'll take care of you."

Williams said he did not return. Instead, he came to Leahy and Burger.

On the following day County Attorney

Templeton charged a prominent Pawhuska cattleman and another man with conspiring to prevent Williams from testifying as a State witness. Thus, Matt Williams exposed what was going on behind the scenes as Hale and powerful friends used threats and money to prevent damaging testimony. The expression "old Mexico," as different from the State of New Mexico, was a cow-country expression. City folks said Mexico.

As court convened that day, Ernest Burkhart listened with a studied nonchalance, a pose he had recently assumed, while Leahy started reading from a transcript of Burkhart's testimony before the Guthrie grand jury. Leahy read how the defendant told of driving to Ripley to tell Ramsey to tell Kirby to blow up the Smith house while Hale was in Texas.

Hamilton, hammering away with the customary claim of federal mistreatment of prisoners, objected, claiming Burkhart was not actually at liberty when he made the statements.

Judge Worten overruled and recalled the jury.

At noon big news broke out of Washington. Federal Judge Cotteral of the western Oklahoma federal district court was reversed. The U.S. Supreme Court, defining "Indian country," ruled the federal government had jurisdiction in the Henry Roan murder, committed on restricted Indian land in Oklahoma. Authority of the United States to punish crimes by or against tribal Indians in the "Indian country" in Oklahoma continued after the admission of the state as before. "Indian country" applied to a restricted Indian allotment, and there was no difference between a "restricted" and a "trust" allotment. "It follows," the high court concluded, "that the judgment sustaining the demurrer to the indictment is erroneous and must be reversed." That was the gist of *U.S. v. Ramsey et al*, 271 US 467. The murder had occurred on the restricted allotment of Rose Little Star, who had not received a certificate of competency authorizing her to sell. The ruling changed the direction of the Osage investigation, taking it out of Hale-dominated Osage County.

In Oklahoma City an elated Roy St. Lewis said he would refile the indictments in federal court and requested immediate issuance of the high court's mandate. St. Lewis said he'd been criticized severely by many attorneys for appealing Judge Cotteral's decision that the federal court lacked jurisdiction in the case.

That wasn't all. Unknown to Hale's battery of attorneys the third blow was about to fall this same day.

CHAPTER THIRTEEN

The day turned sultry and hot, the sky changed to a darker hue, threatening, oppressive. An approaching storm, its thunder growling off toward the southwest, threw a darkness over the courtroom, jammed for the afternoon session.

Trial observers were still whispering over the Supreme Court's ruling when, surprisingly, in a case replete with the unexpected, the State called Kelsey Morrison as a witness. He entered at once — gaunt, sharp-featured, extremely pallid, high-strung — and was sworn in. Missing on his right hand was part of one finger, shot off in a fray west of Fairfax, September, 1923, when officers went hunting for stills.

The defense looked stunned.

A brief delay ensued while Judge Worten informed the witness that his testimony would not be used against him at his own trial.

"The statement the witness is about to make," Dabney explained, "was given earlier to Mister Leahy and myself at Guthrie, after we advised Morrison he could testify with immunity."

That assurance produced no change in Morrison's haunted expression. Always pale, he looked terribly ashen today. In the silence of a startled courtroom, eyes downcast, he began to testify in a voice barely audible to straining spectators: "Hale talked to me at one time at one of his ranch houses and told me Bill Smith had done him dirty and asked me how much I would take to kill the whole bunch." Morrison paused. After a long interval of thought, a manner he was to follow throughout his testimony, he said: "I told him I would study it. I talked to him later in one of his pastures. Hale wanted me to shoot Smith. Later he wanted me to set fire to the house and shoot Smith and his wife as they ran out."

Morrison's mouth twitched. He kept his eyes lowered, apparently to avoid looking at the Fairfax people who knew him and remembered his incredibly violent marriage to Katherine Cole. "I was out with Burkhart and Hale in a pasture at a later time. Hale asked me if I was going on through with it and that, if I wasn't, he would get someone else. I told him I didn't believe I wanted to do it." Another reflective pause. "He asked me how much I wanted to do the job. I told him I didn't want to do it. I told him I knew who he could get. I said this party would have to have the money down. He said he didn't have it then, but would when the job

189

was pulled. Hale said I was to get three thousand. He said Smith and his wife had a joint will and, if one got killed, both should be killed at once. He said if I did not lose my nerve, Ernest would get it all, and I would be taken care of. He meant by all that Burkhart would get the headrights of the Lizzie Q family . . . Mollie Burkhart, Anna Brown, and Missus Smith." After some more hesitation, Morrison added: "Ernest Burkhart told me it was a good job."

"What was a good job?" Leahy asked.

Another pause. "The murder of Anna Brown."

"Did you kill Anna Brown?"

A still longer pause. "Yes . . . I killed her. I was hired by W.K. Hale in Nineteen Twenty-One. He came to me one day and asked me what I would do for a thousand dollars. I told him 'most anything. He said he wanted me to kill Anna Brown. He paid me six hundred dollars and later bought me a car."

After his initial surprise, Hale had kept a fixed, stone face except for a faint amusement now and then.

Tom White listened with growing anger and disgust. Although he and Frank Smith had promised Morrison nothing at Guthrie, and thus had learned nothing, Morrison's later immunity was worth it to strip away Hale's veneer as the "Indian's friend."

★ ★ ★

June 2nd, looking like a dance-hall sheik, tall and slim, straight black hair slicked back, Morrison nervously entered the witness box for cross-examination. Howard rose to confront him.

Morrison said he was 28 years old and had lived in Osage County six years. During that time he had not worked at all.

"Then how did you live?"

"I was married to an Osage."

"Have you ever been addicted to narcotics?"

Morrison flushed through his prison pallor. "No."

"You made a statement to Edwin Dabney and T.J. Leahy?"

"They were trying to get me to confess to Anna Brown's murder."

"Instead," Howard boomed, "they were trying to get you to testify against Hale and Burkhart, weren't they?"

Morrison grinned. "Yes, they were. They told me, if they used me as a witness against Hale and Burkhart, I wouldn't be prosecuted for the things I testified to. I told them I wouldn't say anything about the murders unless I got immunity. . . . I killed Anna Brown sometime in May, Nineteen Twenty-One, about two-thirty in the morning, near Fairfax."

"Why can't you say the exact day of the month?"

191

"I was pretty drunk. Bryan Burkhart and I carried Anna down to the cañon where I killed her. My ex-wife, Katherine Cole, accompanied us to the cañon. Then we got her drunk and took her home."

That explained to Tom why Katherine Cole, at the Bryan Burkhart preliminary, had testified she heard no shot. Later, Matt Williams, there with Shorty Wheeler to deliver whisky, testified to hearing screams and a shot.

"We got Anna drunk to kill her," Morrison went on in a flat tone. "Bryan helped me carry her down to the ravine. She was layin' there drunk. We held her up in a sittin' position. I shot her. She fell over, and we left at once."

"When did you sober up after the murder?"

"When I went to the pen."

"When was that?"

"In June last year."

This far, attacking Morrison's credibility, the defense had accused him of using drugs and established that he was an alcoholic of long standing.

At Hale's ranch house before the murder, Morrison said he had told the cowman he was ready to kill Anna Brown. "He told me to get rid of that squaw, meaning my wife. I told him I didn't have a gun. He gave me his."

Here, Tom White thought, was Hale revealing his utter contempt for the Osage people on whom he preyed by calling Katherine Cole a lowly squaw and further exposing his *modus operandi* — hiring others to do his killing while he always remained the genial public benefactor, something he repeated, when he'd hired John Ramsey to kill Henry Roan. Everything was finally coming to the surface. Yet Hale was still far from being convicted.

Morrison said Hale had told him to put a bullet through Anna Brown's head and leave her with a whisky bottle beside her. That way, if her body wasn't found soon, it might be thought she had died from drinking poisoned whisky, which would not be unusual, and the bullet might be overlooked. "Anna Brown's body was found where I killed her. I shot her in the top of the head with an automatic."

"Where did you go after the murder?" Howard asked.

"To see Bill Hale. We told Hale we'd left the whisky as he directed." Morrison said he had stayed all night at Hale's place, that some woman was there, he didn't know who. He said Hale had told him he was going to send a cowhand to ride the pasture after a few days, and he would find the body. "Hale had loaned me six hundred dollars. He said if I killed Anna Brown I wouldn't have to pay it back. Two days later Hale gave me another six hundred. About three weeks later he gave me a car for the other four hundred. I later got broke, and he signed notes for one thousand for me. He paid the notes. I did not repay them. I sold him some notes and mortgages. He paid me two thousand for some business property in Fairfax later."

"Anna Brown had never done you any harm?"

Morrison dropped his gaze. "No."

"Then you killed her solely to get the money for it?"

"Yes." W.E. Smith had some knowledge of Anna Brown's murder, Morrison said. "Two or three weeks after her murder, Smith told me he knew Hale and Ernest Burkhart had Anna killed."

"Did you tell Smith you had killed Anna yourself?" Howard asked.

Morrison smiled and shook his head. "I did not." But, Morrison said, he did warn Hale of Smith's suspicions. "Hale said it would be a good policy to kill Smith. I told Hale that, if I thought Smith knew too much, I had better kill him, too. I told him I would think it over. Hale said Smith accused him of stealing cattle and hogs and was dirty. And they were having trouble over a debt."

Yet, Morrison testified, as if his contradictory self were speaking, he had no wish to kill Smith, who had done him favors. He continued to refuse to kill the Smiths, although

Hale had raised the payoff from $1,600 to $3,000 since Anna Brown's murder. Morrison said another reason he refused was because, after he and Katherine Cole divorced, he had married Bill Stepson's widow and didn't need the money. "But Smith had been good to me, and I wouldn't have killed him for money."

Mrs. Stepson, a white woman who had inherited an Osage headright from her dead husband, had died in July, 1923, while undergoing an operation. When her will was admitted to probate in county court, the Fairfax *Osage Chief* reported with pique that Morrison, instead of the two children, was given the bulk of the estate. Had Morrison had a hand in Stepson's death? Yes, said some Fairfax old-timers, but without proof.

After Morrison had finished his astonishing story, boyish Dick Gregg repeated his assertion at the Hale-Ramsey preliminary that Hale had tried to hire him to kill the Smith family.

Next the State sprang Blackie Thompson as a surprise witness against Burkhart. Appearance of the dark, balding man sent a stillness over the courtroom. Apparently Fairfax residents knew about him.

"Curly Johnson and I saw Burkhart," Thompson said, "and he told us he wanted the Smiths bumped off. He said there were some diamonds in the Smith house. He told

195

us he would give us a Buick car and a thousand dollars." The fortune of Lizzie Q, mother of Mrs. Ernest Burkhart and Mrs. W.E. Smith, was mentioned, Thompson testified. "I said I would take the car and see about the other later. I got caught with the car and got five years. Burkhart said he had the car insured and wanted me to take it. I pleaded guilty to the theft of the car to protect Burkhart."

June 3rd, a sad thing happened: the death of a child, Anna Bigheart, four. Little Anna, named after Anna Brown, was the youngest of the three children of Ernest and Mollie Bigheart. She had been adopted as a baby by Joe and Bertha Bigheart, the latter a cousin of Mollie's, a somewhat bizarre exchange which Burkhart had explained by saying that Mollie, ill at the time, was unable to care for the infant. After the adoption, Joe Bigheart died, and the Burkhart child inherited half of his estate. Bertha and Joe had no other children, so the child stood to inherit half of Bertha's estate, estimated at $150,000, in the event of her death, the other half going to Bertha's parents. At that time, federal agents were advised, a rumor was circulating that the Hale-Burkhart faction intended to do away with Bertha and her parents so the adopted child could inherit the entire estate.

Today, Mollie slipped away for the services

in Pawhuska and returned, solemn-faced, to renew her vigil of faith beside her husband. Otherwise, it was a dull day for the sensation-hungry.

Dick Gregg refuted he was offered clemency from his sentence in Kansas state prison for testifying against Hale and Burkhart. More emphatically, he denied sending his father to Hale with an agreement whereby Gregg would remain silent if Hale paid $2,500.

June 4th, hard-boiled John Mayo began testifying calmly, no indication that he was about to unleash a bombshell. "Ace Kirby came in one night with an oil can. He told me about getting some caps and fuses. I kept insisting it wasn't enough money. He said he had another man he could get."

Mayo repeated seeing Henry Grammer hand a roll of bills to Kirby after the Smith house explosion. Asked why he didn't inform officers of the planned murders, if he knew in advance, Mayo replied: "I knew better. I'd been murdered the way the country was then."

Then came the uproar.

"My wife was over to see me," he said, "and told me about Mister Springer and another gentleman trying to bribe her to get me not to testify in this case. There were some people fooling around my wife," he said heavily.

Springer bounded up instantly. "Your Honor, I demand that a commission be appointed to investigate this ridiculous charge. What this witness said is absolutely false. I want myself cleared."

Judge Worten agreed to the commission, although one's being appointed would never be reported, and ordered Mayo's accusation stricken from the record. Mayo's statement revived the old story in Fairfax that Springer had threatened rancher Sol Smith with a gun at Guthrie before he went into the grand jury room.

As the action eased, a Fairfax attorney testified to drawing up a joint will for William and Reta Smith, with the survivor to inherit. By this the State succeeded in establishing that the Burkharts stood to gain more if the Smiths died at the same time. Instead, Smith had survived for a few days, and the estate went to his kin.

Now Leahy questioned Burkhart concerning a deal with Blackie Thompson.

"Wasn't the plan for Thompson to steal the car and for you to collect the insurance?"

"No," Burkhart declared.

The State rested before noon, and Howard began presenting his opening statement for the defense. "It's the purpose of the State," he said, "to show W.K. Hale was the mastermind. But evidence will show that W.K. Hale and Ernest Burkhart were law-abiding citizens and had only a speaking acquaintance with John Ramsey." That W.E. Smith did nothing for a living. That Smith stayed drunk and was a bad character. That Hale helped financially rather than hold enmity against him. "Hale was a big-hearted man. The proof is in the checks he wrote." That there was nothing mysterious about when Hale saw Al Spencer and Dick Gregg at Ike Ogg's place. "Hale and Rowe went to Billingsley's home to get some horses. They stopped at Ogg's for a drink. Spencer and Gregg were there. The only conversation they had was in reference to roping, as both Hale and Spencer were fancy ropers."

June 5th, Ernest Burkhart could have been reciting memorized passages as he nonchalantly testified again. Just denials. "Furthermore, I never told County Attorney Templeton I was afraid of my uncle just before I was to testify as a State witness in the Hale-Ramsey preliminary."

Hale, the next witness, demonstrated even more confidence and poise than usual. At his entrance the courtroom became quiet, and the crowd squirmed and gawked to get a better view of the cowman. Neatly dressed in a brown suit, light-colored shirt, and blue tie, he nodded and smiled at several individuals as he glanced about. Then, going on erectly, he shook hands with all his attorneys.

On the stand, in a loud, clear voice, with frequent glances at the jury or the court reporter, he testified on behalf of nephew Ernest: "The first time I met Ace Kirby was in a pasture where Kirby was running a still. I met Kirby two other times, but there was no talk about murder cases. I met Blackie Thompson one time. Later, in Fairfax, he had to introduce himself to me before I knew who he was. Thompson," Hale stressed, "was then on *furlough* from the state pen." Hale was still on the stand when the Saturday session closed.

June 6th, with a show of injured innocence, Ernest Burkhart gave a Sunday interview to the Tulsa *World* from his cell in denial of testimony by outlaws Gregg, Mayo, and Thompson. "It's just a frame-up by a gang of convicts to get out of the pen. I don't know a thing about Smith's murder. We always got along fine together."

"What makes you think these men will gain their freedom by testifying against you?"

"Well, T.B. White and Frank Smith told me they wouldn't prosecute me if I'd testify against Uncle Bill. They promised to turn me loose."

June 7th, Hale, always the main attraction, returned to testify. He spoke directly to the intent jury, leaning toward them, looking at them straight on, appearing relaxed and neighborly. He'd had virtual free run of the county jail, including visits to the women's quarters.

"I was downtown in Pawhuska when I read in a Tulsa paper there was a warrant for my arrest," he said. "I went immediately to the courthouse and surrendered. I was taken to Guthrie." Federal officers, he went on, his tone implying the ridiculous, accused him of murdering William and Reta Smith and their servant girl, Smith's first wife, Reta's sister; Lizzie Q, Anna Brown, Henry Roan, plus other unsolved murders he enumerated. Hale said he went home after a picture show the night of May 21, 1921, the night the State contended Anna Brown was murdered. He said he saw Ernest and Bryan Burkhart about 9:30 P.M. He had known Anna Brown for years. "We were mighty good friends. I had just sold her house and made three thousand on the deal."

He discounted a wide range of accusations against him, from giving the Brown death weapon to Kelsey Morrison to trying to recruit Al Spencer or Dick Gregg to kill the Smiths. "I never told Ernest Burkhart to see John Ramsey and have him get Ace Kirby to blow up the Smith house while I was in Texas."

Leahy presented in evidence a check bearing Hale's signature made out to John

Ramsey in August of 1923.

"That was for feeding cattle for me," Hale explained.

Now, for the first time, Hale gave his version of the disputatious $6,000, which the State contended Hale had refused to pay and figured in Hale's motive to have Smith murdered.

Hale said it was the other way around. Back in 1918 Smith told him he'd got into a mix-up with a woman and a federal officer had threatened to turn him in for a penitentiary offense unless Smith dug up some money. First, Hale loaned Smith money, then Ernest. Smith repaid everything. "Smith told me he was afraid Reta would find out about his mix-up, divorce him, and he'd lose his payroll."

Off-stage, while Hale was repeating claimed methods of "torture" used in vain to make him confess — "They shocked me with electricity." — "Don't you smell flesh a-burnin'?" — "I was blindfolded by White." — "Smith said he'd make me sign a statement yet." — "I heard a six-shooter click." — "They pulled a mask over my face, placed me in a chair, and shot a little juice into me." — the Supreme Court granted the Department of Justice's request that a mandate be sent immediately to federal Judge Cotteral, ordering the trial of Hale and Ramsey for the murder of Henry Roan.

This speed-up, coming two weeks after Judge Cotteral's reversal on the jurisdiction issue, was forty-five days ahead of the usual schedule of handing out mandates, attorneys said. It meant that, despite the maneuvers of a shrewd defense staff, Hale was being inexorably drawn toward the situation most dangerous to him: trial before a federal court, away from familiar Osage County and his shield of influence. And, unforeseen by Hale and his staff of attorneys, another reversal was looming fast, this time close around them, from a quarter they assumed under control and no longer a threat.

It began late that afternoon of June 7th. Ernest Burkhart was walking from the courthouse to his cell in the county jail. Throughout the session he had listened to his uncle's forceful denials and claims of mistreatment by federal officers. He had lost his scoffing nonchalance. He looked tired.

When the curious crowd drifted away and prisoner and guard walked alone, Burkhart, with a glance around, quickly passed a note to the deputy sheriff.

"Don't look at it now," Burkhart said, and they went on. After the deputy had delivered his prisoner, he saw the message was addressed to T.J. Leahy, the well-known and highly esteemed Pawhuska attorney now on the prosecution staff.

Soon thereafter, Leahy read: **See me**

tonight in the county jail. Ernest Burkhart.

Leahy frowned. Now what new shenanigan of Burkhart's was this? Nevertheless, after dark, Leahy drove to the county jail.

Burkhart said quickly: "I'm through lying, Mister Leahy. From this minute on, regardless of the outcome of this trial, when I'm put on the witness stand, I'm going to tell the truth and nothing but the truth." He shook his head in desperation. "I don't want to go on with this trial any longer. But no matter what happens, I'm going to tell the truth from now on."

Leahy regarded him with no little doubt. Not so long ago Burkhart had made a statement to him in Arkansas City, swearing to its truth and volunteering to be a witness against Hale and Ramsey, only to back off completely through fear. Could Burkhart be trusted a second time?

"Being with the prosecution," Leahy said, "I'm in no position to advise you. Why don't you tell your lawyers?"

"I can't tell 'em. No, that wouldn't do." Was he still afraid?

Leahy considered a moment, questioning.

"Get in touch with Flint Moss for me," Burkhart pleaded.

Leahy knew Moss, a Tulsa attorney. Retained early by the Burkhart defense, he had withdrawn without taking part in the case.

Still Leahy hesitated. "Why don't you telephone him?"

"I can't. I'm absolutely helpless here. My only chance is for you to get him for me."

"Well," Leahy said, "I can do this. I'll telephone Flint Moss that you want to see him."

Late that night Leahy located Moss, who consented to see Burkhart the following night at 9:30.

June 8th, looking pale and ill, John Ramsey appeared for his first lengthy testimony. He had testified briefly the day before concerning two recanted confessions, just long enough to claim agents had abused him with electric shocks at Guthrie. Immediately, in Washington, Oscar Luhring, assistant U.S. attorney general, issued a sharp denial that agents used third-degree methods on Ramsey.

"I was tired," Ramsey complained in a doleful voice. "My head was awful weak and bad from flu . . . and I had rheumatism awful bad. . . . They accused me of killin' Curly Johnson. I always understood Curly died from an overdose of dope."

Springer asked him why he had signed one statement.

"I was afraid not to. I knew I couldn't stand any more of the treatment I was gettin', or would get, if I didn't sign. I thought they were going to put the juice to me. I asked to sign it before they gave me the juice."

At Springer's urging, Ramsey denied killing Henry Roan and playing a rôle in the Smith murders.

Carefully the defense opened testimony intended to prove that Bryan Burkhart couldn't have figured in Anna Brown's murder. Duke Burkhart, another brother, testified that on the night of May 21, 1921, a party that included Anna had supper at the Ernest Burkhart home in Fairfax. Bryan took Anna home. Later, others of the party attended a Fairfax picture show while Ernest and Bryan played pool. Everyone stayed all night at Ernest Burkhart's home.

Solemn-faced, speaking low, Mollie Burkhart told the same story.

Mrs. W.K. Hale testified that, in company of her husband and daughter, Willie, she had met the Burkhart party that night. Homer Huffaker, Fairfax bank president, also told of seeing the group.

In another slant, the defense called Ralston rancher John Morris who testified: "I met Hale on the road talking to John Gregg. I heard Gregg ask Hale for money and threaten that his son would testify against him."

Like an echo, cattleman Lou Oller, who had voiced threats against federal agents at Guthrie and drawn Agent Street's challenge, upheld Morris's story.

The last defense witness of the day was a

lanky, tight-lipped, brown-haired young man, Bryan Burkhart.

"I was arrested in Nineteen Twenty-One for the slaying of Anna Brown," he said, "but the case was dismissed." He verified brother Duke's account. "I did not leave Ernest's home that night," he swore. "I never did meet Kelsey Morrison or his wife that night."

"Did you hold Anna Brown while Kelsey Morrison shot her?"

"I did not."

The day ended on that flat denial.

In the prosecution's eyes, there was no denying the social gatherings that evening at Fairfax. That left plenty of time for Anna Brown to be murdered about 2:30 in the morning, for Bryan Burkhart to join Kelsey Morrison, and for Hale to be at his ranch near Gray Horse, a few miles east of Fairfax, and give Morrison the murder weapon — which side would the jury believe?

Flint Moss, the Tulsa attorney, arrived at the county jail that night as he promised. Ernest Burkhart repeated to Moss what he had told Leahy. He was finished with lying. He wanted to tell the truth. He also explained his actions. First of all, he hadn't thought his rôle in the Smith case amounted to murder. "I never thought I'd be brought to trial, and I didn't think I'd be convicted, if I did face trial." But he had seen and felt the chain of evidence drawing tighter around him. Now, if not convicted, he felt he would be charged with perjury.

"I'm sick and tired of all this. I want to get out in the clear. I want to admit exactly what I did . . . which I didn't think was so serious at the time . . . and take my medicine."

Moss could see only a straight, hard road. "Change your plea to guilty. End the trial. Throw yourself on the mercy of the court."

There was no talk of immunity. Burkhart asked for none.

"All right," Burkhart said. "I'll leave it up to you to do what you can do for me."

June 9th, only a few spectators were in the courtroom when the trial resumed. Flint Moss sat to one side. The jury filed in and attorneys took their usual places.

Burkhart entered, grave of face, walking stiffly. But instead of sitting with his attorneys, he went directly to Judge Worten and spoke in a guarded tone. In moments he stood back, breathing deeply, all eyes fixed on him, as if everyone sensed another dramatic turn was about to break.

"Counsel will please come to the bench," Judge Worten said. He spoke to them briefly in a low murmur, then State's attorneys turned away and, with Burkhart, entered the judge's chambers. After Worten ordered the jury out of the courtroom, Freeling, Howard,

Hamilton, and Springer held an animated conference with the judge.

Some minutes had passed when State Attorney General Short appeared in the chamber doorway and said: "Burkhart wishes to see Flint Moss."

Moss rose and went to the judge's office. After about five minutes, Burkhart and Moss came out, followed by the prosecution staff, and the grim defendant made his way to the bench.

"I wish to discharge the defense attorneys," Burkhart said gravely and distinctly. "Mister Moss will now represent me."

"You gentlemen of the defense have heard Mister Burkhart's request, and it will be granted," Judge Worten said.

Moss said: "If the court please, I respectfully request a recess. I believe this case can be disposed of quickly."

Worten nodded. "Court will be recessed until ten-thirty."

The courtroom hummed. Was Burkhart going to plead guilty after switching sides again? It looked that way. A scrambling broke out as some spectators hurried out to pass the apparent news.

Meanwhile, Burkhart, Moss, and the prosecution gathered in the county attorney's office. Someone went for Mollie Burkhart, still waiting loyally in the courtroom. As she came in, her husband smiled at her and closed the door. Moss began preparing a statement.

By 10:30 the courtroom was overflowing. Burkhart's appearance quieted the crowd, many of them Osages.

"Mister Burkhart wishes to withdraw his plea of not guilty and enter a plea of guilty," Moss told the court. Burkhart stood at his side, facing the judge.

"Is this your desire, Mister Burkhart?"

Into the dead-quiet hush, Burkhart replied: "It is."

"Do you change your plea voluntarily?"

"Yes."

"Have state or federal officers offered you immunity if you changed your plea?"

"No."

"Have prosecution attorneys agreed to extend you clemency if you changed pleas?"

"No. Any clemency I may get will have to come through my own attorney, Mister Moss. He advised me to do the right thing."

"Before your plea of guilty can be accepted, Mister Burkhart, there are other questions the court must ask you. Is your statement from the witness stand that federal officers forced you to sign a statement in Guthrie true?"

"It is true they kept me up several hours at night, when I was tired, but it is not true that Frank Smith stuck a gun in my side and that they prodded me with electric wires."

"Was your statement before the grand jury where you related going to Ripley in Bill Hale's automobile to see John Ramsey and have him see Kirby and get him to blow up the Smith house while Hale was in Texas . . . was that true?"

Burkhart replied solemnly: "Yes, that part of it is true."

"The defendant will be allowed to enter his plea," Worten said.

Mollie Burkhart, at the defense table, watched impassively.

Now followed a face-saving gesture for the defense, as if protocol must be observed. After the jury was recalled, Moss addressed the court: "I feel counsel for the defense ought to be vindicated. Burkhart told me that at all times he never told his lawyers the truth, and denied he had driven Hale's car to Ripley to tell Ramsey to tell Kirby to do the job of blowing up the Smith house."

Judge Worten agreed. "I don't think defense attorneys have known the truth until now. They acted as they saw fit for their client."

The prosecution hardly shared such generous opinions. In effect, the defense had "kidnapped" Burkhart, the State's key witness, in open court at the Hale-Ramsey preliminary, taken him to Fairfax where Hale's relatives and friends had influenced him to change his story. Hale himself had been allowed to rush back to the judge's chambers where, in his domineering way, he had no doubt intimidated his pliant nephew to get back into line. The defense had virtually run wild that day in county court. And, lately, there was firebrand Springer, who had allegedly tried to bribe a witness. His rôle throughout the trials was constant, if not effective, as a hurler of threats. With Burkhart's confession died the $250,000 damage suit against the agents.

It was over swiftly. As Worten thanked and discharged the jury, the courtroom erupted into excitement. Some onlookers crowded around Burkhart and shook his hand.

On this same day Tom White discovered Hale's powerful influence was not limited to the bountiful cattle ranges of Osage County and the State of Oklahoma. It extended as far as the halls of Congress, aimed like a gun barrel of dishonor at himself and other agents in the case. Tom and Edwin K. Brown were in Luhring's Washington office of the criminal division of the U.S. attorney general. They were discussing the Burkhart trial in progress at Pawhuska, and whether he could be convicted in Osage County.

Simultaneously Senator W.B. Pine of Oklahoma was raising the roof over in the attorney general's office. It had been called to his attention, the senator roared, that federal agents had used third-degree methods while wringing confessions from John Ramsey and Ernest Burkhart and attempting to make W.K. Hale, a leading citizen of Osage County, confess. Hale himself had testified to undergoing such improper methods. "I demand the immediate discharge of T.B. White, the agent-in-charge, and all other investigating agents in this case."

Just as the senator finished, Director J. Edgar Hoover entered the office. He waved a telegram. "Burkhart," he said, "has just discharged his attorneys, pleaded guilty, and told of his part in the Smith murders. He's ready to testify against Hale and Ramsey in the Henry Roan case."

The startled senator left soon after, explaining he must have been misinformed by his Oklahoma constituents. To the senator's credit, his name did not appear again in the case.

Judge Worten docketed the case against Hale and Ramsey in state district court for September 20th, the delay caused by a shortage of court funds. Hale was bitter, but still confident. "Burkhart's confession is a frame-up," he told the press. "They'll never force him to spend a day in the pen. I'm ready to go on trial with a plea of not guilty and stick to it."

In vast contradiction, on June 21st, Judge Worten sentenced Ernest Burkhart to life imprisonment in the Oklahoma state penitentiary. As the pronouncement fell, Burkhart turned, and there was an expression of relief on his face. Bryan Burkhart was out on bond, pending trial in the Anna Brown case.

Had Ernest's plea, paradoxically, freed his wife from death? Information reaching federal agents indicated that Mollie, who often complained of being ill, was dying from what was believed to be slow poisoning. At her death, Ernest would have acquired the entire fortune of the Lizzie Q family, with the exception of Reta Smith's estate, which had been passed to her husband's heirs.

Left unanswered was another terrible question. In his agonized moments of consciousness after the explosion, William Smith, trapped in the burning wreckage of his home, his dead full-blood wife beside him, had told Fred DeNoya and other rescuers: "Mollie and the kids are here somewhere." Did Ernest Burkhart, having set the Hale-to-Ramsey-to-Kirby order in motion, know that his wife and two children would be there? Friends of Burkhart's insisted he did not, but did not say where he was that night. They also said that once Burkhart sided permanently with the prosecution, his uncle began setting off a backfire of rumors aimed at discrediting his nephew in Fairfax.

CHAPTER FOURTEEN

Oklahoma's most sensational murder trials might shift to the larger arena of federal court in Guthrie as Roy St. Lewis, U.S. attorney for the western district, filed an application for delivery of Hale and Ramsey to federal authorities. But it was Judge Worten's firm intention to try the defendants in Pawhuska, and he refused St. Lewis's request June 24th, citing the expense to be incurred on both sides. "For the state at this time to surrender them to the federal authorities for trial on another charge, and then back here again on the Smith case, it seems to me would be for the state to be doing these men an injustice."

A pause set in while U.S. officials maneuvered for a firmer grip on Hale and Ramsey. This uncertainty held until Luhring arrived July 2nd from Washington for a hurried conference with St. Lewis, Edwin K. Brown, and federal agents. Next day St. Lewis and Luhring applied for a writ of prosecution sworn out before Judge Cotteral.

Moving swiftly at night, Tom White and Frank Smith and Charlie Davis, the former Fairfax "insurance salesman," and a deputy marshal drove north. Destination: Pawhuska. At two o'clock in the morning they pulled up in front of the Osage County jail where Hale and Ramsey slept. Quietly they aroused Sheriff Freas and served him warrants.

"We've got a writ for you, too," Tom informed the sheriff, understanding the man's position as an elected official.

Freas, with discomfort, read the writ ordering him to show cause why Hale and Ramsey should not be delivered to federal agents. Truly he was in a fix. If he honored the writ, he was violating Judge Worten's order holding the pair for state trial. If he didn't, he was bucking a federal court order. After some moments, he said: "They're your prisoners." This would further damage his political future in Hale sectors of the county. Soon after sunup, then, Hale and Ramsey were disconsolate prisoners in Guthrie's Logan County jail.

An expected storm broke in the defense camp. Howard, fuming, said the writ amounted to no more than a hearing. "We'll show at Guthrie that removal of Hale and Ramsey was illegal in that it violated Judge Worten's order to hold the defendants for trial in state courts."

Acting fast, the defense next filed application with Worten for return of the pair to state custody. The judge denied it. Although they had been taken without his knowledge, he said he felt further orders would not be obeyed.

Sheriff Freas was in more hot water as the defense sought a citation of contempt against him for releasing the prisoners. Judge Worten took this matter under advisement.

Losing no time, St. Lewis reinstated the old charges against Hale and Ramsey, countered by the defense with a motion to quash the indictments. Judge Cotteral overruled the motion and ordered the defendants arraigned. Again it was parry and thrust when the defense requested removal of the trial to Osage County.

That was the last strung-out try. Cotteral overruled, heard the pleadings of not guilty, and, over a flurry of objections, scheduled the trial for July 26th.

At last, after seven months of adroit tactical movements by both sides, Hale and Ramsey were to face prosecution in federal court for the murder of Henry Roan.

As the trial neared, every hotel room in Guthrie was taken, and smoke-filled lobbies became crowded again, a reënactment of last January's grand jury session. The same undercurrent of tenseness returned with the old fear as subpoenaed witnesses watched and waited.

During the waiting, the theorizing was endless, quietly spoken. Was W.K. Hale the pleasant mastermind, operating behind a front of respectability and friendship while he sent trusting Osages to their deaths and so bringing immense fortunes closer to his grasp? Hale's attorneys and friends scoffed at the government's charges. Genial Bill Hale was no killer. A shrewd trader, he could have swapped an Indian out of his last blanket. It wasn't necessary for him to have those Osages murdered. He had plenty of money.

Federal agents agreed Hale was well-heeled. He was also money-mad. Much of his fortune had been swindled from Osages. Observers predicted a drawn-out fight over Ramsey's repudiated confession to agents in Roan's murder. Ramsey's situation was comparable to Ernest Burkhart's at the start of his trial in the Smith case.

Like bait, the defense dropped this lure into the pool of speculation: Roan wasn't killed in Sol Smith's pasture. He was shot elsewhere and his body taken to where it was found. Therefore, the federal government had no jurisdiction. The Roy Bunch angle, public knowledge in Fairfax and revived by Hale supporters, was aired. Would the defense try to pin Roan's murder on the former Fairfax butcher, now married to Roan's widow?

What about the array of legal minds in the all-out court battle? How did they stack up? Judge John H. Cotteral, heavy-set, balding, with ten years of experience on the bench, had presided over more than a dozen murder trials. For the prosecution: Roy St. Lewis, youngest U.S. district attorney in the nation, would go under fire for the first time, but had worked behind the scenes with agents since the defendants were indicted in January. At his side were Edwin K. Brown and O.R. Luhring, assistants to the U.S. attorney general, and Oliver R. Pagan, government indictment expert. State Attorney General George Short and his assistant, Edwin Dabney, would have chairs with the prosecution. Dabney, an earnest, forceful lawyer, had led the questioning in Burkhart's trial. And again in the line-up was T.J. Leahy, calm and formidable, himself an old-timer in the Osage, lawyer, banker, stockman, former county attorney, confidante of Indians and whites alike. Largely instrumental in bringing about Burkhart's startling plea of guilty, Leahy was gaining in stature as a prosecutor. Just two weeks ago he had been appointed an assistant U.S. attorney general to serve without compensation in charge of all Osage cases in federal court. Completing the staff was hard-driving Osage County Attorney C.K. Templeton, invited by the government to assist.

S. Prince Freeling, former state attorney general, would lead the defense. He had taken little part in Burkhart's trial, other than in conferences with other team members. Having campaigned over the state many times, he was better known to jurors than any lawyer on either side. Up to two years ago he had been in most of the state's big criminal trials, usually as a prosecutor. J.I. Howard, Freeling's law partner in Oklahoma City, had taken an active rôle in Burkhart's trial, cross-examining witnesses. A vigorous courtroom lawyer, he boomed his questions. The day before the trial he and Freeling had spent several hours with Hale in the Logan County jail. W.S. Hamilton, Hale's other attorney, was a former clergyman. Newsmen saw him as "ministerial in appearance, but cutting in cross-examination." Quick on his feet, Hamilton had shouted that Burkhart was his client the moment Burkhart entered the courtroom in the Hale-Ramsey hearing, a move that had resulted in Burkhart's changing sides. J.M. Springer, Ramsey's attorney, "is no lamb," a Tulsa reporter wrote. "He is noted for the ferocity of his attack. He has been the point of every defense wedge launched so far."

For a while it was believed that Moman Pruiett, flamboyant Oklahoma defense attorney, would join the staff. Pruiett had won acquittals for 303 of 343 accused murderers. He conferred with Hale, saying Hale had asked him to, but did not call again. The defense was set.

A skirmish broke out when Freeling asked for separate trials, arguing that a joint trial could not be impartial and the evidence wasn't applicable to both. St. Lewis retorted that the offense was a joint one, and the evidence of one would be admissible to the other. Judge Cotteral denied the defense motion, and examination of jurors began.

Hale looked less vigorous than at his nephew's trial, although still genial. Ramsey looked unchanged, care-worn, and weak.

Mollie Burkhart, a government witness, came limping through the corridors of the federal building in semi-modern dress, Indian shawl, and braided hair. Other loyalties had changed. The Burkharts' housekeeper, a relative of Hale's and Mollie's constant companion when her husband was on trial, now sided with the defense.

A man in Western dress was observed trying to engage federal witnesses in conversation. This occurred several times. Tom White had agents take into custody for questioning a close associate of the late Henry Grammer.

Attorneys exhausted the first jury panel, and another of 100 venire-men was called. Now and then a question stood out.

"Do you know W.K. Hale? Did he ever lend you any money?"

"Did you know Henry Roan?"

Federal officials' outright assertions of attempts to tamper with witnesses were reflected in St. Lewis's questioning.

"Has any person approached or talked to

you regarding this trial?" Often he mentioned a rancher-friend of Hale's.

"We have several persons under surveillance we believe are trying to get to witnesses," Edwin K. Brown told reporters.

It soon became apparent the prosecution was dismissing prospective jurors who, like Hale, had left Texas to settle in Oklahoma. St. Lewis scratched thirteen former Texans.

Springer, reviving the old tactic of an all-powerful federal government against two unsung Oklahoman cowboys, sarcastically inquired of jurors whether they would be influenced by the imposing array of government counsel.

Late the third day a jury was completed: five farmers, a lumberman, a cotton gin operator, a plumber, a railroad worker, a butcher, a merchant, and an auto dealer.

July 29th, as final battle lines were drawn, Tom White knew that encounters during the Hale-Ramsey hearing and Ernest Burkhart's trial were mere patrol clashes, a prologue to the principal, no-quarter slugging match about to be enjoined.

"The stage is set," the Tulsa *Tribune* said, "and the curtain rises slowly on the great tragedy of the Osage."

Court convened quietly. Tom sat at the prosecution table with J. George Wright, Osage Agency superintendent. Suddenly Springer demanded that Agents White and

Smith be barred from the courtroom.

"The motion is overruled," Judge Cotteral said. "Proceed."

Tom could have smiled except for one reminder. The defense was launching the same line of attack he knew would be followed all through the trial, a continual claim of duress used to get Ramsey's voluntary confession. Freeling wasn't changing strategy.

It was time for opening statements.

Leahy rose and walked slowly to the jury box. "Gentlemen of the jury," he said, "William K. Hale is charged with aiding and abetting in the killing of Henry Roan, while John Ramsey is charged with the killing. The government expects to show the following facts . . . Henry Roan was a full-blood Osage Indian on the tribal rolls. He was found dead in an automobile in the first part of February, Nineteen Twenty-Three, on a tract of land belonging to Rose Little Star, another Osage, and under the jurisdiction of the government. George Pratt of Fairfax saw the car and reported it to officers, who then found Roan lying dead on his side, a wound back of the left ear and another in the right eye. He had been shot once. A justice of peace examination and coroner's jury was held. Doctors examined Roan. Evidence will show that prior to this W.K. Hale had obtained from the Capitol Life Insurance Company of Denver a twenty-five-thousand-dollar policy on Roan's life . . . payable to Hale. Roan was a heavy drinker. Prior to this he had attempted suicide. Hale knew of these facts. He tried to get a policy from Mutual Life Insurance Company, but the company rejected the policy on the Indian. Hale brought Roan to the office of the examining physician of Capitol Life and saw Roan examined. Hale paid the first premium. After he got the policy on Roan's life, the Indian again attempted suicide. Hale said if Roan died within a year, he couldn't get the policy, but if Roan died after a year, he could collect it."

While Leahy spoke, Hale listened with a little smile on his face. Ramsey fanned himself and chewed a toothpick.

"Hale discussed the killing of Roan with his nephew, Ernest Burkhart," Leahy continued. "Hale and Burkhart visited Henry Grammer. John Ramsey was present. Hale then told Burkhart . . . 'There's the man who will pull the job for us. He's safe and he can be trusted.' "

Leahy said Hale, becoming impatient, pointed out Roan to Ramsey as the Indian he wanted killed, promising to buy Ramsey an automobile and pay him $500. He bought the car before the killing, then Ramsey and Roan drank whisky together, and Ramsey asked Roan to meet him in this pasture out of Fairfax known as Sol Smith's pasture. They sat on the running board of the car and drank whisky. Roan got back in the driver's seat and sat down. Ramsey, on the left side of the car, fired his gun in the base of the head of Roan, killing him instantly.

"Later, Ramsey met Burkhart in Fairfax and asked for Hale. 'If you see him, tell him I killed that Indian about thirty minutes ago. I'm going back home today.' Burkhart gave the message to Hale." In closing, Leahy said: "Hale attempted to collect the life insurance on Henry Roan's policy. Gentlemen of the jury, we expect a verdict of guilty without qualification."

The defense chose to present its statement later.

A delay ensued when the prosecution called its first witness, George Pratt. His name was called again and again in the corridors. But the Fairfax youth could not be found. Was he afraid to testify?

Instead, Marshal Bob Parker was called. He described how he and Jim Rhodes, another officer, had found Roan's body after Pratt had hurried to town with the news.

On cross-examination Howard tried to establish Roan's cap was folded under his head, and there was a clean handkerchief around his neck. These tender touches, the defense implied, indicated the mysterious hand of a woman. Was it the first step in the direction of Roy Bunch? But Officer Rhodes didn't remember a white handkerchief.

For a while, as Rose Little Star testified, it seemed the prosecution might have difficulty proving the crime was committed on restricted Indian land or Indian country. A full-blood, unfamiliar with the white man's ways, she said she didn't know whether Roan was killed on her land or not. Neither did she know its boundaries. But St. Lewis introduced a deed in trust for the Osage nation covering the land set forth in the murder indictment. Then the Osage county clerk identified tribal records and land titles and county records showing Little Star's deed to the land where Roan's body was found.

The next witness was prominent in the Osage and known to every Osage on the rolls, Agency Superintendent Wright. Had Rose Little Star been granted a certificate of competency? No, he said. She was a restricted Indian and, therefore, subject to government supervision of her affairs. So the persecution established that Roan was killed on restricted land.

Coroner H.E. Wilson, 70, a well-educated man, told of the inquest over Roan's body, discovered at 4 P.M., February 6, 1923. The fear haunting Fairfax Indians came alive as he spoke further. "We soon realized it would take tremendous efforts before anything could be done. The majority of the sources through which officers conducted their investigation seemed purposely misleading and unreliable. Soon after, the Smith house was blown up and Smith, his wife, and a servant girl killed. It was apparent that concentrated efforts were being made to murder wealthy Osages. Fairfax found itself in a reign of terror. Conditions got so bad several Osages left for California, Mexico, Canada, and distant states."

On July 30th, the stifling courtroom was a kettle of short nerves. By night the hotel lobbies hummed. Was Bill Hale guilty? Some declined opinions, even in private, for there was this reminder for the future. When the case was over, if Hale went free, the federal agents would be gone. What then?

The Hale-Burkhart faction was turned out in full force. Bryan Burkhart, charged in Anna Brown's murder and free on $25,000 bond, was bunking with relatives at the Ione Hotel. Hale continued his ever-bold front, posing on the courthouse steps with wife and daughter for a public photo. As usual, he wore a neat suit, light-colored shirt, and tie.

All eyes noticed Mollie Burkhart, solitary, trusting, in black shawl and gingham dress, rings on her fingers. Sometimes — many times — she sat apart in a corner of the hotel lobby, keeping a dignified silence. Few people approached or spoke to her. Not far away clustered those loyal to Hale and

Burkhart, laughing and chatting, confident of acquittal. Mollie had lost standing with her husband's people just as he had. She and Ernest were all wrong now, and the rumors planted in Fairfax tearing at his past seemed to be growing. But despite his confession of complicity in the explosion that killed her sister, she remained loyal to him. If called, she would testify for the government. It was not generally known that Henry Roan was her first husband.

As the trial resumed, Everett Smith, Fairfax undertaker, related being called to Roan's home in 1921 and finding him bleeding from a chest wound. Smith took Roan to the hospital in an ambulance.

The defense lodged one pertinent question. Had Smith noticed anyone else around the place?

Yes. Someone was in the house, but he didn't know who it was.

Apparently the defense sought to break down Leahy's assertion that Roan had attempted suicide twice, and, instead, someone had shot Roan, leading back to Roy Bunch.

"Call Ernest Burkhart."

He entered hesitantly, taken aback at the size of the staring crowd. His expensive black boots glistened. His suit looked freshly pressed, and he wore a white shirt and bright necktie. Led by Leahy, he was soon into his story.

"I have been with Hale quite a bit in my life," he said, at the same time avoiding the intent, half-smiling gaze of his uncle. "I have known John Ramsey since Nineteen Twenty-Two, when I met him at Henry Grammer's ranch. The first time I recall talking to Hale about Henry Roan was when Roan shot himself in the fall of Nineteen Twenty-One. Hale said he had a policy on Roan, and, if he killed himself before a year, he wouldn't get the insurance."

It was obvious to Tom White that Hale was trying to fluster his nephew. Burkhart lost his poise, looked down, and shifted his hands. In a tight voice, he related going to Grammer's ranch with Hale. "We saw Grammer and Ramsey. Hale and Grammer talked privately. When we left, Ramsey was working across the road. Hale said . . . 'There's a fellow you can depend on. I believe I could get him to give Roan poison whisky or shoot him and drop the gun behind him. He's tried to commit suicide twice and nobody would think a thing about it.' "

Freeling interrupted and asked to confer with his associates. Then it was Springer who faced the bench. "Burkhart is under life sentence for murder and is incompetent. We object to his giving testimony."

"Overruled."

Immediately Hamilton offered the identical objection. Judge Cotteral, his voice sharp, again denied and told Burkhart to proceed.

There was a plan, Burkhart said. Because Ramsey didn't know Roan, Hale was going to point out Roan to him. Because Ramsey didn't have a way to get around, Hale was going to buy him a small car and, in addition, give him $500. "Hale was to take Ramsey to Ponca City to buy the car. I saw Ramsey riding around in the car before Roan was killed."

"Now after Roan was killed, did you have a conversation with Ramsey?" Leahy asked.

"I did. About half an hour after Roan was killed."

"Now, Ernest Burkhart, state when and where that was."

"In January, on the street in Fairfax."

"What did Ramsey say?"

"He asked me where Hale was, and I said I didn't know. He told me to tell Hale 'the Indian job was done.' He said he was going to Ripley for a few days. I asked him when he did it, and he said about thirty minutes ago."

"Did he say what Indian?"

"He said Henry Roan. I asked him where it happened, and he said in Sol Smith's pasture."

"Now, after that, did you talk to Hale?"

"I told him what Ramsey told me to tell him. I said Ramsey killed Henry Roan. Hale wanted to know where Ramsey was, and I told him he'd gone to Ripley. Hale said he should have stayed around and there would have been no suspicion."

Hale continued to stare at Burkhart, giving him the eye, as Tom White saw it. But Burkhart had a stronger grip on himself now.

"After the body was found, did you have another conversation?"

"I did. Hale told me he had paid Ramsey five hundred dollars. He said he had already given him a car and bet he wouldn't have a dollar in thirty days."

"Any further conversation?"

"Later Hale said Ramsey told him how he had done it. Hale said he had told Ramsey to shoot Roan and drop the gun by him and there wouldn't be anything thought about it, as Roan had tried to commit suicide twice, but that Ramsey had taken the gun." As for any conversation about insurance money, Burkhart said: "Hale said the company would pay the insurance. They would have to . . . they couldn't turn him down."

Hale, Burkhart stated, said the plan was to pin Roan's murder on Roy Bunch, since the two had fought over Roan's wife and Bunch had married Roan's widow.

"Now," Leahy pressed on, "tell the court a conversation you had last January with Ramsey in the federal building here."

A storm of defense objections halted Burkhart's reply. Ramsey's statement wasn't admissible! He'd been forced to talk!

Judge Cotteral excused the jury to hear arguments.

Hamilton charged that agents had used improper methods to get Ramsey's statement. "Ramsey's confession was voluntary," St. Lewis fired back. "It's the burden of the defense to show otherwise."

Agent Frank Smith, called next, was relating the meeting between Ramsey and Burkhart — "Ramsey replied . . . 'Yes, he told it all. I guess it's on my neck. Get your pencil'." — when suddenly Ramsey startled the courtroom with a burst of high, mirthless laughter. Smith, never pausing, said: "I wrote the statement myself as Ramsey told the story. He said he didn't care to read it and signed it. Tom White was there. I repeated to Ramsey what I wrote."

St. Lewis turned to the defense. "Your witness."

Springer rose to the attack, shouting, venting his opinion of federal agents, and whirled toward St. Lewis as the district attorney cut in with: "Your Honor, I know it's hard for some lawyers to act the part of a gentleman. But I ask counsel for the defense to treat Mister Smith as a gentleman."

Judge Cotteral smote for order and got it.

But the clash didn't end. Springer raised his voice at Smith.

"Stop bellerin'," Smith drawled, "and I'll try to answer you."

Already Springer was off on another tack. "Didn't you try to change the transcript of the testimony taken by a stenographer during the Hale-Ramsey hearing at Pawhuska?"

"*I did not*," Smith shot back, and looked straight at the defense table. "But Mister Hamilton was hanging around the court reporter. We had some men keep an eye on him."

Hamilton's chair grated with the words. He sprang up, lean face challenging and furious. He began shouting and waving his arms, which caused more confusion, and Judge Cotteral called it a day.

It was clear to Tom White, leaving with the prosecution staff, that Hale's attorneys were still abusing witnesses and getting away with it. Today's federal courtroom had scarcely more decorum than a brawling trial in Osage County. A dirty fight lay ahead; it would get dirtier as the trial progressed.

The Tulsa *World* caught the taut atmosphere pervading the scene of the trial. "Never has this original state capital been so mortally afraid. No accusations against Hale are made here in the streets. His friends, and they are legion, keep their silence; his enemies, and they are legion, hold their tongues. Witnesses are stoic. No blood has been spilled here. No threats have been hurled openly. But you can't speak freely. You don't want to express yourself. Is it because whispering tales have preceded the trial that careless talkers have been silenced? Is it because people who know so much of the Osage Reign of Terror have left no forwarding address?"

July 31st, Judge Cotteral excused the jury again and began a hearing on the admissibility of Ramsey's confession to the jury. Frank Smith returned and tangled with Springer over defense allegations. Objections by St. Lewis only slowed Springer momentarily as he continued to browbeat Smith. "You won't answer my direct questions because you know we're going to impeach your testimony."

Smith glared back. "Pardon me, Mister Springer, but part of your records are incorrect."

Freeling took up the needling. Smith denied using a battery on Ramsey. So the infighting went. The defense didn't deny that Ramsey had talked. But Ramsey hadn't been properly fed — nor allowed proper rest — had been subjected to shocks with a battery, allegations designed to kick up clouds of doubt on how agents had obtained the statements. Would Judge Cotteral be swayed in Ramsey's case as Judge Worten had been in ruling Burkhart's admissions at Guthrie were not voluntary, although admitting his conversations with Leahy?

Tom White took the stand. Leahy asked him to relate Ramsey's statement relative to Roan's murder. In even tones, Tom testified:

"Ramsey said early in Nineteen Twenty-Three Bill Hale came to Henry Grammer's ranch where Ramsey was selling whisky. Grammer told Ramsey . . . 'Bill Hale has a job he wants you to do.' Ramsey said it depended on what the job was, and Grammer replied . . . 'It's to bump off an Indian'."

"What did Ramsey reply to that?"

" 'That's different'."

Ramsey sat tight-lipped as Tom testified the prisoner had not been abused or forced to make a statement against his will.

"Did Ramsey complain about being closeted with agents?"

"He did not, and Ramsey himself asked to see Burkhart in private."

Parrying, the defense called a Stillwater farmer, a member of the grand jury that had indicted Hale and Ramsey. He said Ramsey's confession did not bear his signature when presented to the jury.

St. Lewis acted fast. That afternoon the farmer was arraigned on a complaint of perjury before the U.S. commissioner. Pleading innocent, the man said he had known Springer and Hamilton twenty-five years.

As the first bitterly fought week ended, a marked impression prevailed, gathered on the streets and in the jammed hotel lobbies of shuffling, restless people from the Osage: gone was January's blustering talk. Nobody seemed eager to voice an opinion. Was it fear?

CHAPTER FIFTEEN

August 2nd, called Monday to counter the testimony of Agents White and Smith, Ramsey was testifying as the hearing moved on without the jury. He spoke in a steady voice, his lined face pained, making motions with his hands. At times he would duck or flinch or show fear, as if dodging a blow. He was putting on quite a show equal to his Pawhuska performance, Tom White thought. Some new expressions had been added and others improved. He was getting good at it.

"I asked to be alone with Ernest. I said . . . 'Ernest, what did you mention my name for?' He said . . . 'You will sign it.' I said . . . 'What will I tell them?' He said . . . 'You won't have to tell them anything. They will fix it.' He said they'd made promises to him after forcing him to sign a statement with a gun. 'They just want you to convict Bill Hale,' Ernest said."

Ramsey talked faster, his story flowing, and Tom White, knowing the torture routine, sensed the payoff accusation was near.

Ramsey made a sudden, violent motion. "Somebody brought something in and placed it against my head. Somebody said . . . 'It goes the other way.' It was taken off and two prongs put on the back of my head. I thought at first it was a gun and was thinking what was best to do. When they moved it, I thought it was an electric shocker. One time they brought in what I thought was a battery. About an hour later they took the riggin' away. They said . . . 'I guess you are ready to sign up.' I told them I had no information. Smith went out and came back with a paper and said . . . 'Sign here.' I signed. He went out and came back with another paper and said . . . 'Sign this.' I never read the statement before I signed it. I never dictated a statement."

As for the new car, he needed it "to get back and forth from home" to Grammer's, "where I was doin' carpentry work." None of the car money came from Hale, he said.

Springer asked why Ramsey had signed the statements.

The aggrieved look returned. "I had to sign because I couldn't stand the treatment and punishment. They threatened to put the electricity to me. I'd have signed anything to get some rest. There is no truth in the statements . . . I never killed anyone. As far as I know, Bill Hale had nothing to do with killing any of them."

The defense called the grand jury foreman and a juror, a cattleman. Both claimed Smith said the statements were not signed.

As if expecting that, St. Lewis read from grand jury testimony that showed Agent Smith had two statements from Ramsey, both signed, whereupon the foreman said he "might be confused."

Then Edwin K. Brown, Smith, and Tom denied unsigned statements of Ramsey were presented to the grand jury and each denied Ramsey had been tortured or threatened. So far, it was the word of federal men against Hale's friends.

August 3rd, Judge Cotteral had a ruling ready when court convened. Ramsey's confession to federal agents was made voluntarily and could be introduced as testimony, although the jury would have to decide its admissibility.

What looked like a prosecution victory fell apart when Burkhart, ever unpredictable, blurted out that Agents White and Smith had told Ramsey: "Would you rather be prosecuted for murder or be a witness and make a statement?"

The jury, just admitted to the courtroom, was excused, and Leahy, speaking for the prosecution, said he was shocked and asked the witness if he wasn't confused.

Burkhart reflected and said he was mixed up and asserted J.M. Springer had told him at Pawhuska that Ramsey had said it. And then Burkhart said a number of Hale's friends had tried to influence him before he was to testify in the Hale-Ramsey hearing. He'd been urged to do whatever W.S. Hamilton told him to do.

Leahy asked why Burkhart had employed Hale's attorneys.

Burkhart said he had tried to retain Flint Moss of Tulsa, but Hamilton had told him Moss had backed out of the case.

"We introduce this line of testimony," Luhring told the court, "to show that sinister influences were brought to bear on Burkhart and made him commit perjury on the stand at Pawhuska."

After Judge Cotteral admonished the defense to expedite its case, Howard asked what the witness did for a living? Like many squawmen, Burkhart said loafing or hanging around pool halls. Before marrying Mollie, he had worked as a taxi driver.

Howard's tone turned nasty, tinged with self-righteousness. "If you knew all these things, why didn't you notify officers that Roan was about to be killed?"

"I figured the best thing for me was to keep my mouth shut." In the next breath Burkhart was into his interrogation by federal agents. "T.B. White asked me what I knew about the Roan case. I said I knew all about it. I told them Roy Bunch was innocent."

It was typical of Burkhart that nearly every time he found himself the central figure in the trials, something went smash.

Hale was staring hard at his nephew. Burkhart looked confused, under strain, and suddenly he said: "T.B. White advised me to tell it all. He said he would have the murder charge against me dismissed if I signed a confession. White promised me immunity from prosecution."

Tom White felt a thrust of angry astonishment. Burkhart hadn't been promised a thing. Neither had Ramsey. What in God's name had got into Burkhart? Was he wavering again in fear? Was it Hale's stare?

Tom glanced at the defense table. Hale, who had watched the previous day's proceedings with less outward confidence than usual, was jubilant.

August 4th, although Burkhart continued under fire, with the defense claiming he knew nothing but hearsay, he had regained his composure.

Springer charged in, throwing accusations. "Didn't you go to Ripley with Curly Johnson and plan the bank robbery there?"

"No."

"Didn't you steal automobiles with Blackie Thompson?"

Burkhart admitted buying a car from Thompson. That was all.

Despite varying on some details and admitting he had contradicted himself on others through confusion, the government's star witness stood steadfast in his main assertions: that Hale discussed hiring Ramsey to murder Roan; that Hale was to give Ramsey $500 and a car; that Ramsey informed him of Roan's murder soon after the crime; that Hale told of paying Ramsey after the killing. Even Springer couldn't shake Burkhart on these major points.

Agent Smith followed and related Ramsey's confession, heard for the first time by the jury, after Judge Cotteral denied a motion to exclude it. However, the court ruled, Ramsey's statement could not be used against Hale. Smith also threw new light on the Roan death weapon. It was, he said, a .45 automatic which came from Grammer's ranch, where there was a regular arsenal.

August 5th, a slower tempo set in, but to spectators the trial was a holiday. Seats were hard to find within minutes after a session opened. The curious, local and Osage County, arrived early with fans and sack lunches, holding their stations through noon recess. Guthrie's hotels enjoyed turn-away business. Long, expensive cars from Indian country lined the streets, causing overalled farmers to pause and ponder the make, speed, and cost.

Government attorneys fretted about the trial's slow progress, three days spent determining the admission of Ramsey's confession and the defense's lengthy cross-examination of prosecution witnesses. Having learned to expect a clash every time a federal agent was cross-examined, spectators inched forward when Freeling, a veteran at impressing a jury, faced Frank Smith.

"Did you not advise Ramsey to get another attorney, to discharge Mister Springer?"

"I told Ramsey that Springer was Hale's attorney, not his own. I had seen Springer's tactics in these cases and knew he was really representing Hale. I am sorry for the way Ramsey has been handled in this case."

Springer, a smile playing across his face, now chuckled aloud, and Edwin K. Brown protested to the court: "Springer is laughing behind Freeling's back. It's not proper."

"The court," replied Judge Cotteral, his own patience running thin, "cannot control the facial expressions of counsel."

Smith was on the stand three hours. When the firing ceased, his square-jawed testimony remained unchanged: Ramsey's confession contained only what he had told agents, in his own language and without coaching; Ramsey had not been threatened or forced to sign.

St. Lewis called Tom White next as he moved to bolster the validity of Ramsey's confession.

"Did you question John Ramsey in January,

this year, when the case was being presented to the grand jury?"

"Agent Smith and I talked to him."

"Will you tell us what you did?"

"I introduced myself and Smith and told him we were investigating the Osage murders. Ramsey appeared nervous. He admitted working for Henry Grammer and serving a sentence in the Oklahoma penitentiary for cattle theft. I said to him Grammer was a king bootlegger, and Hale was connected with the murders. We said . . . 'Hale and Grammer have taken advantage of you and your circumstances. You go to the penitentiary, they get the money. Hale got twenty-five thousand dollars for the murder of Roan while you got one thousand.' We told Ramsey we had a story from Burkhart implicating him in the killing of Roan. Ramsey said he didn't believe us. We brought Burkhart in to see him, and Ramsey asked him if he'd told all. Burkhart said he had. Smith and I withdrew from the room for a few minutes. When we returned, we asked Ramsey if he believed Burkhart had told us everything. Ramsey said he did and told us to get our pencils."

Tom denied offering inducements to Ramsey or threatening him and described the substance of Ramsey's agreement with Hale. "Ramsey dictated his confession to this effect to Smith. He signed it himself, voluntarily. I had telephoned Agent John Wren, in Fairfax,

243

to bring Ramsey here to help the government further its investigation of the Osage murders."

Springer bounced up, pointing at Tom, accusing him in a loud voice: "By what right did you have Ramsey brought to Guthrie from Fairfax to question him?"

"Burkhart told me Ramsey killed Roan. The information we had from Burkhart was sufficient reason for questioning Ramsey."

Springer snorted. "You had no legal right to accuse or question Ramsey in the Roan murder."

There was a pause until Tom said: "I have never grilled any man under investigation as you have grilled witnesses and me, Mister Springer."

August 6th, when presenting the government's opening statement to the jury, Leahy had explored the motive for Roan's slaying, citing the $25,000 life insurance policy issued on the Osage naming Hale as the sole beneficiary, a curious arrangement which the editor of the Fairfax *Osage Chief* had called attention to on the front page as long ago as October, 1923, when Hale had sued for payment in federal court against Capitol Life of Denver, Colorado.

Agents backtracking the suit over the policy, issued July 14, 1921, learned that Capitol had charged fraud and misrepresentation. Roan was an "habitual drunkard and had a guardian," facts the company said had been concealed. On the insurance application, Roan was listed as a "farmer and stockman." That Roan owed Hale $6,000 on a house in Fairfax, as claimed by Hale in his suit, was attested to in Roan's petition for a guardian, which federal operatives had examined. But there was no evidence Roan owed a whopping $25,000! Why not a policy to cover the actual amount of Roan's indebtedness? Or why not just collect through the usual procedure of filing a claim against Roan's large estate, which Capitol asserted Hale had already done and been paid by the administrator of Roan's estate, Mrs. C.E. Ashbrook, of Fairfax.

Moving now to present in evidence events leading up to issuing the policy, the prosecution called its lead-off witness, F.W. Reynolds, who had sold the disputed policy. Roan, he said, came to him in the summer of 1921 and asked to take out a $25,000 policy.

" 'I don't have the money to pay the premium,' Roan told me. 'But Bill Hale will handle the policy and be willing to be the beneficiary'."

Hale brought Roan to see him when Roan signed the application, Reynolds said. "I told them I wasn't sure about it, that generally the beneficiary must be a blood relative. I didn't know then that Roan was under a guardianship or had been rejected as a bad risk by another insurance company a few months before. I delivered the policy to Hale. It contained the one-year contestability clause."

Hadn't Roan mentioned he was indebted to Bill Hale, a friend for years, who had helped him out several times, Freeling countered.

Correct.

Dr. W.H. Aaron testified that Hale was present at Roan's examination and remarked that Roan owed him about $8,000.

Tom White, hearing that, mused how fast Roan's debt to Hale kept going up from the original $6,000, which Capitol said Hale had already collected through the estate.

Dr. W.H. Goss, an examining physician for Mutual Insurance, where first Roan had sought a policy, made a prophetically grim crack at Roan's examination. He said he had jested with Hale — "You aiming to kill this Indian?" — then assured the court he had been only joking.

Backing up before the fury of Hamilton's grilling, the doctor said lamely he couldn't remember exactly who was with Roan.

The prosecution brought in John McClain, a Mutual agent, who said his company rejected Roan's application. Later, at Hale's request, he examined Capitol's policy on Roan's life.

"It was a poor policy from my company's

point of view," McClain said. "I didn't like to say much out of respect for the other agent, but I knew the questions in it had been answered falsely."

Black-haired Matt Williams followed, a man with a rough past, now a key witness. His importance had increased since testifying in Bryan Burkhart's preliminary and his charges that two of Hale's friends had tried to bribe him.

Early in 1923, he testified, he and Hale had talked at Ralston. " 'There will probably be a deal pulled off pretty soon,' Hale said and told me he had a twenty-five-thousand-dollar insurance policy on Roan and there would be a rich widow left. I told Hale the widow wouldn't do a man much good because Roy Bunch had the inside track. Hale said Bunch would be run out of the country because the murder would be placed on him." It was about January, 1923, Williams said, that Hale had told him he had Ramsey lined up to do the job.

Springer and Freeling seemed to relish taking turns working on the one-time Ralston saloonkeeper.

Had he ever been in jail?

Why, yes. He had served three prison terms for peddling whisky.

How many times had he been married?

Three times and was contemplating a fourth plunge into matrimony.

The defense was still pecking away at Williams's reputation when adjournment came. During the afternoon, rumors circulated about a mystery witness the government intended to call.

August 7th, staged in 100-degree heat, the trial dragged on, still slowed by the overlong cross-examinations. Since the beginning, witnesses had averaged about one a day.

Springer continued the attack to discredit Williams, implying that he had received unusual privileges while traveling the Southwest with federal agents, all expenses paid.

"I'll tell you why I requested the company of government officers," Williams replied coolly. "I was afraid for my life if I testified against Hale. I've kept silent about the Roan case because I was afraid I'd be bumped off. If I told what I knew at the time, it would have been like committing suicide. I was afraid of Bill Hale and his influence."

"These agents took you about anywhere you wanted to go in the United States, didn't they?"

"Nope. I'd like to go out to California," Williams said longingly, setting off a ripple of laughter the judge squelched.

"How much expense money has the government been allowing you daily since the grand jury investigation?"

"Four dollars?"

"What services did you render the government for that?"

"I'm rendering it right now. But the expense money don't have anything to do with my testimony."

Springer stepped away, then abruptly confronted Williams. "Isn't it true that you were admitted to an insane asylum?"

"That's true," Williams admitted, and turned pleadingly to Judge Cotteral. "Your Honor, I'd like to explain that." Cotteral allowed the request, and Williams said that, as a heavy drinker, fighting the whisky blues, he had read that the Vinita institution was a fine place to get cured. His brother had filed the insanity complaint to have Williams admitted. "Judge," Williams said gravely, "the charge was alcoholic insanity, and I was discharged after thirty days. That's the truth."

Tom White was called to explain the government's policy in caring for witnesses. "I assigned agents with Matt Williams to protect him from being killed. Williams told me he feared for his life. Agents traveled with him to keep his whereabouts unknown. Williams asked the government for protection."

St. Lewis was calling his witnesses rapidly now. After Burkhart and Marshal Parker, a Ponca City auto dealer told of when Ramsey had purchased a Ford roadster for $465.50. St. Lewis next introduced the car's registration record.

Then out of the wings stepped a new face, the rumored mystery witness — young Dewey Selph, Leavenworth convict and a fellow prisoner of Ramsey's last January in the Guthrie jail. He took the witness stand to smash Ramsey's claims of third-degree methods being used to force his confession.

Would the witness please tell the court of a conversation he had with Ramsey?

"We talked in a cell," Selph said. "I told Ramsey it looked like he'd got himself in a bad jam. Ramsey said . . . yes, that there wasn't anything for him to do but go up there and tell the truth. Burkhart had gone and told the whole thing. Ramsey said Hale got him to murder Roan."

St. Lewis, with a dramatist's flair, chopped the scene off at its peak. Selph was the last prosecution witness.

At 10:30 St. Lewis rested.

"May the court please," Freeling said, addressing the bench, "the defense would like to request adjournment until Monday."

But the day was yet young. Judge Cotteral, in no mood for further delays after often urging the defense to expedite its case, crisply denied the motion.

Springer approached the jury for his opening statement in behalf of Ramsey. Tom White, alongside Frank Smith, folded his arms and leaned back, ready for the usual tirade against government officials and two federal agents in particular.

"For the last four years," Springer said, "Ramsey's been an invalid. Evidence will show that January Sixth the government sent one of its agents, who took him to Guthrie without authority. Ramsey was then under a physician's care."

Racing back and forth before the jurors, Springer shook his fists and pointed accusingly. "Tom White and Frank Smith intimidated Ramsey. Evidence will show that these two *agents* . . ." — he placed a slurring emphasis on the word — "accused him of every crime in Osage County and kept this cowboy closeted from one P.M. until six A.M. To get rid of White and Smith, Ramsey signed a confession which says Roan was killed with a Forty-Five, when actually he was shot with a Thirty-Eight or Thirty-Two."

The .45, Tom remembered, wasn't mentioned by Ramsey until after he had confessed.

By now Springer was shouting. "They gave him the choice of being a government witness or a defendant! He was lodged in a cell here without a bed, bedding, or heat, and kept like a dog. They tortured Ramsey. They said they'd give him one more chance before giving him the juice."

As for the disputed car, Springer said Grammer owed Ramsey enough money for that. "Hale had nothing to do with the matter. Moreover, Ramsey and his wife were visiting in Fairfax on Sunday, January Twenty-Eighth, and stayed until Tuesday. Ramsey was sick."

Springer was outrageous but also forceful, Tom White admitted. The jury might believe the sickly Ramsey was elsewhere at the time of Roan's murder.

Freeling, with an air of old-school dignity, rose to speak for Hale. His tone calm and conversational, he pictured Hale as a hard-working, impulsive man who formed quick judgments. Hale had tried to help his nephew, Ernest Burkhart, a rather shiftless fellow. "Their natures were different. Burkhart had married the grass widow of Henry Roan."

Was Freeling implying that a white man disgraced himself when he married an Osage? Was the statement a reflection of Hale's own feelings? Agents on the case in Fairfax said Hale, privately, had expressed only contempt for Indian blood.

"Evidence will show Roan was a competent Indian," Freeling said. "Hale and Roan were good friends. Hale sold him cattle and feed. Roan wanted Hale to buy his headright for fifty thousand dollars. There were never two better friends. At one time Hale sold him thirteen thousand dollars' worth of cattle. A cattleman's friendship is strong. At one time another man owed Hale thirty-five thousand dollars without even a note as security. Roan asked Hale to take an insurance policy on his life and to pay the premium. Roan owed Hale twenty-three thousand dollars. They embodied all the indebtedness and premium in a note of twenty-five thousand dollars."

Tom White thought wryly, concerning the defense's explanation for the size of the policy, why it was written for $25,000 instead of the $6,000 indebtedness stated by Roan in his application for a guardian. How fortunate that everything figured out at exactly $25,000!

"The last time Hale saw Roan was in Fairfax. Roan asked him for a loan of twenty-five dollars to go to Henry Cornett's to purchase whisky. Hale warned him. Roan said he would hide the whisky in a pasture. Hale gave him the twenty-five dollars in the presence of another man."

Like an orator, Freeling paused for effect. "Roan learned of the infidelity of his wife, Mary, with Roy Bunch. They stayed in the country a few days. Roan asked officers to find his wife. Roan's unhappiness prompted him to attempt suicide."

So it was out, Tom White saw. The defense was basing its case on the old Bunch rumor, first circulated around town by Hale, and checked out by agents as baseless.

"The second alleged suicide attempt by Roan was not an attempt," Freeling went on.

"Bunch and Roan were gunning for each other. The two fought several times. On the night of January Fourteenth, Nineteen Twenty-Three, evidence will show that Bob Parker and two officers were passing Roan's house and saw Bunch trying to get inside. One officer shot at him twice. He dashed into a neighbor's. Bunch said he had whisky in the house."

Freeling had the jury hushed. "Bunch purchased a pearl-handled Thirty-Eight revolver. Hale had no motive for killing Roan. Proof will show Bunch had the strongest motive in the world for killing Roan. Bunch walked by the undertaking parlor time after time when Roan's body was brought in . . . Roy Bunch and Henry Roan went often to Henry Cornett's to buy whisky. Bunch was seen in a car near the fatal cañon, and not half a mile away came Roan. That was the last time Roan was seen alive." Freeling paused. "We ask you to give us the same respectful attention," concluded Oklahoma's former attorney general.

August 9th, on Monday the defense beckoned Ramsey, and Springer, sentence by sentence, read the confession. Ramsey alternatively shook his head and declared — "No, that's not true." or — "It's absolutely false."

Not once did Ramsey's eyes stray from

Springer to the jury. His face was lined, and he looked ill. He said he had never recovered from an attack of influenza. He moved about wildly at times, nervous and strained. Was this the Springer-orchestrated picture the defense hoped to show, a thin, sickly man being persecuted by a powerful federal government, a lone, sick cowboy fighting against odds? Or did the jury see a guilty but weakened man, a victim of hard times, a hard-used, part-time cowboy, a sometimes carpenter, often a whisky peddler, his stressful economic situation with a large family leaving him vulnerable to the propositions of wealthy, domineering Westerners like Hale and the late Henry Grammer?

Attorney and client went down the list of the government's principal charges linking Ramsey to Roan's murder.

The car? Grammer owed him for carpenter work, Ramsey replied.

"Did Hale give you money and buy you a car for killing Roan?"

"Absolutely not."

Ramsey's version of his now-famous meeting with Agents White and Smith required most of the morning. Why did he sign the statements in the Roan and Smith murders?

Ramsey looked imploringly at Springer, as if recalling agonizing pain. "My God, Jim, I don't think even a strong man could stand

255

up under that treatment. I was simply all wore out, and all I wanted was to get home, away from them." He sank back, spent, and coughed.

"Didn't you realize what you were doing?"

"I knowed when I signed the statements that every word was false and I could prove it if I had to. I had nothing to do with the slaying of Roan."

Leahy drew a grudging admission from Ramsey that maybe Grammer was making a little whisky, but Ramsey denied talking with Hale and Grammer about Roan. That was absolutely false. He denied ever admitting to Dewey Selph in the Guthrie jail that he had murdered Roan.

Heat and cramped seating had spectators restless, but Hale's appearance as a witness fifteen minutes before adjournment settled the crowd. His voice was clear and steady while he sketched his career from the Texas cattle ranges to Oklahoma. He said he was 52 years of old and told of his wife and daughter. With no little pride, he admitted to being extremely successful in the cattle business. He said he owned 5,000 acres of land and leased 45,000 acres in Osage County. He handled approximately 15,000 head of cattle every year.

"I am well acquainted in the Osage country and have extended a tremendous credit since I've been there. I've had cattlemen owe me sums ranging from thirty-five thousand dollars to fifty-five thousand dollars and have never taken a security from them any time for their debts. Several times I've owed that amount myself and have never given any security."

Ernest Burkhart, he said, was his sister's son. "Burkhart married Henry Roan's grass widow and since that time has never worked."

As Hale testified, St. Lewis made five separate objections and was overruled each time. This was merely the warm-up. The cattleman would return to the stand tomorrow.

August 10th, Hale drew another packed house. Some late arrivals from Osage County offered money for seats and found few takers. It seemed that just about everybody wanted to hear the leading citizen of Fairfax. Hale made a bold entry, shoulders back and chin out, the old, exaggerated military erectness to his walk, which to Tom White was like a strut, a manner, with his coolness while testifying, that was fostering his sobriquet as "King of the Osage Hills." Reporters were beginning to write about his iron nerve. He picked up his narrative in direct testimony:

"I made a fifty-dollar loan to Ramsey in Nineteen Twenty-Three. It was to pay hospital expenses of Ramsey's daughter. I also loaned him twenty dollars at one time. He paid it back. I have never owed him anything except for feed. I first met Roan twenty years ago. There were several business dealings with Roan, beginning with smaller deals and finally larger ones. There was some discussion about Roan's head-right, but there was no possibility of buying it, because it was against the law. If it became possible, I was to buy it. He asked me fifty thousand dollars for it in Nineteen Thirteen. If oil production ceased, I would have been the loser. I was to pay him the difference between what he owed me and the headright. Roan owed me several thousand dollars one time for cattle. He gave me a note for twenty-five thousand dollars, which included a note for the premium on an insurance policy I had taken out on him. I had decided to take out the policy as security for the money he owed me."

A policy was sent in once and rejected, Hale said, because the inspector understood Mrs. Roan shot at Roan once. He denied that the doctor had joked with him about "killing this Indian."

Hale outlined numerous business transactions with Roan, charging ten percent interest on small notes, eight on larger ones. "We were good friends, and he sought my aid when in trouble and he needed money. A few weeks before his death he telephoned me and asked me to come out to his house. I went there. He told me his trouble with his wife and family. She wasn't there. The last time I saw Roan was in the First National Bank in Fairfax. Roan appeared sober. He asked for twenty-five dollars to get some liquor. I let him have it."

Hale emphatically denied driving Ramsey to Pawnee to take a train to Ponca City to buy a car, paying Ramsey to kill Roan, or pointing Ramsey out to Burkhart at Grammer's. "There was no way I could profit by Roan's death. I could have profited if he had lived, for I could have bought his headright."

As Tom White listened, he thought how lucky Hale was that Henry Grammer, the kingpin bootlegger whose name ran like a hot wire through the complicated twistings of the Osage investigation, had died in the auto accident in June, 1923, the peak year of the tribal murders, and conveniently soon after the Roan and Smith murders. The presence of Grammer, with all he knew as boss of the county's criminal element, would have been a big hole for the defense to plug. Also dead was Ace Kirby who had blown up the Smith house.

So far, so good, it seemed for Hale's way of visiting with the federal jury. Until Freeling posed a question that asked, in effect, for Hale to describe the third-degree methods Agents White and Smith had used when they attempted to force a confession from him.

Luhring's objection leaped out. Judge Cotteral excused the jury, heard arguments, and sustained, costing Hale the chance to dramatize for jurors the torture session he had acted out at the Burkhart trial. This was the second setback for the defense; the first had been admission of Ramsey's confession. To court observers Hale's claims would have backed Ramsey's claims of being forced to confess.

Hale talked on. He knew Matt Williams, who had operated a saloon in Ralston where Hale traded, but scoffed at any deal on Roan, or saying "there would be a rich widow left."

"Was Roan working prior to his death?" Freeling asked.

Hale's mouth curled. "Did you ever see an Osage work?"

Then came Leahy, bringing disturbing questions and a keen knowledge of Indian legal affairs. Why hadn't Hale filed a claim with Roan's guardian or the administrator of his estate for the $25,000 he asserted was the basis of his application for insurance on Roan?

Hale explained that he and Roan had agreed the amount would go on the headright transaction. However, Hale had presented a $6,000 claim to Roan's guardian and received payments totaling $3,500. Also, after Roan's death, he filed with the administrator a $1,700 claim, which included a note for $1,675 and $25 for cash, the second dated January 15, 1923, shortly before Roan's death.

Hale admitted dealing with Roan and lending him money after Roan's affairs had been placed with a guardian, Mrs. C.E. Ashbrook of Fairfax. Hale said he was constantly lending Roan small amounts, although he knew Roan was a steady drinker.

Had Hale ever noticed a still in operation on Grammer's ranch?

Yes, but Grammer didn't own it, although doubtless he bought the output.

"Weren't you a deputy sheriff at that time?" Leahy asked pointedly, implying Hale should have made arrests.

Hale's reply was all pride. "There was only one sheriff that I didn't hold a commission under."

Listening to the cattle king's testimony, Tom White was struck by the constant reference to whisky, the proven means by which the white man traded the trusting Osages out of their possessions, leaving them bewildered, degraded, and despised by the money-changers who cheated them, while claiming to be good friends.

Turning to the charges against Ramsey, the defense put on the grand jury foreman, who hinted again that federal agents had used force on Ramsey and made a new charge:

Luhring, in the grand jury room had told convict Dewey Selph that they could do a great deal for him.

The other two grand jurors, siding with the defense, the Stillwater farmer and the cattleman, returned to testify that Ramsey's confession was unsigned.

St. Lewis, who had already charged the farmer with perjury, asked the cattleman: "Weren't you reprimanded during the grand jury session for associating with Lou Oller, one of Hale's partners?"

Springer shouted: "This is impudence of the worst kind!" He hurled an objection.

Judge Cotteral quieted both sides and adjourned court.

CHAPTER SIXTEEN

August 11th, the defense began calling character witnesses to construct the framework of an alibi for Ramsey, establishing his whereabouts at the time of Roan's murder. Eleven, mostly farmers, trailed to the stand. They testified to seeing Ramsey at Ripley most of January, 1923, and later Ramsey went with his wife and child to visit relatives in Fairfax. Ramsey was in poor health, they said, unable to work steadily.

St. Lewis was examining a Fairfax witness. Several times he asked the woman to face the jury, and each time Springer objected.

"I want her to face the jury," the district attorney exploded, "because Jim Springer sits there with his feet moving around informing the witness how to answer."

Springer was instantly on his feet, advancing toward the prosecution table. "What's that? I'll . . . I'll . . . ," he muttered.

Judge Cotteral, weary of the wrangling, banged for order, and Springer calmed down. Later he explained a new molar falling out had caused him to jerk his foot in surprise.

If anything, Tom White thought, that was a new excuse for extreme courtroom behavior, and wondered why Cotteral hadn't sat him down. Had Springer's — "I'll . . . I'll . . ." — meant he was going to slug somebody?

St. Lewis recalled the grand jury foreman. To the defense's surprise, the witness said he had refreshed his memory from notes taken during the jury session and wished to retract his earlier testimony. He said he did not hear Luhring make certain promises to convict Dewey Selph.

Springer jumped him. "Didn't Saint Lewis threaten to prosecute you for perjury after court yesterday?"

"No. Nobody threatened me."

August 12th, Sam Tulk, former Osage Agency officer and now Ponca City chief of police, stood for the defense. He was in a car with Fairfax officers Bob Parker and Jim Rhodes when they saw two men around Roan's house. One was peeking through a window. . . . Tulk never finished. St. Lewis objected, and the battle was on over introduction of testimony alleging Roy Bunch, not Hale and Ramsey, was responsible for Roan's death. Cotteral sent the jury out while he heard arguments. In attempting to shift the blame, St. Lewis said, not only must a motive be shown, but also an *overt act*.

Then Judge Cotteral ruled. Testimony relative to Roy Bunch's possible implication in Roan's death was admissible. The jury was called back, and the defense began unfolding its sensational sequence that Bunch, who had married Roan's widow, was the guilty man.

With Freeling examining, Tulk said one of the two men seen around the house was Bunch. The two hightailed it when shots were fired. Yes, Tulk had seen Mrs. Roan and Bunch driving around before Roan was murdered, and, when Roan's body was brought in, Tulk had noticed Bunch walking back and forth in front of the undertaker's.

Tulk's testimony sounded damaging until Leahy started breaking down the inferences. What did the officers find when they rushed up to the house after firing shots at the two men who had fled? Was anyone inside the house? Was Roan?

No. Roan wasn't in the house.

Weren't there other persons besides Bunch outside the undertaking parlor? In fact, hadn't a great many Fairfax people — just about the whole town — gone down there to view the body after the news spread?

Yes, there were others out there, walking up and down.

"Call William Copeland."

The witness identified himself as assistant cashier at the First National Bank of Fairfax. Yes, Hale and Roan did extensive trading together, much of it transacted at the bank. He identified Roan's signature on the controversial $25,000 note drawn on behalf of Hale.

In Tulsa, the same day, the *World* reported, two familiar Fairfax names appeared as defendants when the federal government filed suit in federal court to recover $49,514.52 on behalf of Charles Fletcher, an Osage Indian. Some $19,000 was sought from C.E. Ashbrook, Fletcher's guardian, and $15,000 from each of the two men who had given surety on Ashbrook's bond. One was W.K. Hale. The suit was among twenty the federal government was filing as a consequence of a recently passed Congressional act that allowed Osage guardians to collect only $1,000 quarterly and denied them any part of their wards' proceeds from land.

August 13th, apparently advancing its stand that Roan was killed and his body hauled to Sol Smith's pasture, another way of accusing Bunch, the defense called Russell Beree, a Smith ranch employee.

Two or three days, or maybe a week or more, before Roan's body was discovered February 6th, Beree said he saw a mysterious car drive up to the ranch one night. Beree's wife said someone left the ranch and approached the car. The purpose here, reporters wrote, was to plant the theory that someone from the ranch, with Bunch and Mary Roan as accessories, murdered Roan and had his body taken to the cañon and left in a car.

Not all defense testimony went so smoothly. A former Fairfax woman, young and vivacious, now living in Ponca City, related seeing Bunch and Mrs. Roan together.

St. Lewis asked her: "Were you ever married to that full-blood Indian boy sitting in the courtroom?" He gestured to a young Osage, who stood up.

"Yes."

"How long were you married to him?"

"One year."

Did Bill Hale and Ernest Burkhart drive with her and the Indian to Pawnee to witness their marriage, a hasty one, St. Lewis hinted?

They did, she said. But her husband was "sober as a judge," when she married him, and she had lived as his wife thereafter.

Wasn't there some trouble over a divorce?

With a slow nod, the pretty witness admitted that her husband sued her twice before she agreed to a divorce. She finally gave it to him for $15,000.

One more question, please. Did Hale receive part of the divorce settlement?

Oh, no. She had no agreement to pay Hale or Burkhart anything.

Dismissed, smiling demurely at the ogling crowd, the shapely witness went outside where her shiny new car was parked.

F.S. Turton, former manager of the Big Hill store in Fairfax, told of hearing a commotion downstairs and hurrying there and finding "Roy had Henry down. He had hold of his head, punching it against the cement floor. Another man and I separated them and put Henry out of the store. It was only a few minutes until he came back again. Roy Bunch hid in the icebox. We put Roan out again. There were plenty of butcher knives down there, but Roy did not use them."

The moment had arrived for the defense to wheel up its main gun, Henry Cornett, rancher and friend of Hale's, a tall, light-haired, cowboy-looking man of about fifty, currently appealing a thirty-year bank robbery conviction.

Did Roan come to Cornett's ranch to buy whisky, then Bunch with Mrs. Roan on the same day late in January, 1923? Yes, they did. Roan was alone. Please tell the court what happened.

"I saw Roan at my ranch about a week or ten days before he was found dead," Cornett testified. "Roan was pretty drunk. Curly Johnson was staying at my place, making and selling whisky. Johnson got in the car with him and drove down the creek, north. Henry then went north. You can go that way to the Sol Smith pasture, where the body was found. I saw Bunch and Missus Roan about twenty-five minutes after Roan left. Bill Taylor was with Bunch in the front seat. Curly had come back. He got on the running board with them, and they went down to the creek. When they came back, they took the road south. The two roads merge a few miles away. I never saw Roan alive after that. Curly carried a Thirty-Eight Special while at my place."

Questioned by St. Lewis, Cornett denied telling federal agents he would assist the prosecution if they would help him out.

More mystery, more insinuations followed. A prominent Fairfax bootlegger testified that on the night Roan was believed murdered he saw Bunch drive a car into the country and in the car were two people covered up. On another occasion, the witness said, he broke up a Roan–Bunch fight.

A housekeeper for the Roans testified that during all the time Roan was missing, Bunch lived at the house.

A Big Hill clerk said he sold Mary Roan a .38 revolver in 1920, bolstering the defense claim that Roan was killed with a .38, not a .45 automatic as the prosecution claimed.

As the last witness stepped down, observers said the defense appeared more confident than at any period of the trial.

The Bunch theory wasn't new, the prosecution pointed out. Agents had investigated it long ago and found it without foundation.

"It is very probable," St. Lewis told reporters, "that Bunch will not take the stand to reply to charges against him by the defense."

In addition to the courtroom drama, a

local theater was showing newsreels of the principals and attracting packed houses.

August 14th, persisting in trying to trace the elusive .38 revolver, the defense questioned Marshal Bob Parker. Had he ever taken a gun from Bunch?

Parker said he had never taken a .38, but he had found a weapon of that description in a car Kelsey Morrison was driving. Later, Bunch claimed the handgun, saying he had left it in a pool hall and Morrison had taken it.

Roy Cook, Fairfax pool hall owner, testified that Roan had chased Bunch into Cook's pool hall. But Bunch had hid. Roan had been drunk.

C.E. Ashbrook, First National Bank cashier, whose wife was Roan's guardian two years before his murder, said Hale and Roan were good friends. Hale gave or loaned Roan money when Mrs. Ashbrook refused. Ashbrook identified Roan's signature on notes for $25,000 and $1,675.

"Did Hale ever file claim with the estate for the twenty-five-thousand-dollar note?" Leahy asked.

"No."

What had been an uneventful and methodical presentation by the defense to involve Bunch suddenly changed late in the day with a jail-cell statement from Henry Cornett, claiming Curly Johnson had killed Roan. Cornett, described by the Tulsa *Tribune* as a witness "who openly vows loyalty to Hale," was "sore as hell" at federal agents, claiming he had been "framed" on a bank robbery charge. "Curly Johnson told me he killed the Indian and was to get $10,000 for the job," Cornett declared. "He told me if I would keep quiet, I would get half. I told him I didn't want any of that money. I ordered Johnson off my place." That wasn't all, Cornett said. Later, Johnson tried to kill him!

Cornett claimed further that his two nephews, helping on the ranch, went south on the day Roan and Bunch and Mrs. Roan came to the ranch. They saw the Bunch car pass, then Roan, then Johnson. He said Roan's body was found about two miles south on the same road. A day later Cornett said a nephew informed him what they had seen on the road, the cars passing. Cornett said he then confronted Johnson and drew the confession from him.

Cornett closed on a much-worn accusation: he was promised freedom if he testified for the government. One of the higher-ups had approached him right there in Guthrie and asked him if he would be willing to lay down if everything against him was dismissed.

To Tom White, Cornett's story was simply more mudslinging to discredit the government. It was a poor statement in several ways. Curly Johnson wasn't around to deny or admit his confession, and at no time did Cornett name Bunch as Johnson's employer. If these claims were true, why hadn't they been introduced in court? The defense insisted Cornett would have so testified, but Judge Cotteral would have barred the testimony.

"All bunk!" was St. Lewis's only comment.

Meanwhile, Roy Bunch and wife Mary remained available as federal witnesses. Bunch openly stated his innocence and denied any connection in Roan's death. As for stories about Bunch's and Mary's being seen on the road to Cornett's whisky ranch, government attorneys asked if it was unusual at that time, when other residents also often drove out there?

August 16th, still building on a .38 revolver as the Roan death weapon, the defense called a former tenant couple of the Roans. They related taking a pearl-handled handgun from a bedroom that Bunch had occupied after Roan's death and hiding it under the house. It was there, the woman said, when Marshal Parker and Agent John Wren came for it last January. Her husband said he found spots under the handle that might have been rust or blood.

Wren testified he found no spots.

Incisively Leahy brought his broad knowledge of the Osage country into play as he questioned these two defense witnesses.

Weren't they working for Hale now? "Yes," the woman replied, "we're living on Hale's place near Gray Horse."

Leahy questioned the husband about cattle Hale had sold Roan, the condition of the stock, and their eventual disposition.

With reluctance, the witness said some of the cattle were driven to a pasture and he never saw them again, and that some of the cows were aged.

Continuing its strategy to place Bunch near Roan not long before his disappearance, the defense called a former pool hall operator.

"I drove out to Cornett's to get some whisky about eight days before Roan's body was found. On the way I met Roy Bunch between Sol Smith's north and south pastures." At Cornett's he said he saw Curly Johnson drive up from the east, the direction that led to Roan's body.

Freeling now called Hale, apparently for a whitewashing. What was his connection, if any, with the wedding referred to by the prosecution between the young white woman and the Osage youth?

Shrugging genially, Hale said he was a good friend of these Osages and he and Burkhart had accompanied the couple at the groom's request. Hale paid for the marriage license and gave the justice of the peace his fee. The Indian wasn't drunk. Hale denied profiting from the divorce settlement.

Always the Indian's friend, Tom White said to himself. It had paid Hale well over the years.

As court adjourned in the late afternoon heat, the end of the rough-and-tumble, accusatory trial seemed in sight.

August 17th, Freeling rested early for the defense, leaving the prosecution three principal targets to smash at in rebuttal: Ramsey's alibi that he was ill and couldn't have been in the vicinity of the crime or in Fairfax when Roan was murdered; validity of the $25,000 note Roan reportedly gave Hale; and the elaborate structure built around the Bunch murder allegation.

Leading off, a former ranch neighbor of Henry Grammer's punched Ramsey's alibi around. From about January 8, 1923, until the end of the month, James Balleau said, at a time when the defense claimed Ramsey was in Ripley except for a brief visit with relatives in Fairfax, Ramsey worked intermittently for him doing carpentry. The witness said he had seen Ramsey with a new Ford roadster a short time before Roan was killed. Ramsey left frequently in the car.

Mrs. Flora DeArmand, Pawhuska court reporter, took the stand and qualified as an expert witness for the government. Leahy then presented the $25,000 note Roan was said to have signed to Hale.

"Has there been an erasure on the note?"

"Yes, the month in the date."

"In your opinion what change?"

"The letters J-A-N-Y have been written over and a little to one side of June."

Leahy argued that the alterations, from June 24, 1921, the same date the application for the insurance on Roan was signed, to Jany. 24th were made in order that the note would appear to have been drawn long before the actual time it was written.

St. Lewis questioned William Taylor, a Fairfax mechanic, who denied having gone with Bunch and Mary Roan to Cornett's ranch in pursuit of Roan a few days before Roan's frozen body was found.

Taylor also hit at Ramsey's alibi when he told of having a drink with Ramsey at a pumping station near Fairfax on January 14th, a day when, according to the defendant and other defense witnesses, he was ill and confined to his home in Ripley.

Taylor was cool under cross-examination. But suddenly Springer shouted accusingly: "You know as a matter of fact that you three people . . . Roy Bunch, Mary Roan, and yourself . . . killed Henry Roan!"

Taylor's instant denial was all but lost in St. Lewis's protest. "Every time a government witness takes the stand, Springer accuses him of murder."

The objection was sustained. Question and

denial were stricken from the record. But, as Tom White saw it, Springer was sowing doubt and confusion while keeping the spotlight of evidence off Hale and Ramsey.

There was a pause. Adjournment looked near. Had the government exhausted all its witnesses? But St. Lewis had the strategy of saving his aces for late in the day.

A former Fairfax postmaster testified to seeing Ramsey and Roan together in a café. When? A short time prior to Roan's death.

"Call Missus Fannie Lasley, please."

A composed Indian woman entered, her voice just a murmur as she took the oath. The defense table was stirring in surprise. What was this, another slap at Ramsey's careful alibi?

Rather leisurely, St. Lewis led Mrs. Lasley into her story. She lived in Fairfax. What did she and her husband formerly do there?

"We operated a rooming house. The Royal Rooms."

St. Lewis held a ledger now. He showed it to the witness. "Was this the register used at the rooming house?"

"Yes."

After a storm of objections, Judge Cotteral admitted the register in evidence and instructed the jury to determine its worth.

Did the register show a John Ramsey stayed at the rooming house in January, 1923? It did, she said. And what dates show

John Ramsey registered there? Her reply was the 19th and 21st.

Unasked, she suddenly said somebody had used an eraser on the register, trying to change the dates Ramsey was there. "My husband and I kept the records, but the changes are not in either of our handwriting. They have been changed by someone else."

The battle heated up as Springer cross-examined.

"Does the witness recognize the man sitting over there?" he asked, pointing at Ramsey.

"No."

"Does the witness recognize him as the person whose name appears on the register as John Ramsey?"

She shook her head. "No, I don't remember his face."

The witness stepped down, and it appeared the defense had at least blunted her testimony.

But St. Lewis had another shot left. "Call John V. Murphy."

Murphy, a young federal agent, told of taking Mrs. Lasley to the U.S. marshal's office to see if she recognized Ramsey as the person who had registered at her rooms. Ramsey and the Hales were there.

"Missus Lasley shook hands with the Hales," Murphy said. "But Ramsey walked over to the window and looked out."

"Exactly what did Ramsey do when Missus Lasley entered?"

"Ramsey turned his back when she walked into the room."

CHAPTER SEVENTEEN

August 18th, corridors of the federal building soon filled as the end of the trial loomed. Throngs started gathering on the courthouse lawn. When word was telephoned to the Osage that final arguments were about to begin, Indians and whites gunned their automobiles southwest.

St. Lewis hadn't finished tearing at Ramsey's alibi. An employee of the pumping station near Fairfax testified seeing Ramsey there, drinking with others on January 14, 1923, thus backing up mechanic William Taylor's testimony. Ramsey and others had sworn he left Fairfax on January 10th and went to his home in Ripley and remained there two weeks until he visited relatives in Fairfax.

A Guthrie police officer, in charge of the city jail, when Ramsey was held there last January, contradicted Springer's cries of mistreatment — namely, no food for two days before Ramsey was served breakfast — and he said the jail was warm.

Five witnesses including W.C. Spurgin, Fairfax auto dealer and a leading citizen, declared Matt Williams had a good reputation for veracity. The triple-murder Smith case flashed out of testimony when Spurgin said he was interested in the prosecution of Hale and Ramsey "because they blew up a house across the street from me, and I want to make Fairfax a safe place for my wife and children."

There was also a parting blast at the defense's Roy Bunch accusation. H.E. Wilson, the long-suffering, long-frustrated Fairfax justice of the peace, testified that the pearl-handled .38 revolver, made so much of by the defense and which a Roan tenant had turned over to officers in January, 1926, couldn't possibly have been the Roan death weapon — the courtroom fell so still Tom White could hear an Indian boy popping his chewing gum — because, Wilson said in his cultivated voice, the gun was in his court's possession when Roan was killed in late January, 1923. The court had it from September, 1922, until May, 1923.

It was time for final arguments. St. Lewis, in the first major trial of his career, would open for the prosecution, then Leahy. Luhring would deliver the final plea. For the defense, Howard would present arguments for both Hale and Ramsey, then Springer for Ramsey, followed by Freeling, Hale's attorney.

As St. Lewis faced the jury, his dark eyes flashing, his movements had the effect of a curtain rising on the closing scene of the

Osage murders, which had attracted national attention for months. For Tom White and other federal agents, who had taken continual abuse since before the Hale-Ramsey preliminary, the case stood for more than the United States vs. W.K. Hale and John Ramsey. Something more far-reaching was involved. It meant Indian vs. White Man in Oklahoma, Courage and Justice vs. Fear and Intimidation.

"Hale was the ruthless freebooter of death, whose purpose was the debauchery of the Osage tribe," St. Lewis said, and defended the absence from the witness stand of Roy Bunch, a grave spectator today. Bunch knew nothing of the Roan murder; therefore, any testimony by him would be immaterial. He ridiculed defense claims that Roan was murdered and his body taken in a car to the pasture. "It was ideal, this lonely place where Roan was lured. The real killer is in this room, and his name is John Ramsey. Don't let them throw dust in your eyes by seeking to shift the blame."

Ernest Burkhart, St. Lewis said, a constant target of the defense, "is a man whose mind is at ease because he has relieved his tortured soul of a terrible secret and now seeks repentance and forgiveness."

Reading Ramsey's confession to the jury, St. Lewis said it alone was enough for conviction. He defended Agents White and

Smith in securing the confession. "Roan signed his death warrant when he signed the life insurance application for the twenty-five-thousand-dollar policy which Hale took out for him. This is the death flag," St. Lewis shouted in conclusion, waving the policy before the jury.

Howard pictured Hale as a jovial man of the open range and campfire, hospitable, generous with his money, a friend of the red man, imbued with the common spirit of the men who had settled Oklahoma. Booming his charges, Howard struck hard at the character of Ernest Burkhart and Matt Williams, and denounced the activities of federal agents in the case. He asked why Bunch had not been placed on the stand to say that he did not do it. Bunch was seen with Mrs. Roan innumerable times before Roan's body was found. Bunch had broken up Roan's home. Howard declared the car in which Roan's body was found in Sol Smith's pasture was placed there.

Hale listened closely, the same confident smile worn during the long days of the trial playing across his ruddy face. Ramsey looked pale and ill. At times, observers noted, he was almost lost sight of during the rise and fall of oratory. It was usually Hale. Seldom did the defense refer to Ramsey. Was he virtually a forgotten man as Frank Smith had testified?

★ ★ ★

August 19th, a tense hush settled over the perspiring spectators as the closing arguments continued. Every seat in the courtroom was taken. Stylishly dressed white women sat next to colorfully clad Osages, all squeezed into the long seats.

Leahy, a wide-jawed, clear-eyed Irishman, nearing sixty, approached the jury, speaking in a forceful, yet unhurried voice.

"Federal agents," he began, "have worked against tremendous obstacles as faithful servants of the government. What reason had Tom White and Frank Smith to go out and fix this crime on W.K. Hale and John Ramsey? Is it a crime for the government to investigate these murders? Burkhart told me what he knew about the Roan murder after keeping silent three years through his relationship with Hale. Matt Williams told what he knew, keeping silent until this year because to tell would have been like suicide."

Leahy plunged on. "I'm not accusing these attorneys of corruption, but their manner of handling Ernest Burkhart throughout these cases had the effect of making him back down from testifying against W.K. Hale, until, at last, he brought himself out of his dilemma by pleading guilty in the Smith case."

Leahy recalled when W.S. Hamilton had halted the Hale-Ramsey preliminary and de-

283

manded to talk privately with Burkhart before he testified for the State. How Hale's friends had crowded into the judge's room around Burkhart, and later at Fairfax told him to rely on the advice of Hamilton, who was not his attorney, but Hale's. "When Burkhart finally pleaded guilty, he told the truth."

Tom White was aware of an absorbed listening by the crowd. Many had known Leahy for years, knew his reputation as a respected attorney and county prosecutor. He was the one man a desperate Burkhart had appealed to when he faced up to his ultimate decision. But would the jury be impressed?

Leahy laid open Ramsey's alibi, stressing that only Ramsey's relatives had testified to it. He held up the rooming house register and displayed it to jurors, calling attention to entries by a John Ramsey two nights in January, 1923. "If you can find he lied about his alibi, can you believe anything Ramsey has testified to?"

Leahy scored Hale for selling cattle at high prices to a drunken Indian to whom he repeatedly gave money for booze. Citing the handwriting expert's testimony on the note, he said it was re-dated back from June to January so as not to look suspicious.

As Leahy wound up his argument and Springer took the floor, Tom White knew a barrage of accusations was coming.

"Burkhart will never serve a day in the state penitentiary and his perjured and false testimony is merely part of the price he's paying for his liberty!" Springer opened up. He whirled on Leahy, waving his arms, shouting: "You know it, too!"

Leahy came up fast, on his feet. "That is untrue and *you know it*, Mister Springer."

St. Lewis broke in to say that Burkhart had been taken to Pawhuska where he would be a witness September 20th against Hale and Ramsey in the W.E. Smith case.

Sneering, Springer denounced Tom White and Frank Smith and Edwin K. Brown, assistant U.S. attorney, pointing them out individually, claiming third-degree methods used on Ramsey. "Has the time arrived," he shouted, "when human life can be taken away so cheap on the perjured testimony of these thugs who call themselves federal agents or on that given by convicts or ex-cons?"

So far, Springer had been careful not to hurl insults at agents outside the courtroom. If he did, Tom White knew there would be swift retaliation, particularly by Alex Street, a former Ranger.

Freeling, in his old-school style, began with a lengthy analysis of the government's evidence, saying it rested solely on the insurance policy and the testimony of Burkhart and Williams, one a convict, the other a former convict. He charged that citizens were being deprived of their Constitutional rights.

A graying, heavy-bodied man, Freeling now fired the main barrel. "We dared Roy Bunch to come in court and try to deny that which we have proven. Why are Roy Bunch and Mary Roan not here to face this jury? I do not know who fired the fatal shot, but I do know that Roy Bunch above every other man wanted Henry Roan to die. The lust and avarice prompted by his illicit love affair with Mary Roan was far more motive for seeking Henry Roan's death than was the insurance policy held by Hale."

Freeling bowed. Luhring would deliver the last closing argument tomorrow.

Out of San Antonio, Texas, this same sweltering afternoon came an Associated Press report of Osages still fleeing from fear of a stalking death. Tribesmen were in search of new homes. If the colonization plan developed, an estimated eight hundred Osages might settle on 500,000 acres in southwest Texas. A delegation was studying the proposal.

Tom White frowned at the news. More signs of panic. Like the " 'fraid lights" still stringing Indian homes at night in the country. Full-bloods, particularly, were afraid Hale might go free. If so, what happened then?

August 20th, in a forceful address that the *Tribune* said attorneys declared was the greatest closing argument heard in Oklahoma in twenty-five years, O.R. Luhring, assistant to the U.S. attorney general, fixed the date of Henry Roan's murder either January 29th or 30th, 1923. "Roan's car was seen in the cañon on Sol Smith's place with a dead Indian in it on January Thirtieth. The testimony of two brothers, who were out setting their traps, shows they first saw the car one week before the Pratt boy found the body and reported it February Sixth. This and the testimony of Henry Cornett and his nephews that they saw Roan alive January Twenty-Seventh was offered by the defense. I thank the defense for the dates."

Luhring, formerly a U.S. representative from Indiana, had a distinguished courtroom manner to go with his frost-white hair and athletic frame.

"I wish to state publicly that the Department of Justice and I appreciate to the fullest extent the work these federal officers have done in the interest of law and good government. This case is an unusual one, not a common murder case, and that is the reason I have been sent here to participate in the prosecution. The Osages aren't in Osage County by choice. They are here through the actions of the government. And, yet, the richest tribe of Indians on the globe has become the prey of white men. The Indian is going. A great principle is involved. You have heard defense counsel criticize such government officers as Edwin K. Brown, T.B. White, and Frank Smith. Every move these servants of the government has made has been with my approval."

Luhring let his gaze range over the jurors. "You have heard the astounding statement of Mister Freeling and Mister Springer that Hale's name never came up into this probe until Burkhart mentioned it. Why, the government had known about Hale for six months!"

Freeling jumped up, objecting violently. Cotteral sustained.

"Hale," Luhring continued, unruffled, "sat there and heard Roan lie while being examined for a twenty-five-thousand-dollar insurance policy. It is absurd to say he had no motive. Hale is a thief who preyed on ignorant Indians. That is how he amassed the fortune his attorneys speak of so proudly. All his transactions reek of fraud."

Hale was grinning. Luhring might as well be discussing the Kansas City steer market.

Speaking sharply, Luhring denounced Hamilton's conduct at Pawhuska when he took Burkhart into private consultation before he could testify for the State. "Never in all my experience have I heard of such a thing as happened there. Later, Burkhart wove a story in Hale's favor, but on this stand I know he told the truth."

As Luhring pressed on, praising the veracity of Matt Williams and Dewey Selph, he had the attention of all but one juror. "You don't believe the United States is bribing witnesses, do you?" Luhring asked, speaking directly to the juror. "If they wanted to fix up a story for Matt Williams to tell, why didn't they say he saw the shot fired? His testimony is meager. You can't help believing it is true."

He described for the jurors the plight of Burkhart, "one day the pampered pet of the defense, safe in their good graces until he told the truth, now an outcast. There is no limit to which Hale and his friends will not go to protect Hale."

Luhring seemed to have forgotten his pointed reference to the one juror until he paused, his tone turning grave. "The jury is the safeguard of the people, but put one man on a jury who is *fixed* . . . who has a personal interest . . . and he will defeat the whole purpose of government."

Luhring checked himself again, his eyes moving across them. "Recently I had occasion to prosecute men on a jury because a rich man had influenced them. Gentlemen, all the government asks is to perform your duty."

At 3:15 P.M. the jury got the case with Judge Cotteral's terse instructions, stating in part: "You must establish that Roan was shot on a restricted allotment of an Osage Indian.

If, however, it is found he was not killed there, that is ground for acquittal in this court. If you find without a reasonable doubt that Ramsey with malice aforethought unlawfully murdered Roan, you will convict him of murder in the first degree, otherwise, acquit him. If you find Hale procured Ramsey to do the slaying with malice aforethought, you will find him guilty of murder in the first degree or acquit him. The alleged confession has been introduced. The oral statements said by officers to have been made have been denied. You must decide whether they were, and whether the written statement was procured voluntarily or involuntarily. Witnesses have been called who have been convicted of crimes. You must decide whether their testimony is credible. There is no majority verdict. You must agree one way or the other. Murder in the first degree is punishable by death, but the jury may add life imprisonment."

Early in the evening the jury sent out for a microscope. Only one construction could be placed on the request: Jurors were examining Mrs. Lasley's much-smudged rooming house register.

By the following day and no verdict, wagers in Guthrie jumped five to one for a hung jury. Strong as the government's case was, observers said, many factors favored the defense. It had presented a confusing number of issues to the jury, especially the Bunch murder theory. It had succeeded in dragging out the trial. Grand jurors were split over whether Ramsey's confession was signed or not, and Ramsey's emaciated physical appearance had aroused sympathy.

Another element was the pioneer attitude toward the American Indian. In this instance, a jury of white men trying a white man for the murder of an Indian. "It's a question in my mind," a prominent member of the Osage tribe told a Tulsa reporter, bitter as predictions of a hung jury mounted, "whether this jury is considering a murder case or not. Whether a white man killing an Indian is murder. That, or just cruelty to animals."

The jury was put to bed Monday night after deliberating thirty-three hours. Friends and relatives of Hale and Ramsey still waited at the Ione Hotel. Attorneys and federal agents and witnesses stayed close, awaiting the news. Judge Cotteral was known to permit juries to remain out as long as seventy-two hours. The great expense incurred by both sides was another factor in not calling the jury yet.

Railbirds from the Osage winked knowingly. It was just like they'd figured: Bill Hale's influence reached plumb into federal court.

About an hour before noon on August

25th, there was a stir of excitement in the federal building. St. Lewis and defense attorneys Howard and Hamilton were hurriedly summoned. Hale and Ramsey appeared under guard. Court convened before only a knot of spectators and news reporters, who learned the jury was coming in after being out five days.

Hale was pale, uneasy; his deep-set eyes had a burned-out look. It was the first time he had shown strain. Ramsey, as usual, looked worn, thin, ill.

A weary tension etched the faces of the rumpled jurymen as they filed in. The defendants eyed them for some sign; apparently there was none. When the shuffling ceased, Judge Cotteral asked if there was any possibility of reaching a verdict.

"Judge, Your Honor," came the tired voice of the foreman, "there is no possibility of a verdict. We've taken sixty-four ballots, and we're still deadlocked." Several jurors nodded in agreement.

Judge Cotteral turned to the defense. What were its wishes?

Freeling, Hale's main counsel, wasn't in the courtroom, and Howard said he would agree to dismissal since it appeared a verdict wasn't possible.

The government?

St. Lewis, flushed with suppressed anger, replied: "I think there are some good men on this jury, and I think there are some who are not so good. Whisperings have come to me from Oklahoma City and Tulsa about this jury that some have been fixed. I usually disregard such whisperings, but I am inclined to think there are some friends of Bill Hale on this jury. I ask, therefore, that the jury be dismissed."

With stunning swiftness, the trial was over. Cotteral dismissed the jury and ordered the defendants held for U.S. marshals.

Hale and Ramsey, smiling broadly, were escorted back to the county jail. St. Lewis walked angrily to the Ione Hotel. The jury was deadlocked in a six to six mistrial. "The King of the Osage Hills" still wasn't roped, tied, and branded.

CHAPTER EIGHTEEN

W.S. Hamilton of the defense took pointed exceptions to St. Lewis's remarks about fixed jurors and friends of Bill Hale's on the jury, but the aggressive district attorney did not back down and expanded on his statements.

"There was too much studied indifference to government testimony," he told the press. "Too many whisperings of a conspiracy to defeat justice and too many letters received by federal officers giving alleged information of a packed jury."

It was the darkest period of the Osage investigation, a greater setback than when Ernest Burkhart, in fear of his life and yielding to the pressure of relatives, had swapped camps at Pawhuska. The case had a much broader sweep than determining the killer of trusting Henry Roan, Tom White and Frank Smith agreed. If left here, the issue unresolved, or if a second trial ended in acquittal, Osages could expect to live under the same cloud of fear or worse. And what of those courageous white people who had testified for the prosecution? Hale would emerge stronger than ever. A man of his nature would not forget who had stood against him. Would Hale and Ramsey be tried next in state district court at Pawhuska for the W.E. Smith murders? That appeared likely until on September 2nd federal and state authorities agreed to retry the Roan case in federal court on October 20th in Oklahoma City.

Meanwhile, the U.S. Supreme Court denied a rehearing for Hale and Ramsey, and Judge Cotteral denied bail for both defendants, confining them to the county jail in Guthrie. But the Osage probe was too quiet, out of character, judging by past events. An outbreak of fresh accusations against federal agents was overdue.

One erupted September 28th, as Kelsey Morrison was appearing before Judge Cotteral on a liquor possession charge. When the prosecution asked a penitentiary sentence for the offense, Morrison accused Agents White and Smith of framing the Anna Brown confession on him. A considerable achievement, Tom White observed, amused, since Morrison had refused to discuss the murder with him and Frank Smith at Guthrie. Not until Leahy and Dabney had talked to Morrison later had he agreed to testify with immunity at Burkhart's trial.

Judge Cotteral fined the erstwhile Romeo squawman $250 and sentenced him to ninety days in the county jail.

J.M. Springer of the defense was also

having problems. A federal grand jury recommended action against him for allegedly attempting to influence witnesses to commit perjury on several occasions. In its report the jury recommended that Roy St. Lewis swear out a formal complaint charging Springer with contempt of court. What with a second trial looming fast, and the prosecution girding for a final showdown, no charges were filed against the Stillwater firebrand.

Soon after this Springer had fistic troubles in Fairfax. William Taylor, the young mechanic whom Springer had accused of Roan's murder with Roy Bunch and Mary Roan, saw his needler on the street. Quick, hot words. Perhaps a sneering retort. Fists flew. Springer returned to the Smith-Williams hotel, "severely beaten, but not believed seriously hurt," the Associated Press reported. Taylor was charged with assault and battery and released on $20 bond.

The second Hale-Ramsey trial opened October 20th before a different presiding judge, John C. Pollock, of Topeka, Kansas. Nearly five weeks of exhausting trial work had rendered down much of the fat off the hard-fought case. Judge Pollock, a strict adherent of proper court procedure and one eye on a heavy docket, denied separate trials and seated a jury the first day, whereas three days had been needed at Guthrie. One reason was evident: prosecutors asked no questions regarding capital punishment.

Hale appeared his usual public self, confident, energetic, nodding and smiling at acquaintances as he entered the courtroom. However, he sat with a serious face during the jury selection. Ramsey paid scant attention, leaning back in his chair and staring about the room. Mrs. Hale and daughter Willie were in attendance.

T.J. Leahy gave the opening statement for the prosecution, citing events leading up to Roan's death. Tom White noticed a changed atmosphere as proceedings moved along. Judge Pollock demonstrated early he would allow no detailed testimony not bearing directly on the case and little duplication.

A parade of serious faces, by now as familiar to court followers as actors in a hometown play being repeated by popular demand, passed to and from the witness box, uttering remembered lines. Many times Springer's abusive questions were overruled by the court when St. Lewis objected.

On the second day Judge Pollock admitted Ramsey's confession as evidence, speeding up the trial. Ramsey listened with a set smile while Leahy read. Hale's countenance was sober.

Judge Pollock denied requests by Springer and Hamilton that the jury be removed for hearing the confession. Ramsey was never threatened or given "electric shots," Tom

White and Frank Smith repeated. No attempts were made to "break Ramsey's will."

Ernest Burkhart, brought from McAlester where he was serving a life sentence for his rôle in the Smith case, underwent three hours of grueling cross-examination. He stuck to his testimony in the Guthrie trial: that Hale had told him Ramsey would kill Roan and that Hale gave Ramsey $500 and a car to kill Roan.

Freeling sought to shake Burkhart's credibility. "Why did you change your testimony in your trial at Pawhuska?"

"I testified falsely at Pawhuska because you said you'd beat the case," Burkhart replied firmly.

At every indication of delay, Judge Pollock cleared the snarl and the trial proceeded. Abuse of federal agents and government witnesses ceased; in fact, it was not allowed. At noon on Saturday, October 23rd, St. Lewis startled spectators with the announcement: "The prosecution rests."

In only three and a half days the trial was as far advanced as after three weeks at Guthrie. Some government witnesses who had testified previously had not been called, including Matt Williams. Apparently the defense had succeeded in convincing the jury to disregard his testimony in the first trial.

Two events outside the court caused a whir of excitement. An Oklahoma City attorney was caught giving whisky to a Osage Indian witness. In Fairfax another alarm swept the edgy town when a full-blood Osage died unexpectedly while trying to use the telephone in a filling station. The man's family demanded a coroner's investigation and autopsy, which indicated death was due to natural causes. Just the same the death reflected the jittery feeling pervading the Osage while Hale and Ramsey were on trial a second time.

Ramsey came on stage to a courtroom packed to the doors. Contrary to his usual nervousness, he appeared at ease while sticking to his story that agents used duress to force a confession from him. Luhring tripped him up on several dates. He refused to recognize as his own two signatures of "John Ramsey" on the register of the Royal Rooms, signed on dates he had already testified he was home in Ripley.

Judge Pollock admitted the signatures as evidence.

"Hale, the last defense witness," reported the *Daily Oklahoman*, "appeared elusive on the stand, thoroughly at ease and refused to be tripped by Luhring. Although the smile he had during the Guthrie trial is not evident, his reserve and bold front continue to impress court observers."

Was another mistrial in the offing?

At this time a new career in law enforcement opened up for Tom White, assigned to take charge of the federal penitentiary at Leavenworth, Kansas, as acting warden during a probe of the prison administration. Sworn in, he returned to Oklahoma City to find the trial racing to conclusion, unaware that he would return to his new duties in time to complete an ironic finality to the Osage investigation.

It was October 27th, when the defense rested, still stubbornly and desperately asserting that Roy Bunch had murdered Roan.

Building evidence in rebuttal aimed right at Ramsey, the government called a new face, Frank Wooten, former Osage County cattle buyer now living in Mexico. In the summer of 1923, he said, while being driven on a country road by the defendant, Ramsey told him Hale had given him the car in which they were riding, a Ford roadster. Agents Wren and Davis testified they heard Ramsey, in the federal building at Guthrie, say he used a .45 to slay Roan. Mechanic Bill Taylor told of seeing Ramsey at a pump station near Fairfax in January.

After only eight days the jury received the case. The first trial had taken thirty-one. The jury, Judge Pollock instructed, could return only three possible verdicts:

Both defendants guilty.

Both not guilty.

Or Ramsey guilty and not Hale.

The jury could set punishment for either man found guilty at life imprisonment or death.

Somewhat surprisingly to the prosecution, Judge Pollock ruled the jury could consider that Roy Bunch might have killed Henry Roan. Pollock said the alleged confession of Ramsey implicated only Ramsey. "The fact that Ramsey was questioned by federal officers does not mean the confession was involuntary."

Twenty hours later on October 29th exciting news circulated among the waiting trial followers: the jury was ready to report. The courtroom filled rapidly. Hale and Ramsey entered under guard and sat down with their attorneys. Hale had his chin up, a characteristic bold front, as he watched the court clerk. Ramsey's mouth twitched. The jury filed in, followed by Judge Pollock.

When all were seated, the judge asked: "Gentlemen of the jury, have you arrived at a verdict?"

"Yes, sir," said the foreman, in relief, passing the paper.

Pollock read for a long moment, then handed the verdict to the clerk.

So silent was the courtroom that the ticking of a wall clock sounded unusually distinct. Every small sound seemed magnified.

Hale and Ramsey leaned forward to hear. Hale's face expressed a guarded eagerness. Ramsey's was a mask.

"We find," the clerk began, clearing his throat, "the defendants guilty of murder in the first degree and recommend they be confined to prison for life."

Ramsey bent slightly forward, mouth twitching, a strained look in his eyes. Hale sat straight, showing no emotion.

Judge Pollack told them to stand before the bench to be sentenced.

They rose together, Hale's quick movements those of an active man, Ramsey slowly drawing himself up. They stood side by side. Now Hale seemed stunned, his face impassive. Ramsey moistened his lips. He swallowed hard.

"My disagreeable duty in sentencing you," Judge Pollock said, "is made easier by the law, for it gives me no alternative. You have been tried by a jury of your peers and found guilty of taking the life of an Indian. Therefore, I sentence each and both of you to spend the rest of your natural lives in Leavenworth Penitentiary." He paused. "Have you anything to say, Mister Hale?"

"No, sir," Hale answered, his voice strong and steady.

"And you, Mister Ramsey?"

Ramsey shook his head. He seemed dazed, unable to believe that Bill Hale's lawyers had lost.

A few days later defense attorneys claimed they had evidence that would clear Hale, which St. Lewis branded "as the usual effort to lay the blame on a dead man." Reporters understood the dead man was Curly Johnson, late Osage County bank robber and boot-legger, whose name had been brought up before in the case. The court allowed Hale time to arrange his business affairs. He had disposed of much of his property, selling 2,000 acres of grazing land. His home ranch of some 1,200 acres of grazing and farmland would be managed by his son-in-law, Willard Oller. Mrs. Hale was to make her home with the Ollers.

A group of Hale's die-hard friends gathered at the county jail on November 16th on the eve of his departure. "Tears came to the eyes of Homer Huffaker, president of the Fairfax First National Bank, and S.S. Mathis, manager of the Big Hill Trading Company," the *Daily Oklahoman* reported. Some observers wondered if Hale's conviction in Roan's murder would affect the company's revenue, since Osages spent freely there, and Hale was known to have an interest in the store.

The Big Hill was among a group of firms that had met with the Osage Tribal Council in 1921 to deny that bills presented to the agency for payment were padded, the Pawhuska *Journal-Capital* reported. For years Osages had complained that merchants over the county charged more to Indians than white people. On the other hand, merchants

303

complained that Osages were often slow to pay and, when collecting, difficult to find. Sometimes a pressing creditor would get the put-off reply — "Pay you payment." It meant in three months and was a quasi-humorous saying in the Osage.

During the trials the defense had often attempted to discredit and smear federal agents, expressly singling out Tom White and Frank Smith, Springer ever in the fore of the attacks, shouted taunts, jibes, accusations, sneers. Taking them for nearly a year hadn't been easy for the two Texans, but now by a queer turn of fate matters were reversed and the scales of justice balanced. Escorted by U.S. marshals, Hale and Ramsey were received at Leavenworth Penitentiary on November 17, 1926. As guards met the arrivals from Oklahoma and admitted them inside the penitentiary walls, a tall man approached.

Hale looked up in surprise. "Why, hello, Tom," he sang out genially, his nerve unbroken, in the tone of meeting an old friend.

"Hello, Bill," Tom White answered. Only two days ago he had been appointed warden. The Texans shook hands, somewhat slowly.

Ramsey said — "Howdy." — and Tom spoke to him. They shook hands, then Tom turned the prisoners over to checking officers. It was done.

EPILOGUE

Grateful Osage Indians, through their tribal council, passed a resolution thanking all who had assisted in the drawn-out investigation and prosecution. Not forgotten were the often-maligned federal agents. Out of the light shone in court on the murders came tightened inheritance laws to protect tribal members. No person convicted of killing an Osage "or convicted of causing or procuring another to take the life of an Indian," such as in the Roan case, could inherit or receive any interest from the estate of the decedent, "regardless of where the crime was committed." In addition: "None but heirs of Indian blood could inherit from those of one-half or more Indian blood." An exception was made for existing marriages.

Still, Hale continued to fight for another trial, and in March, 1928, the Eighth Circuit Court of Appeals reversed his conviction and remanded the case for a new trial. The appellate court reversed the case, the *Daily Oklahoman* said, largely because the trial court failed to grant Hale a separate trial from that of Ramsey, whose confession "may have operated to the prejudice of Hale" and that a severance should have been granted. The decision likewise vacated Ramsey's sentence.

Hale's attorneys shrewdly got a change of venue to the northern federal district, which placed the trial in Pawhuska, obviously reasoning the former cattle king would stand a much better chance on his own range. Roy St. Lewis made a countering move. He resigned as U.S. attorney for the western district and was appointed an assistant to the U.S. attorney general to prosecute Hale and Ramsey again.

As the trial approached in January of 1929, antics familiar to prosecutors enlivened the case. One man was charged with intimidating Matt Williams. A half-brother of Hale's, T.C. Hale, was alleged to have attempted to bribe a prospective juror. Judge Franklin E. Kennamer announced he had heard rumors of "a very grave nature" relative to the case.

Freeling was missing from Hale's line-up of no fewer than eight attorneys. Four were Pawhuskans, including W.S. Hamilton. T.J. Leahy joined St. Lewis on a staff of five.

The government had steadily strengthened its case. No longer afraid after Hale's conviction at Oklahoma City and seeing the government intended to follow through aggressively a second time, more witnesses came out of the brush with additional evidence, much of it sensational. A new witness, cattleman Ross Erickson of Latham, Kansas, said Hale wanted one of Erickson's ranch hands "to take care of John Ramsey" because Hale was afraid Ramsey might talk. Erickson testified Hale also made reference to Ernest Burkhart and his brothers and that he would like to "get them to Mexico before they talked." Again, Burkhart testified about the plot to murder Roan, saying Hale told him Ramsey "should have shot him in front" to make it look more like suicide, and dropped a gun near Roan.

The bulk of the defense's testimony was aimed at placing Roan's murder on Roy Bunch. Boldly denying all accusations, Hale testified Roan was worth much more to him alive than dead and considered the proposed purchase of Roan's headright a good business deal. Hale was found guilty a second time of complicity in the Roan case on January 26, 1929, and sentenced to life in Leavenworth Penitentiary. Eleven jurors had voted for the death penalty, so Hale had escaped finality by one.

Ramsey went on trial November 14th at Pawhuska, after a defense maneuver failed to have Judge Kennamer disqualified. The Tulsa jurist was known as a tough judge.

Roy Bunch became a witness for the first time and denied conspiring to take Roan's life. Again, Burkhart testified Hale hired Ramsey to kill Roan so Hale could collect the $25,000 life insurance policy. As in

Hale's trial, new witnesses punctured Ramsey's alibi.

O.C. Webb, a Fairfax telephone operator in 1923, testified Ramsey came to the telephone office and first called a woman in town. Webb said he listened in on their conversation, evidently an old diversion, and heard Ramsey ask: "Is he ready to go?"

"Yes, he's about under," Webb said the reply had been.

Next, Webb said, Ramsey had called Hale and informed him. "I have Henry ready to go."

"Be sure not to fail me," Webb quoted Hale.

Then, Webb testified, Ramsey assured Hale: "You know you can depend on me."

Five other witnesses came forth to say Ramsey had talked to them about killing Roan, adding to the government's case. Ramsey attempted to shift the blame on Bunch, Burkhart, and the dead Curly Johnson.

John Ramsey was convicted again on November 20, 1929, his life sentence rating a banner headline in the *Journal-Capital*. The jury had acted swiftly, going out at 10:40 P.M. and returning the verdict at 1:25 A.M. The government had asked for the death penalty.

"I talked to Hale and Ramsey on many occasions," Tom White recalled. "Hale never let on that he was guilty, and he never lost that strut and domineering attitude. But he did complain about money he'd spent on his defense. He told me he'd paid Springer ten thousand dollars in attorneys' fees and court expenses, and he was almost broke."

Evidently resigned and short of funds, Hale dropped all appeals in May, 1929. He became a trusty on the prison farm and remained a prisoner until July 31, 1947, when he was paroled, over the Osage Tribal Council's protests. One provision of the release was that he could not return to Osage County. Ramsey was freed the following November.

Osages smelled political influence behind Hale's parole, signed by President Truman, a surprising turn in view of Hale's bloody reign as the "Indian's friend." He was released to the custody of his daughter, now Mrs. Willie Cohen of Wichita, Kansas, and under the jurisdiction of the federal probation officer there.

As the years passed, bits about Hale drifted back to Fairfax. He was here and there, tending bar in Montana, selling "hot" diamonds in Dallas. In West Texas, he tried to renew old contacts among cowmen, and even handled some stock on commission. But his past trailed him even out there, and he never made a comeback. W.K. Hale died in August, 1962, at age eighty-seven in a Phoenix, Arizona, nursing home and was buried at Wichita.

John Ramsey was paroled later and reported living in Oregon.

J.M. Springer's shouted prediction that Ernest Burkhart "will never serve a day in the state pen" proved wrong by some thirty years. When he entered the Oklahoma penitentiary, Governor M.E. Trapp held office. The touchy issue of parole was hanging fire when Governor Henry S. Johnston was elected. Some Fairfax sources believed Johnston's impeachment hurt Burkhart's chances for early clemency.

Tom White, Roy St. Lewis, and T.J. Leahy were among other officials recommending parole for Burkhart shortly after Hale's conviction. White wrote Governor Trapp:

He told us the truth when we were on the wrong track, and all he had to do was just sit silently by and see us take the wrong case (Bert Lawson) to court.

The government had no case without Burkhart. Hale and Ramsey could not have been convicted without his confession and testimony. His confession led to Ramsey, until then not a suspect in Roan's slaying, and also helped exonerate Roy Bunch, an innocent man, of murder rumors that Hale had generated in the Roan case. Clemency efforts didn't succeed until December 30, 1937, over the protests of the Tribal Council and Hale.

Burkhart's freedom was short. His parole was revoked August 19, 1940, when convicted in the $7,000 burglary of the home of Mrs. Maggie Morrell Burkhart, now wife of his brother Bryan. An old snare took hold. Maggie was a restricted Osage Indian, so Ernest Burkhart faced a federal prison term. Fearing his uncle, he asked to be sent to Atlanta prison instead of Leavenworth, and the request was granted. Oklahoma authorities then placed a detainer on Burkhart. Therefore, when released from Atlanta in August, 1946, he was returned to the Oklahoma penitentiary. Not until late 1959, twelve years after his uncle's release, did he apply for parole.

Partly deaf, stooped, thinning hair snow white, he appeared before the board. Taking note of his clean prison record and testimony against Hale and Ramsey, the board voted unanimously to grant him freedom. Osage tribal leaders protested again and lost.

"I was just an errand boy for my uncle," Burkhart told the board. "He wasn't the kind of man to ask you to do something . . . he told you." For a moment Burkhart might have been back on the witness stand at Pawhuska, wavering under Uncle Bill's flinty gaze. "The headrights had nothing to do with the bombing. Hale was feuding with Bill Smith over some adjoining ranch land." No mention was made of the $6,000 debt Hale refused to pay Smith, or of Smith's probing Anna Brown's murder, or of Hale's plan to blow up the house and concentrate the family wealth in Burkhart's name.

A.L. Jeffrey, former Osage County assistant attorney, and municipal counselor for Oklahoma City when Burkhart was released, said that back in 1926 Burkhart had told a different story. "Burkhart told me he was afraid his uncle would eventually kill him, his wife, and their children to gain control of the headrights."

Paroled, Burkhart left immediately for New Mexico where a $75-a-month job awaited him, the last central figure in the Osage murders to leave prison.

Brother Bryan fared much better. In 1927 Osage County officials dismissed charges against him in Anna Brown's murder after Kelsey Morrison was convicted in nearby Washington County. Morrison eventually won an appeal on the grounds that improper evidence was used against him. Gravitating back to the Osage and its deadfalls after being released from the Oklahoma state prison in January of 1931, he was killed in a downtown gunfight with Fairfax officers and the sheriff.

No charges were ever filed in the puzzling death of George Bigheart in Oklahoma City, nor that of his attorney, W.W. Vaughn. Fairfax old-timers said a known tough character who "hung around" the ranch of a friend of Hale's was believed to have kicked

312

Vaughn out the window of his Pullman berth. Why? Because Vaughn had possession of incriminating evidence, which also vanished that night.

After Ernest Burkhart's release, the old suspicion that had never quite died surfaced again in Fairfax. Had he known that Mollie and the kids would be in the Smith house that night? Marshal Bob Parker gave an unequivocal no when asked. Mollie had remarried and died in 1937.

Author Marilyn Mullins, who wrote a four-part series on the murders for the *West Texas Livestock Weekly*, quoted Mollie's personal physician as recalling that she was "taken to her bed" at every report Burkhart might be paroled. Had Mollie, a loyal wife during the trials, learned that husband Ernest had also plotted her death and the kids' that night so he could inherit everything?

Two other actors with minor, yet important, rôles in the unfolding drama of the Osage played their tough-guy parts to the end. Boyish, blue-eyed Dick Gregg, former pal of the late outlaw Al Spencer and once approached to kill the Smiths, escaped from Kansas state prison. An outlaw to his last reckless moment, he died in a shoot-out with state officers west of Tulsa on August 29, 1929. Blackie Thompson escaped at McAlester and fled to Texas. There, involved in a robbery and murder, he was tried and convicted. While on death row awaiting execution at Huntsville, he escaped and died in a shoot-out with county officers near Amarillo. Thompson had figured in Ernest Burkhart's confession when he urged him to talk to federal officers and not take the rap, after Burkhart had at first refused to discuss the case with Agents White and Smith.

Warden Tom White's problems with Oklahoma outlaws were far from over when the Osage trials ended with hard-fought convictions. Already forming in the seething discontent of four thousand federal prisoners crowded into facilities for one thousand eight hundred at Leavenworth existed elements for the sternest test of his life, an experience that was to affect him for years, yet without bitterness or hatred for convicts.

Bursting into the warden's office with smuggled rifles, shotguns, and explosives, seven desperate men, five of them Oklahoma hardcases, made a break for freedom on December 11, 1931. Through the kitchen window in the warden's home, Bessie White, petite, brown-eyed, the mother of two sons, saw the grim procession marching across the grounds, Tom, a gun at his back, a captive of his own prisoners. Terrified, she watched the band of armed men pause, look around, then continue on as the prison gates swung open, a decision Tom had made when the convicts threatened to light a stick of dynamite if guards tried to stop them.

She felt the sickening pump of her heart, unable to move, and then she ran outside after them as fast as she could, her heart cold, until she saw them get into a waiting car and roar away. She stumbled and stopped, frozen with fear. Would she ever see Tom again?

Tom White was on a ride of death. All the while he prayed for a little time, hoping he might yet stall the escape. But no chance came. They kept taunting him, threatening to kill him. He became reconciled to dying. His captors ditched the car and seized another.

A young couple was strolling along the country road, a brother and sister, as it turned out. The convicts forced them into the crowded car, shouting about hostages. Soon they could see a car in pursuit. After a twenty-mile chase on muddy roads, apparently having eluded pursuers, they suddenly stopped. They started talking about killing the couple.

"I know you're going to kill me," Tom said, trying to reason. "But don't shoot these two. They're not in this. Let 'em go. Why make them suffer?"

"We'll kill you first, Warden. How's that?"

Somehow the moment passed, while his captors talked wildly about what to do. Then, as if on impulse, shoving and punching him, they made Tom stand outside the car. This time they were going to kill him. He knew it, he saw it. He rushed Grover Durrell, former Al Spencer gang member and mail train robber, grabbing for the convict's shotgun. Tom twisted and almost had it, but the butt struck the side of the car, and he lost it.

Will Green, another Oklahoma outlaw, ran around the car, and Tom saw the snout of a shotgun swinging toward him. Unable to dodge, he threw up his left arm just before Green fired, taking the blast below his elbow and in the chest. Tom staggered back, but held his feet, dazed. Closing in savagely, Green smashed the barrel across Tom's head and knocked him down. In the excitement the sister and brother ran free. The convicts left Tom for dead and sped on to a gun battle that took three of their lives.

Next day, in a Kansas City, Missouri, hospital, Bessie White slipped into her husband's room and asked what to tell reporters clamoring for details.

"Just tell them the truth," he said.

Tom White recovered to retire with Bessie in El Paso, Texas. He lived to be ninety, passing on in late 1970. In all his years as a lawman, beginning as a Texas Ranger and heading the investigation of the Osage murders, one of the U.S. Bureau of Investigation's most complicated and difficult cases, he had never killed a man. For that he was proud.

ABOUT THE AUTHOR

FRED GROVE has written extensively in the broad field of Western fiction, from the Civil War and its postwar effect on the expanding West, to modern quarter horse racing in the Southwest. He has received the Western Writers of America Spur Award five times — for his novels *Comanche Captives* (1961) which also won the Oklahoma Writing Award at the University of Oklahoma and the Levi Strauss Golden Saddleman Award, *The Great Horse Race* (1977), and *Match Race* (1982), and for his short stories, "Comanche Woman" (1963) and "When the *Caballos* Came" (1968). His novel *The Buffalo Runners* (1968) was chosen for a Western Heritage Award by the National Cowboy Hall of Fame, as was the short story, "Comanche Son" (1961).

He also received a Distinguished Service Award from Western New Mexico University for his regional fiction on the Apache frontier, including the novels *Phantom Warrior* (1981) and *A Far Trumpet* (1985). His recent historical novel, *Bitter Trumpet* (1989), follows the bittersweet adventures of ex-Confederate Jesse Wilder training Juáristas in Mexico fighting the mercenaries of the Emperor Maximilian. *Trail of Rogues* (1993) and *Man on a Red Horse* (1998) are sequels in this frontier saga.

For a number of years Mr. Grove worked on newspapers in Oklahoma and Texas as a sportswriter, straight newsman, and editor. Two of his earlier novels, *Warrior Road* (1974) and *Drums Without Warriors* (1976), focus on the brutal Osage murders during the Roaring Twenties, a national scandal that brought in the FBI. Of Osage descent, the author grew up in Osage County, Oklahoma during the murders. It was while interviewing Oklahoma pioneers that he became interested in Western fiction. He now resides in Tucson, Arizona, with his wife, Lucile.

The employees of Thorndike Press hope you have enjoyed this Large Print book. All our Thorndike and Wheeler Large Print titles are designed for easy reading, and all our books are made to last. Other Thorndike Press Large Print books are available at your library, through selected bookstores, or directly from us.

For information about titles, please call:

(800) 223-1244

or visit our Web site at:

www.gale.com/thorndike
www.gale.com/wheeler

To share your comments, please write:

Publisher
Thorndike Press
295 Kennedy Memorial Drive
Waterville, ME   04901